FOOTFALL

Snow is falling. An old woman reads alone in bed . . . there is the sound of breaking glass and footsteps on the stairs . . . When Cambridge academic Cassandra James learns that her friend, Una, has been found dead, she is shocked, then suspicious. Was it a bungled burglary? Una had tried to ring Cass just before she died, and she'd changed her will, depriving the Cambridge Literary and Philosophical Institute of her library of Victorian literature. Why? And it seems that there is another Cassandra James running around Cambridge getting her in trouble! The line between appearance and reality is blurring . . .

Books by Christine Poulson
Published by The House of Ulverscroft:

DEAD LETTERS
STAGE FRIGHT

Christian Poulson was born and brought up in North Yorkshire. She has written widely on nineteenth-century art and literature and her most recent work of non-fiction was a book on Arthurian legend in British Art 1840-1920. She lives in a water-mill in Derbyshire with her family. This is her third novel in the Cassandra James series.

CHRISTINE POULSON

FOOTFALL

Complete and Unabridged

ULVERSCROFT
Leicester

First published in Great Britain in 2006 by
Robert Hale Limited
London

First Large Print Edition
published 2009
by arrangement with
Robert Hale Limited
London

British Library CIP Data

Poulson, Christine.
Footfall
1. Women college teachers- -Fiction. 2. Murder- -
Investigation- -Fiction. 3. False personation- -
Fiction. 4. Detective and mystery stories.
5. Large type books.
I. Title
823.9′14–dc22

ISBN 978–1–84782–824–8

Published by
F. A. Thorpe (Publishing)
Anstey, Leicestershire

Set by Words & Graphics Ltd.
Anstey, Leicestershire
Printed and bound in Great Britain by
T. J. International Ltd., Padstow, Cornwall

This book is printed on acid-free paper

Acknowledgements

Visits to Bromley House in Nottingham, the Portico Library in Manchester, and to the London Library (of which I have long been a member) have given me some fascinating insights into the world of independent libraries. I am grateful to their staff and I salute them all. The Cambridge Literary and Philosophical Institute and its staff exist only in my imagination, alas, as does St Etheldreda's College.

Thanks are owed to Claire Blundell Jones, Peter Blundell Jones, Sue Hepworth, Jude Marsh, Amanda Rainger, Christine Shimell, Bob Tanner and Jonathan Waller for their support and criticism. They have saved me from many a blunder. I want to thank Roger Fosdyke, too, for advice on some aspects of police proceedure.

The chapter titles are also the titles of nineteenth-century novels or short stories. Their authors are listed in a postscript.

PROLOGUE

Over and over again I've tried to reconstruct that last day of Una's life. In many respects it was probably a day like any other, punctuated by the small pleasures that the elderly come to rely on: *The Times* crossword, a glass of sherry before lunch, afterwards an espresso made in her special machine.

Except it wasn't quite a day like any other because she was worried enough to leave the house to catch the last post at five o'clock. It was bitterly cold and her arthritis was troubling her. A neighbour saw her struggling along to the post-box. She was leaning heavily on her stick. For me, that's when she really comes into focus.

When she returned from the post-box, she cooked herself a meal. She hadn't let her standards slip. She had spaghetti with a bolognese sauce and a green salad washed down with a glass of red wine. I respect her for that salad. I know I'd never make something like that just for myself, the pasta, yes, but not the salad. She left the dishes for the cleaner who would be coming in the morning. She made a hot-water bottle, poured herself another glass of red wine, and went into the hall to the stair-lift. I see her floating up to the first floor like a saint ascending to heaven.

She got ready for bed. It was early, but why not? It was already dark outside and the spacious bedroom that looked out over the botanical gardens was the warmest room in that vast house. She had everything she needed: a radio, a portable TV, a telephone. She never went to sleep before midnight, but usually she enjoyed her long evening reading, thinking, and remembering. That night though would have been different. She was troubled, distracted.

When did she first realize that she wasn't alone in the house? Did it begin with the sound of breaking glass? I can't be sure, but that's how I picture it. I see her raising herself up in bed, slowly, painfully. Did she know right away that someone had broken in? Perhaps at first she wasn't sure. It was so windy: the night was full of noises. It could have been the dustbin lid blowing off. If she had been certain, wouldn't she have rung the police or even one of her neighbours? The phone was right there by the bed.

She always shot the bolt on her bedroom door before she went to bed, so that may have given her a sense of security. And anyway she wasn't the kind of old lady to scare easily. I see her cocking her head, listening for further unusual sounds. I don't think she would have heard the feet coming quietly up the stairs. If I'm right, the first moment at which she was certain that there was someone in the house was when the doorknob turned. It was one of those old-fashioned Bakelite ones. I see her gazing at it, frozen in shock, unable to move or make a sound. Did she know immediately that this wasn't just a straightforward burglary? I'm sure she did. I think in those few seconds she knew it all.

I see them both, the intruder on one side of the door, she on the other, for both of them the whole world narrowed down to this single spot: narrowed down to the first floor of a big Victorian house in Cambridge, and finally to a doorknob turning. The intruder wasn't expecting anyone to be at home. There's a thud, another thud. The old woman sees the door begin to quiver and then to shake from the impact of a shoulder on the other side.

And that breaks the spell. She reaches for the phone. She punches in a number, her hand surprisingly steady, praying that it will be answered. Even an answering machine would do. It doesn't matter much if she dies, it has to come sooner or later, but there is something she must do first. The wood is splintering, the bolt is coming away from the door. She hasn't got long. She wishes she had said more in the letter. The phone is ringing at the other end. It's all right she tells herself, the person she has chosen is intelligent, even without this last contact she will work it out, and she will know what to do.

Now the door flies open. She looks straight into the face of the attacker.

And at that moment the phone is picked up at the other end.

1

The Half-Sisters

Half-sisters and step-sisters feature in many Victorian novels. They allowed a dramatization of nature versus nurture, a theme that was of the deepest possible interest to writers and thinkers from the mid-nineteenth century onwards. Darwin's *On the Origin of Species by Means of Natural Selection*, published in 1859, and *The Descent of Man* in 1871 were merely the —

No, that wasn't right. There was nothing 'merely' about *On the Origin of Species*. I leaned back in my seat and drummed my fingers on the table. I stared at the glowing computer screen as if it might come up with the next word of its own accord. 'The most important . . . ?' No, that wasn't right. 'Landmarks?' Yes.

Darwin's *On the Origin of Species by Means of Natural Selection*, published in 1859, and *The Descent of Man* in 1871 were landmarks in a —

In a what? Controversy? No. 'Debate?' Yes!

in a debate that first gathered momentum with the geological discoveries of the —

And I was away, my fingers racing across the keyboard. I'm one of the few British academics I know who touch-types instead of pecking at the keys with two fingers. All the same I couldn't keep up with the words that were unscrolling in my head with the speed of messages from a ticker-tape machine. I was so absorbed that I didn't hear Giles coming up behind me.

When he cleared his throat and said, 'A word in your shell-like?' I jumped in my seat.

'Sorry, Cassandra, I didn't mean to startle you,' he said.

'What? Oh no, it's fine,' I said vaguely, still half in the nineteenth century.

I had to resist an urge to put my hand over the screen of my laptop. It wasn't private exactly, but I hate people reading over my shoulder. I shifted round in my chair so that I could look up at him without craning my neck. I hadn't noticed until now that the last of the daylight had gone. Beyond the light cast by my desk-lamp, darkness had gathered in the corners of the room. Giles's bumpy forehead and longish, lank hair looked a little sinister lit from below.

'I was hoping we could have a chat,' he said, giving me a smile that exposed a lot of gum.

'Well . . . ' I glanced at my watch. It was ten to five. I had to pick Grace up from the nursery at six.

'Surely you've got time for a cup of tea? I've just put the kettle on. And I've got a chocolate fudge cake from Fitzbillies.'

'Oh, well, in that case . . . '

'See you in five minutes in my office?'

I nodded. When he had gone, I switched off my lap-top and tidied up my notes on Geraldine Jewsbury, an influential nineteenth century writer and reviewer, author of *The Half-Sisters*, a key text for this chapter of my book. Her papers are held by the Institute and were the reason I was spending my study leave there.

The Institute is housed in a fine Georgian building in Downing Place. From where I sat facing the window I could see lights on in the laboratories that rose slab-like across the way. The room I was working in had once been a servant's bedroom and now contains the

Institute's collection of pre-1950 travel literature. Hardly anyone came up here, which was why I'd been able to commandeer it as a temporary study. It was none too warm even with a plug-in electric fire. I'd had to resort to wearing fingerless mittens. Now that I'd stopped typing, my fingers were cold and there was an ache somewhere around my left shoulder-blade.

I went over to the window and stood there, massaging my shoulders. Orange light from the street lamps revealed dirty heaps of snow lining the narrow road below. There wasn't a soul in sight down there. The busy streets of central Cambridge were only a stone's-throw away, but the silence was profound. I could have been alone in the world, suspended in a globe of light above the dark street.

It was time to go down and join Giles, but something kept me there. I felt lethargic, disinclined to hurry. I'd had some bad nights lately, nursing Grace through chickenpox. The gilt lettering on the spines of the books gleamed in the light from the desk. I picked a book at random off a shelf, opened it, and inhaled the musty, aromatic smell of old paper and dust. The title-page was yellow round the edges and flecked with brown, *To the Foot of the Rainbow: Twenty-five Hundred Miles of Wandering on Horseback through the South-West* by Clyde Kluck-horn. The book had been published in 1928 and when I turned back to the flyleaf, I saw that it had last been taken out in 1934. This was one of the things I loved about the Institute: in most other lending libraries this book would have been de-accessioned long ago; here no one would dream of throwing it out.

If I'd had the faintest inkling of what was to come, maybe I would have lingered even longer, savouring those last few moments of peace. But I shut up the book and put it back on the shelf without the slightest premonition of the grief and the trouble in store.

★ ★ ★

On my way down I was joined by Florence, the Institute cat, a piratical-looking creature, mostly black with a white face and a black patch around one eye. There's been an Institute cat since 1824, when the place was founded by Josiah Johnson, a wealthy Cambridge corn merchant. It's really the Cambridge Literary and Philosophical Insti-tute, but it's always known as the Institute or the Lit and Phil. The Institute cats are noted for their longevity, as indeed are the librarians: Florence and Giles were the last in a short, but distinguished line.

Florence followed me down the elegant wooden spiral staircase that connects the book-lined gallery to the reading-room below. Most of the superb collection of Victorian literature is housed in a utilitarian extension, architecturally undistinguished, that extends back from the building towards St Andrew's Street. But the original building still has the atmosphere of a private house. The reading-room was once the drawing-room. It's light and airy with a domestic charm all its own. The fine proportions, red armchairs, white plaster-work and rather bad Georgian portraits give it an air of leisured opulence. It's only when you look more closely that you see that the paintwork is scuffed, even flaking in places, and that the plush is wearing thin on the chairs.

The librarian's office is a grand name for what is just a corner of the issue hall, screened off with half-walls below and frosted glass panels above. Portraits of previous librarians in wing collars look down from the walls. On a tray on the desk was a china tea-pot, a saucer of lemon slices, two cups and saucers. Resting beside it was a large gold cake-box with 'Fitzbillies' inscribed in art deco lettering. I wondered what had warranted a visit to the best cake shop in town.

'Take a pew, take a pew,' Giles said.

I watched him fussing around with cups and plates. When I'd first met him he had put me in mind of the Reverend Slope, the libidinous hypocrite in *Barchester Towers*. I had no idea why. Was it that there was something a little unctuous about his manner? That impression hadn't survived long: now that I knew him better, I liked his toothy smile and found his eccentricities endearing.

'You like your tea on the weakish side, don't you, Cassandra?'

'Please. And no milk.'

I settled back in my chair. There was a discreet meow and Florence sidled out from under it. Giles opened a desk drawer and took out a carton. He poured some of the contents into a saucer and put it down for the cat.

'I thought they couldn't digest milk,' I remarked.

'They can't. This is special lactose-free stuff.' Giles looked a little shame faced. 'I spoil her, I know.'

I laughed. 'I'm a cat lover, too. So, what did you want to talk about?'

'The trustees want to know if you are willing to have your name put forward to fill the vacancy left by the death of Professor Wilson.'

'It would be an honour,' I said, and I meant it.

It was one of those moments that makes you realize that you've come a long way. The Institute is part of the social and intellectual fabric of Cambridge, one of the few institutions that really do span both town and gown. Over the years the roll-call of trustees has been an illustrious one. Somewhere at the back of my mind I couldn't help being surprised that someone should think I was grown-up enough for this.

Giles handed me my tea. 'You're just the sort of person we need. New blood, someone *young*.'

I couldn't help smiling. Only in academic life is one regarded as a mere stripling at forty.

'The bureaucracy here grinds slowly, as you know,' Giles went on. 'Don't expect to get elected before the summer.'

'Just as well, from my point of view,' I said, realizing that I hadn't considered how I was going to fit this in with all my other commitments. 'Just now every moment of the day is accounted for. Things will be better when I've finished this book.'

'Is there much left to do?'

'I've got two more chapters to write. I've just started one on half-sisters and step-sisters

12

and then there's one on twins. Problem is I've got a deadline in six weeks.'

'Oh, publisher's deadlines ... ' Giles shrugged. 'They surely don't expect to get it on time.'

'Except that this is the third and it's tied into production schedules. I lost time through Grace having chickenpox, but I should be OK as long as nothing else goes wrong.'

Giles picked up a paper-knife. He seemed about to cut the string on the cake box. He sighed and put the knife down. This switch from euphoria to gloom was typical. 'I wouldn't blame you if you had reservations about becoming a trustee, quite apart from lack of time. There are plenty of problems — money, of course. And the question of how far to modernize. You know, when I took over last year, I didn't realize quite how much resistance to change there'd be.' He crossed one leg over the other, revealing a couple of inches of white, hairy calf. A foot in a well-polished brogue swung gently. 'There's so much I want to do. We simply have to have the catalogue computerized.'

I couldn't argue with this. I liked the old-fashioned card index and the ancient leather-bound catalogues, the pages greasy with much thumbing, but they weren't likely to gladden the heart of a modern librarian.

Giles brooded over his tea. 'It's a great pity the frontage onto St Andrew's Street was ever leased off.'

'I don't think there was much choice at the time.'

It had happened in the sixties during one of the Institute's periodic episodes of financial crisis. As an independent library, the Institute didn't receive any public funds and the subscriptions were nowhere near enough to keep the place afloat. Luckily, part of the building fronted onto the main shopping street and this had been rented out to a building society on a long lease.

Giles brightened. 'Oh, but it'll be great to have you on board.' He raised his teacup in a salute. 'And I mustn't make too much of the problems. Sooner or later there will be a big infusion of cash and some very nice additions to the collection. Can't say too much at the moment.'

He picked up the paper-knife again and this time he got as far as cutting the string on the cake box. The sides fell away to reveal a sumptuous cake, dark brown and gleaming with butter icing. Giles carved out two large slices and manoeuvred them onto plates.

I glanced at my watch. It said ten to five. That was what it had said the last time I'd looked at it. I looked more closely. It had stopped. My heart gave a little lurch.

'What time is it, Giles?'

'Let me see. It's twenty to six.'

'What! I'm supposed to collect Grace at six.' I got to my feet. 'I'm going to be late.'

'The cake — '

'Sorry, Giles, I've got to dash.' I snatched up my coat and bag.

'I wanted to ask — would you and Stephen like to come for dinner one evening?'

'That would be great — look, I've got to go — '

'Sunday?'

I was on my way out of the office by now. I cast one last longing look at the cake. 'Assume it's OK unless I let you know.'

I was hurrying down the stairs to the street, trying at the same time to struggle into my coat and holding my hat in one hand, when I heard footsteps behind me. I turned to see Michelle coming down the steps two at a time. She's Giles's other assistant, and an ex-student of mine whom I taught in Sheffield five or six years ago. She's a dishwater blonde with something odd about the pupil of one of her eyes that makes you look twice. It's a strange shape, as if the black had leaked out into the iris, but it didn't detract from the appeal of a face that was alive with interest and responsiveness. I try not to have favourites, but every so often it's hard to avoid. On her part I suspected a touch of hero-worship. No big deal: teachers get used to their pupils regarding them as more (or, sometimes, less) than human.

'Cassandra, I wonder if I could have a word,' she said breathlessly.

'Can it wait? I'm in a tearing hurry.'

She was staring at my shoulder, the one that wasn't yet in my coat.

'Michelle? Can it wait?'

She looked up and said, 'What? Oh, yes.' Her eyes dropped to my shoulder again.

I glanced down to see what had caught her attention. There was a snail-like trail of dried snot on my jumper, a memento of an enthusiastic hug from Grace that morning.

'Hell,' I said, 'I've been going around like this all day.'

Michelle laughed. 'When my brothers were little, my mum used to wear her cardigan on inside out until she was out of the house.'

'A brilliant idea. Look, we'll fix something up, OK? Maybe have lunch together? I'll be working upstairs again tomorrow. Come and find me.'

Her face cleared. 'Thanks. That's cool.'

When I opened the door onto Downing Street, a blast of cold air hit me. Cocooned in the warmth and quiet of the Institute, I hadn't taken in the change in the weather. It had begun to snow again, large flakes that chased one another through the darkness. I groaned aloud. I'd come on my bicycle, leaving my car at St Etheldreda's college on the Madingley Road, so as to avoid the traffic in central Cambridge. I'd be soaked by the time I got back there. And the traffic was always much worse when the weather was bad.

I was definitely going to be late.

2

The Way We Live Now

Forty minutes later I was sitting in a queue of traffic, tapping the steering wheel and looking at my watch every few seconds. The heater was on full blast and the car was full of the smell of wet wool. It was even worse than I had feared, because there had been an accident on Grange Road. To add to my discomfort I was dying for a pee. I'd tried to ring the nursery on my mobile, but only got a message telling me that it was closed until eight o'clock the following morning.

At last I pulled into the car-park of the nursery. It's in a pleasant Edwardian house in a cul-de-sac off West Road, behind the University library. All the windows were dark except for one on the ground floor, and the car-park was empty.

Leaving the car at an angle, I jumped out and ran through the falling snow. Both the inner and the outer door were unlocked. They were never open when the children were there. I looked into the room on the left where I had seen the light. It was empty. The little tables and chairs looked forlorn without the children. There was a sound off to one side and when I looked round the edge of the door I saw that the cleaner was there pressing her mop into her bucket. She paused when she saw me. I'd never run into her here before, but I had the disconcerting feeling that I knew her. I had no idea where I'd been seen her before or what her name was, but the colourless hair swept back in an Alice band and the fine-featured face were familiar.

She smiled at me. 'Dr James!'

'I'm looking for Grace, my little girl.'

'But the children have all gone home.'

Then where was Grace? A nightmare scenario began to unroll in my head. I got a grip on myself. The staff would never have let Grace go with anyone who wasn't authorized to collect her. It must have been Stephen.

'But I always collect her on Mondays,' I said aloud.

'This is Tuesday,' the woman said.

I stared at her and it was a moment before the penny dropped. I hit my forehead with the heel of my hand. Of course! Grace and I had both been worn out by her bout of chickenpox: we'd had a long weekend convalescing at my mother's and hadn't come back until Monday night. I'd slipped into my first-day-of-the-week routine, and Stephen hadn't.

'I got into a muddle,' I explained.

'That's all right then,' said the cleaner with manifest relief. She was obviously delighted to see me and expected me to know who she was.

'You'll be pleased to hear that I've kept up my reading,' she said. 'After I wrote that essay on *Great Expectations* I read all Dickens's other novels.'

And then I did know who she was. She'd been in one of my adult education classes the previous year. I could have kicked myself for not remembering.

'I think *Our Mutual Friend* is my favourite,' she went on.

A drop of water plopped off the brim of my hat onto my nose. I brushed it away with the back of my hand. Her name was on the tip of my tongue. One of those little girl names that can seem incongruous on a grown-up woman. She was a bit younger than me, around thirty at a guess. The sensible thing would have been to confess that I had forgotten it, but there was something in her artless enthusiasm that made me reluctant to do that.

I played for time.

'Have you done any more courses?' I asked.

She rested her hands on the top of the mop. 'Did one on modern poetry, but it wasn't nearly as good as the Victorian novel. I've just started one with Dr Jenkins — American literature: Huckleberry Finn and Nathaniel Hawthorne and all that.'

I gestured towards the stairs. 'I wonder if I could use your loo before I head for home.'

'Oh yes, it's that door on the landing — '

It niggled away at me. What was her name? As I came back down the stairs the thought shot into my head: something to do with pantomimes. That was how I'd remembered her name when I was teaching her. Surely not Cinderella or Snow White? Though that might be appropriate for a cleaner in a children's nursery.

She was still hanging around in the hall. She shot me a shy, side-ways look.

'I'd like to do an Open University degree if I can get the money together,' she said.

What on earth was it? Aladdin? Puss-in-Boots? Hansel and Gretel? That was more like it. Yes! I'd got it. Not a pantomime exactly but pretty close: Peter Pan.

'That sounds like an excellent idea, Wendy,' I said, beaming at her. I didn't remember her contributing much in class, but I had a vague recollection of her as a conscientious student.

My mobile rang. I fished it out of my

21

pocket. I knew who this would be. Because if it wasn't my turn for collecting Grace, that meant it was my turn for going straight home to cook the dinner. Sure enough, it was Stephen wanting to know where the hell I'd got to.

★ ★ ★

I drove north-east on the A45 towards Newmarket, leaving plenty of room between my car and the one in front. Only the week before there had been a ten car pile-up when a lorry had jack-knifed on the ice and it was a miracle that no one had been killed. The road had been blocked for hours.

It had first snowed around a month ago, just after Christmas. There had been two or three partial thaws before the big freeze had set in again. For the last few weeks it had taken twice as long as usual to drive out from Cambridge to the Old Granary near Ely where we lived. Stephen and I kept debating whether to move into the small flat we'd kept on in Cambridge. Stephen had been living there alone when we first met. But it was so small, just a *pied-à-terre* really, and we always came back to the question of our cat, Bill Bailey. Pets weren't allowed there.

The snowflakes grew smaller and sparser as

I turned off towards Waterbeach. The roads had been well gritted, but twice I passed cars that had skidded into the ditch and been abandoned. They were already blanketed with thick snow. I slowed down to a crawl as I passed them. The huge, frozen fields stretched away white and flat in every direction. A sickle moon was balanced on the tips of a long line of Lombardy poplars. Tiny lights glinted in distant farm-houses. As I got closer to Ely the curves of the road brought the spotlit tower of the cathedral in and out of view like a beacon glimpsed at sea.

I'd almost reached the turn-off to the Old Granary when I saw the blue flashing light behind me. With a sinking heart I pulled over. The police car stopped behind me and a policeman got out. I wound my window down.

'Are you aware, madam, that one of your back lights isn't working?' the policeman said.

He switched on his torch and played the beam over my front tyres. 'And that the tread on this near-side tyre is well below the legal limit . . . '

Fifteen minutes later, red-faced and furious with myself as well as two hundred pounds poorer, I pulled up outside the Old Granary.

As soon as I opened the front door, two things hit me. One was a high-pitched shrieking and the other was a disgusting smell of burning. I made my way down the short hall with a sense of foreboding. I pushed open the kitchen door and was met by a blast of cold air. Stephen had opened a window to dispel some of the smoke. I paused on the threshold, briefcase in one hand and hand-bag in the other.

Stephen, red in the face and scowling, was in the act of swinging a pan of burning potatoes over to the sink. Grace in her pyjamas was by the fridge pointing implor-ingly up at the handle. She wasn't quite two years old and it was well out of her reach, but that didn't stop her trying. Bill Bailey, our long-haired black-and-white cat, was sitting bolt upright next to his empty food bowl at the far end of the kitchen.

Stephen threw me a glance of mingled annoyance and despair. The pan hit the water in the sink with a fearsome sizzle. The novelty of this made Grace shut up for a moment. Then she noticed me.

'Mummy, Mummy, Mummy,' she said in a voice broken with sobs. She pointed to the fridge door.

'What does she want?' I asked.

'Milk,' Stephen snarled. 'She's already had two glasses with her fish fingers. All right, you little baggage, milk you want, milk you shall have.' He took two long strides to the fridge door and wrenched it open. As if he had set off an alarm, the telephone mounted on the kitchen wall began to ring. Grace, concluding that she had pushed her father too far, retreated rapidly towards me. She wrapped both arms round my leg and whimpered theatrically. Stephen seized a bottle of milk and slammed the door shut with such force that it bounced open. The rack on the inside of the door came away. A second bottle of milk, a glass jar half full of stuffed olives in brine and a glass of water containing a few celery sticks plummeted onto the tiled floor. On the way down the bottle of milk disgorged its content down Stephen's leg. The crash was spectacular.

Bill Bailey shot under the kitchen table. Grace was stunned into silence and so was Stephen. A lake of milk and water and brine spread out across the floor, bearing tiny pieces of broken glass with it. The telephone went on pealing away.

'Oh God', Stephen said, shaking milk off his trouser leg. He squatted down and started picking up pieces of glass. Grace let go of me and headed towards the milk lake. I grabbed her, put her in her high-chair and fastened her harness on, ignoring her squeals of protest. Bill Bailey emerged from under the table. I half stepped, half jumped over the pool and scooped him up just as he was crouching down to the milk and splintered glass. I threw him out into the hall and closed the door after him.

Still the telephone rang.

'For pity's sake answer that,' Stephen said. 'It's driving me mad.'

I snatched up the receiver, thinking that I wouldn't be responsible for my actions if it was someone trying to sell double-glazing.

'Yes?' I snapped.

There was a moment's silence, then a clattering as though the receiver had been dropped at the other end. It was followed by a crash so loud that I thrust the phone away from my ear. When I listened again, I heard a scuffling sound and what might have been a gasp.

Behind me Grace was wailing and struggling against her harness. I was half-aware of Bill Bailey mewing in the hall.

Stephen was still crouching by the milk lake. 'What's going on?' he asked.

I shook my head and held up a hand.

There was silence at the other end of the line. Then the line went dead. I joggled the receiver and listened again. There was still nothing. I hung up.

Grace was still bellowing. I reached into a

cupboard for a packet of breadsticks, ripped it open and handed her one. She clenched it in her fist and stuck the end in her mouth.

'Who was that?' Stephen said, getting to his feet.

'I don't know. It sounded like . . . I don't know what it sounded like. I'm going to dial 1471.'

But before I did that and could discover where the call had come from, the phone began ringing again.

I grabbed the receiver. This time there was nothing at all, simply silence on the other end of the line.

'Hello, hello?' It was hard to be sure, but I thought I heard an intake of breath and then the line went dead.

This time I did manage to dial 1471, but the caller had withheld their number.

I turned back to the kitchen to see Stephen with a bottle of Valpolicella in one hand and a corkscrew in the other.

He smiled at me. 'I thought we might need this tonight and I see I was right.'

★ ★ ★

'Have you put your diaphragm in?'

'Yes, yes, it's all right.'

'Actually I was hoping that you hadn't.'

Stephen took his hand off my waist and rolled over onto his back.

'Oh.'

The mess in the kitchen hadn't been as bad as it looked and the meal, when we finally sat down to it at nine o'clock, wasn't too bad either. We'd given up on the potatoes and had noodles with the lamb casserole that Stephen had found in the freezer. But with this little exchange all my frustration and exhaustion, which had been temporarily banished by food, wine and proximity to Stephen, came flooding back. This was one of those moments when I wished I hadn't given up smoking. Was there after all half a packet somewhere in the house, I wondered, all the time knowing that there wasn't.

'We can't put it off indefinitely,' Stephen said. 'You're forty-one after all.'

'That's nothing these days. Lots of women have babies in their forties.'

Stephen said nothing. The silence was more irritating than if he'd come out and said it: you'll soon be over the hill.

We hadn't closed the bedroom curtains. It's dark out in the Fens away from the street-lights of the city, but tonight the crescent moon shed just enough light for me to see Stephen's face pale beside me on the pillow.

'To be honest,' I said, 'after the kind of day I've had, I scarcely feel I can cope with the child we've already got, let alone another one.'

'We agreed that we didn't want Grace to be an only child.'

'It wouldn't be the end of the world, though, if she was.'

'You haven't changed your mind?'

Now it was my turn to be silent. Stephen hauled himself up, stretched out an arm and turned on the bedside lamplight. I sat up too and we blinked at each other in the sudden light.

'Did you have to do that?' I said, shielding my eyes.

'I just want to know where we stand on this.'

'Look, in theory, I think it's a good idea to have another baby.'

'But a baby isn't theoretical, is it?'

'My point exactly. And looking at in a purely practical way, how do you propose to fit anything else into the day?'

'That's the wrong way to think about it,' Stephen said. 'There's never a right time for having a baby, you just have to go ahead and do it.'

'You mean *I*'ve got to go ahead and do it. What are you prepared to contribute? Are you prepared to cut down on your working hours, stop bringing work home?'

'Me! Look, I do my share!'

'OK, OK.' I slumped back on the pillows. 'Let's not get into a fight about it. We both work hard, but we're always on the brink of chaos. We're only just holding everything down as it is.'

Stephen didn't say anything. The silence lengthened. I turned to look at him and saw that he was grinning.

'Just what is so funny?' I demanded.

'I had a meeting with the boss of that big software company that we've started doing business with. Very formal, everyone was there, accountants, technical whiz-kids. I was in the middle of explaining an abstruse point about patent law, when I felt a sneeze coming. I pulled what I thought was a handkerchief out of my pocket.' He laughed. 'It was a pair of your knickers! They must have got in the wrong drawer. I'd stuffed them into my pocket without looking at them.'

'Do you think they realized?'

'I think they must have done. But nobody said a thing. God knows what they thought I'd been doing in my lunch-hour! But half-an-hour later we'd clinched the deal.'

I laughed. He stretched out an arm and I

put my head on his shoulder. I ran a hand into the hair on his chest, greyer now than when we had met four years ago, and inhaled the familiar scent of Cussons Imperial Leather soap.

I said, 'It really matters to you, doesn't it? Having another baby.'

He rolled over onto his stomach and rested his head on his folded arms. 'I just feel . . . ' he hesitated, searching for the right words, 'I feel there's something missing. Someone hasn't shown up for the party.'

I turned to face him. For a moment I seemed to see the child he was thinking of. I saw another little girl, like Grace, standing on uncertain legs and gripping the edge of the bedroom door.

Stephen turned over so that we were face to face and smiled at me. I smiled back. As he kissed me, he took my hand and laced his fingers in mine. He pushed me back onto the pillow.

I was sinking into a state of pleasant acquiescence when Stephen took his mouth off mine. I opened my eyes.

Stephen held up my hand still clasped in his.

'What's happened to your ring?' he asked.

3

The Portrait of a Lady

It was an Edwardian ring made of silver and set with amethysts, my birthstone. It had been probably made as well as designed by some minor Arts and Crafts artist, and it had cost a small fortune. Stephen had given it to me for my birthday, which had also been our first wedding anniversary. I wore it on my ring finger in place of the engagement ring I'd never had.

This wasn't the first time it had gone missing.

'Grace couldn't have swallowed it, could she?' Stephen asked at breakfast the next morning.

I shook my head. 'She stopped trying to eat everything in sight a while ago. It's much more likely that it's gone the way of your car keys.'

Their disappearance had caused early morning chaos the previous week. We had discovered them two days later in a matchbox. And then there had been the floppy disc slotted into the video recorder.

Grace had taken my ring once before when I'd left it on the edge of the bath after taking it off to wash her hair. I'd just got to her in time to stop her trying to flush it down the loo.

Grace was disembowelling a boiled egg. Sensing our gaze on her, she looked up and beamed at us. Her thistledown fine hair was sticking out in all directions. Unlike me and Stephen, she was at her best in the morning. She gave us a salute with her spoon and returned to her task. More egg was going on her face than in her mouth, but it was easier to wipe her face afterwards than to risk her wrath by trying to help.

'How long did she have?' Stephen asked, pouring himself another cup of coffee.

'I had to go downstairs to get a new packet of nappies, and then I couldn't get it open. I had to look for a pair of scissors. Three minutes?'

'So: motive, means, opportunity.' Stephen ticked them off on his fingers. 'It's not looking good. Grace? Grace?'

She looked up reluctantly.

'Did you take Mummy's ring?' he asked her gently.

'Yes.'

'You did?' Stephen was surprised. She'd denied all knowledge of it before.

'Yes, yes, yes,' she said enthusiastically.

'Can you tell us where it is?'

She nodded and lifted up her arms. Stephen raised his eyebrows at me and went over and lifted her out of her high-chair.

Hardly daring to breathe, we followed her out of the kitchen into the hall. She reached up a hand to the hall table. She could just about curl her fingers over the edge. I lifted her up so that she could reach into the earthenware bowl we keep there.

She plucked out my car keys on their silver key-ring.

'Mummy ring,' she said, lifting them up.

'Thought it was too good to be true,' I sighed.

'Mummy, Mummy, Mummy,' Grace chanted lovingly. 'Mummy ring, Mummy.'

'Look on the bright side,' Stephen said. 'She hasn't had a chance to bury it in the garden and she certainly hasn't hocked it. So it has to be *somewhere* in the house.'

But it wasn't, at least not in any of the usual places. After Stephen had gone, taking Grace with him, I stripped the sheet off the cot, looked under the mattress, and took the duvet out of its cover. I tipped out Grace's box of toys. I sieved through the contents of the waste-paper basket.

Stephen was right, I told myself. It had to

be somewhere. The main thing was to make sure that it didn't somehow get taken out of the house. I made a note to ask Stephen to check his briefcase that evening and that gave me another idea. I searched through my own briefcase and my handbag, but it wasn't there.

I gave up and left for Cambridge and the Institute, doing a detour via Kwik-Fit so that I could buy a new set of front tyres and via the college so that I could collect my mail.

★　★　★

I was still brooding about my ring as I made my way through college to my office. I didn't notice until I was almost at the threshold that the door was open and someone was sitting inside waiting. It's never likely to be good news when a policeman shows up at your place of work, yet the first thing that struck me when I set eyes on Superintendent Jim Ferguson, was how ill he looked. I'd first met him around three years ago during the investigation into the death of my head of department. Stephen knew him and had asked him to get involved. Jim seemed to have aged ten years since then. My next thought was that this had to do with being stopped by the police the previous evening. Of course that was ridiculous. A trivial offence like that wasn't going to bring a Detective Superintendent hot-footing it to my door the next day.

And then I understood what I should have realized right away. He had come to break bad news. Something awful must have happened.

My apprehension must have shown on my face. He said, 'It's nothing to do with your family. Come and sit down, Cassandra.'

My heart was beating fast as I seated myself in an armchair. Jim sat opposite.

'I think you know a woman called Una Carwardine?' he went on.

'Yes?'

'She spoke to you last night.'

I shook my head. 'No. No, I don't think so. I haven't spoken to her for ages.'

Jim frowned. 'At 7.49 last night, a call was placed from her home to your home number. The connection was made. Either someone answered that call or it was picked up by an answering machine or an answering service. Were you at home last night?'

'What time did you say?'

'7.49. The call only lasted for around ten seconds.'

'Oh God.'

'You've remembered now?'

'What's happened? Please tell me.'

'This morning Dr Carwardine's cleaner arrived at her house to find her employer lying at the bottom of the stairs.'

My hands shot up to my face. 'Oh my God!'

'We're treating it as a suspicious death. I'm the Senior Investigating Officer in charge of the case.'

'You mean, someone *pushed* her down the stairs?'

'We think someone broke in expecting the place to be empty. Dr Carwardine was supposed to be away on holiday, the cleaner told us. We don't know why she came back early. It was unlucky for her that she did.'

I felt hot and little black specks appeared in front of my eyes. I put my head in my hands.

Jim said, 'You've had a shock. Shall I call your secretary? Would you like something? A glass of water?'

'No, no, I'll be OK. Just give me a moment.'

When the giddiness had passed off, I told him what had happened, all of it, the difficult day, the muddle over Grace and the nursery, the phone pealing on and on and why I hadn't answered and what I heard when I did. 'She must have been trying to get help. My God . . . '

'The phone lead had been pulled out of the

socket,' Jim said. 'One of the first things I did was to find out if she'd tried to ring someone. That was how I got your number.'

Even as I tried to absorb the horror of it, questions were forming in my mind.

Jim put one of them into words. 'I'm wondering why she tried to ring you? Why not the police — or even a neighbour? Someone near enough to help her. There wasn't a hope in hell that you could get there in time to make any difference.'

'I can't understand it either.'

'How well did you know each other?'

'We first met, oh, it must have been soon after I took up the job here. Six years ago? Seven? We saw a lot of each other then, not so much recently. She'd tried to get in touch with me a couple of times over the last few weeks. She left a message at the college, and I meant to ring, but what with one thing and another — Grace has had chickenpox and I've been so busy . . . I just hadn't got round to it.'

And now I never would. That thought hung unspoken in the air.

Jim frowned and ran the flat of his hand over his head. His hair was fair and cut very short, not much more than stubble. I was struck again by the change in him. The lines on his face had deepened and he looked as if he wasn't getting much sleep. What on earth had happened to make him look like this? When I'd first met him I had found him so attractive. He had been one of those men who radiate sexual energy. And not just that: he really liked women. The combination is rarer than you might think.

He said, 'Maybe Dr Carwardine punched in the wrong number?'

'Well . . . maybe . . . '

'She was an old woman — maybe getting a bit confused?'

I gave a snort. 'Una confused? The last time I saw her, she was more on the ball than I was.'

'And when was that?'

'Oh, Lord, it must be, oh, several months. Maybe even as far back as September? October, perhaps. We ran into each other in the college.'

'I'll speak to her doctor.' Jim looked at his watch. 'I have to go. I'll need to speak to you again and I'll need a statement from you, Cassandra. Someone will be round later this afternoon. If anything else occurs to you, ring me on this number. Any time.' He handed me a card.

'I'm not in the office very much,' I said. 'You'd better have my mobile phone number. I'll keep it switched on.'

He wrote it down and we got to our feet.

There was something I had to ask. 'Can you tell me? Was it — I mean, did she — ?' I couldn't get it out.

He knew what I was asking. 'I can't say officially yet, but it looks as if she broke her neck. She would have been dead when she hit the floor. Wouldn't have known a thing.'

As we walked to the door, I said, 'Will you let me know — '

'If there are any developments? If I can.' Jim hesitated on the threshold. He put his hand on my arm.

'I'm sorry to have been the bearer of bad news. I'd like you to keep quiet about the phone call. And one more thing. Do you happen to know who her next of kin is?'

I shook my head. 'I'm sorry. I know there weren't any children. I don't know who that would be.'

When Jim had gone, the room seemed very empty. Although it was overheated and stuffy, I was shivering. I stood by the radiator and warmed my hands. I had letters and emails to answer and phone calls to make, but all that would have to wait. Already the nagging litany of 'if onlys' was beginning to go round and round in my head. If only I'd gone straight home instead of going absent-mindedly to the nursery, and if only I hadn't been stopped by the police, I might have arrived home in a more collected state of mind. Stephen wouldn't have been trying to cook the dinner and look after Grace at the same time and I would have picked up the phone when Una rang. She had wanted to speak to me and that chance had been lost forever. I'd let her down. I told myself that it wouldn't have made much difference if I had answered it earlier, but that wasn't really true. Maybe I could have alerted the police. From what Jim said, it didn't seem that they would have got there in time to save her life, but at least her body wouldn't have been lying there at the bottom of the stairs all night. Or they might have caught the killer. Of course there was no way I could have known how important that phone call was, but if only . . .

I tried to fix my attention on the scene outside. St Etheldreda's is one of the newer colleges, built in 1920 in doll's house Georgian, all red brick and white paint. In emulation of older and grander colleges like St John's and Trinity it was planned around a series of quadrangles or courts, as they're known in Cambridge, though that term doesn't really do justice to the huge open space that I was looking out on now. Today the shaved lawns and flagged pathways were covered in snow and in the centre the bare branches of an ancient copper beech, far older than the college, were outlined in white. The view from my window led back to Una, too, for the very last time I had seen her, she had been moving slowly across the court, leaning on her stick.

When I arrived at the college she was long retired from her post as Graduate Tutor, but she had still been a Fellow and came in several times a week.

I thought of the evening that had marked the beginning of our friendship. Una had a connection with one of the older Cambridge colleges; her late husband, Terence Carwardine, had been master there. She had invited me as her guest to a formal dinner. My memories of that evening were vivid: the Latin Grace rapidly intoned by an elderly don as wrinkled as a tortoise, the dining-room dark with mahogany panelling, candlelight glinting off the old college plate and the ordeal of finding myself seated next to the Master, whose field of expertise was the eighteenth-century novel.

I know a lot about the nineteenth-century novel — that's my specialism — but I hadn't read Smollett or Sterne for years. As I struggled through the first course, Una threw me glances of commiseration across the table. I can see her now: her big brown monkey eyes set in a net of wrinkles and her bobbed hair, very different from the corrugated perm of so many elderly women of her generation. As we started on the roast duck I was driven to admit that as an undergraduate I had regarded *The Expedition Of Humphrey Clinker* as the dullest novel I had ever read and I had never had reason to revise that opinion. The Master sniffed and turned to his neighbour.

As we left the dining-room for coffee and port and Madeira in the Senior Common Room, Una appeared at my side.

'Do forgive me, my dear,' she murmured. 'I didn't mean to let you in for that. I do so agree with you — a terrible old bore.'

'Smollett?'

She cawed with laughter. 'The Master. They were made for one another. Though possibly, I am being a little hard on Smollett there. Not a favourite of mine, but a fine writer all the same.'

'I was a bit naughty,' I admitted. 'I got fed up with being interrogated as though I was a student at a viva.'

'Sadly it is often the case that great learning doesn't go hand in hand with even tolerably good manners. Never mind. I invited you tonight so that I could get to know you better and I intend to monopolize you for a while.'

She put her hand on my arm. That hand with its carefully tended nails painted red and the big antique rings — one I remember was composed of a huge cluster of little garnets so that it looked like a luscious fruit — that hand was all of a piece with the rest of her: the distinctive perfume, the striking clothes she wore of velvet and chiffon in rich dark colours such as claret and midnight blue. She must have been beautiful in a *jolie laide* sort of way as a young woman and she was still glamorous.

After that evening Una took me under her wing. No one knew more about nineteenth century literature than she did. She and her husband had amassed a huge collection. It contained some choice things — I remembered an evening looking at their Henry James first editions — but it wasn't just the quality of some of the items, it was the quantity, too. When I'd first visited Una I'd been staggered. I've got a lot of books — Stephen says that one day we'll have to move out of the Old Granary and give it over entirely to my library — but it's nothing compared to the Carwardine collection. It covered every spare inch of the huge Victorian house in Brooklands Avenue. Una once told me that the floors had been reinforced to take the weight of the books.

For a while we saw a lot of each other and then gradually it grew less as I struggled to combine teaching, research and administration in my academic career. I met Stephen. I took over as head of department. Then came the birth of my daughter. My life was full to overflowing. When I did see Una we got on as well as ever, but the gaps between our meeting grew longer.

There was a knock on the door. I looked up to see Merfyn putting his head round the door. At the sight of his familiar friendly face, I burst into tears.

★ ★ ★

'What you need is a good strong cup of tea,' Merfyn said.

He plugged in the kettle. I keep tea-bags and so on in my office for times when I work late or don't feel like going to the Senior Common Room. Merfyn sat down opposite me, stretched out a pair of long legs and crossed them at the ankle. In his elderly tweed suit, he managed to look both formal and scruffy at the same time.

We'd been friends for a long time. He's about ten years older than me. As head of department I'm technically his boss, but he still feels to me like one of the older generation. He and his wife Celia married young and have four grown-up daughters. When I first met him he was a glamorous young lecturer in a cape and fedora and I was a shy research student. Now our roles had been reversed. He was still a lecturer, but I'd overtaken him to become head of department. Merfyn was too big to let that bother him and anyway he had never wanted to be in charge. It was sheer good nature that had prompted him to stand in for me while I was on study leave.

'It's shocking, quite shocking. It comes to something when you're not safe in your own home,' he said. 'I suppose someone looked at that huge house and thought it must contain valuable things. Do you want ordinary tea or herb tea?'

'Ordinary, please. It did contain valuable things, didn't it? I mean all those books.'

'The best private collection of nineteenth and early twentieth-century literature in the country is hardly likely to attract your bog-standard burglar, is it? Did that police-man say if anything had been taken?' He put a tea-bag in the little earthenware teapot and poured hot water in.

'I didn't think to ask. I just assumed that whoever it was got the hell out of there when they realized that they'd killed Una.'

46

'They can't have meant that to happen,' he agreed. He leaned forward to pour out my tea. 'Is this strong enough for you? Yes? Good. Celia and I used to see a lot of Una, but somehow that dropped off a bit after she retired. I regret that now.'

'You and me both.'

'It's the end of an era. Una was real old Cambridge and the last of that generation. She and Terence came here in the fifties. They'd been here even longer than I have.' Merfyn grinned. He had come to Cambridge from the Welsh valleys on a scholarship thirty years ago and had never left. 'Did you ever meet Terence?'

He poured out a cup of hot water and put a sachet of lemon verbena in it.

'Not to talk to,' I admitted. I wrapped my hands round my cup.

I had seen Terence Carwardine at one or two conferences when he was nearing retirement and I was a young postgraduate. He had written a ground-breaking book of literary criticism in the sixties and was far too eminent for me to think of speaking to him. I remembered a large man, physically imposing, with a high domed forehead and craggy features. He had died about ten years ago.

'Between you and me, I suspect she was the better scholar,' Merfyn said. 'Wouldn't be the first promising academic career stymied by lack of opportunity.'

'I sometimes wondered about that.'

'Put it down to a combination of bad timing and being a woman. All that post-war 'back to the home' stuff. It was difficult for a woman, especially a married woman, to get a decent academic job in the forties and fifties. But make no mistake about it, she was bright, very bright.' Merfyn waggled the tea-bag around in his cup. 'Was she at Bletchley during the war? I rather think she was. She was wasted here, hanging about on the fringes of academic life — a bit of supervising, a bit of examining — all those part-time, badly paid jobs that Cambridge specializes in. They invariably get dumped on women or postgraduate students.' He fished out the tea-bag and slopped it into the saucer.

'And they're expected to be grateful for it at that,' I said. 'But she did produce some very good work of her own. That book on Sidney's sonnet sequence, for instance.'

Merfyn leaned back in his chair. 'To my mind she never quite got the credit she deserved. And I do wonder if she didn't play a much bigger role in Terence's work than either of them admitted.' Merfyn sighed and the cup rocked in his hand. The bag in the saucer tilted sideways and deposited a few drops on his trousers. 'She certainly played a big part in building up that collection of books. When she started, hardly anyone was thinking of collecting Victorian sensation fiction, Mrs Braddon, Mrs Henry Wood, all that crew. She picked up some real gems for virtually nothing.'

'And now they're back in fashion again. The better ones anyway.'

'And even the bad ones can be fascinating in their own way.'

The tea and the cosy chat about books were having the soothing effect that I guessed Merfyn had intended.

'Second-hand book shops couldn't shift them for love nor money at one time,' he went on. 'A lot of those Victorian three-deckers were sent to be pulped. And really you can hardly wonder. Have you ever tried reading anything by G. R. J. James?'

'No, but I bet Una had. She told me that she'd read — or least skimmed through — every one of those books.' In my mind's eye, I saw them, shelf after shelf, covering virtually every wall from the hall up to the attics. In some rooms there were free-standing book-cases as well. Thousands upon thousands of books . . .

'I wonder what will happen to them all now.'

Merfyn looked surprised. 'You mean you don't know?'

'Know what?'

'I thought it was common knowledge. Everything's going to the Lit and Phil. That's what Una told me. There's family money, I'm pretty sure. And then there's the house. You know how prices have shot up lately, especially in central Cambridge. It must be worth upwards of half a million now.'

4

Great Expectations

'I wish we'd cried off,' I whispered.

'It was too late by the time we remembered and that's that.' Stephen put his finger on the doorbell and pressed it firmly.

It was the weekend after Jim had broken the news of Una's death and we were standing at the front door of Giles's little Georgian terrace-house in Lensfield Road.

'At least it'll be a meal neither of us have had to cook,' Stephen added. He stamped his feet and thrust his hands deeper into his pocket. 'And didn't you say he has a reputation for being a bit of a gourmet?'

'I don't want to have to talk about Una.' I had a hollow feeling every time I thought about what had happened.

'Maybe it won't come up.'

'It's bound to.'

'At least Giles doesn't know about the phone call. In fact, he probably doesn't even know yet that it was murder.'

The article in the *Cambridge Evening News*

had said only that Una had died after a fall at her home.

We fell silent as we heard footsteps approaching. The door was flung open. Warmth and light poured out.

'Come in, come in,' Giles cried.

He ushered us in, talking all the while. 'Cassandra, let me help you off with that coat. Stephen, I am so pleased to meet you at last. Nice of you to turn out on such a filthy night.'

We were borne though the hall on a tide of chat and *bonhomie* and fetched up in the drawing-room. It took me a moment to realize what was unusual about it. There was no electric light. The room was lit by dozens of candles: they were in wall sconces, in candelabra and most impressive off all, about twenty of them were arranged in a glittering chandelier hanging in the centre of the room.

'How lovely,' I said.

Giles beamed. 'I do have electric light in the kitchen and in one or two other rooms, but in here I do without it altogether.'

He was wearing a brocade waistcoat and a bow tie. I was glad I'd made an effort and put on my red and black silk trousers.

A woman was slowly getting up from a *chaise-longue* at the far end of the room. Giles hurried forward, 'No, no, don't get up,

52

Eileen. She's been ill,' he explained. He spoke in a proprietorial way that intrigued me.

'Went into hospital to have kidney stones removed and got one of those superbugs. Such a bore,' Eileen said as she came forward. The candlelight softened the outline of a sharp nose and gave a lustre to large, exophthalmic eyes.

'Should you be on your feet, Eileen?' Giles was hovering anxiously at her elbow.

'Don't fuss, Giles, I'm perfectly all right.' Eileen smiled at me and held out her hand.

'Eileen, this is Cassandra, but you must surely know one another — '

Her hand was cool and firm in mine. I realized that I had met her before.

'Of course, the second-hand book shop,' I said.

'Scarcely that,' Giles said. There was a hint of reproof in his voice.

Eileen Burnham owned Burnham Books in the part of Cambridge known as New Town, just north of the Botanic Gardens, and only a stone's throw from Giles's house. It was open only a couple of mornings a week and it was more like a private house than a shop. It specialized in first editions. I'd been in there once or twice, but most of the stock was out of my price range. I'm not really a collector, anyway: I have one or two nice things, but more by accident than design. I buy my books for reading. My eyes had adjusted to the light now. Business must be booming, I thought, as I took in Eileen's camel wrap-around skirt, plain white shirt, and long chocolate brown cashmere cardigan. That kind of simplicity and elegance didn't come cheap. And neither did Eileen's haircut. Her gleaming helmet of bobbed hair swung as she laughed.

'Second-hand will do just fine,' she said. 'Though it's true that we're not talking piles of dog-eared paperbacks. I like my books to have had just one careful owner.'

She reminded me of someone, but I couldn't think who.

'We see a lot of Cassandra at the Institute,' said Giles. 'She's working on a book on sisters in Victorian fiction.'

'How fascinating. *Little Women? What Katy Did?* Or maybe you're not including American novels?'

'I am when they were popular with a British readership.'

'And those marvellous family sagas by Charlotte M. Yonge?' Eileen said. *'The Daisy Chain? The Pillars of the House?* I've always adored them. They're crammed with sisters.'

Giles beamed. 'I knew you two would have lots in common. I'll get some drinks.'

As Eileen and I chatted, and Giles distributed gin and tonics, I was able to take in more of my surroundings. The walls were painted pea-soup green and the sofa and chairs were upholstered in an elegant regency stripe. Jane Austen would have felt at home there. The room was immaculate and as far as I could see it contained nothing that had been made later than 1900, not so much as a paperback book or a newspaper, let alone a television or a stereo. I wondered how Giles could afford a house and furniture like this on his librarian's salary.

Giles and Stephen were deep in conversation. Occasionally a few words drifted over. 'Skating over the fens . . . ' 'nothing like it since the 1940s'. They had fallen back on the weather and for once it was well worth talking about. After the snowfall on the night Una had died, there had been another partial thaw followed by one of the hardest frosts of the winter. Luckily we had an arrangement with a friendly local farmer, who had cleared the snow from the track that led from the Old Granary to the main road. If it hadn't been for that, Stephen and I would never have made it into Cambridge that evening.

My eye was caught by a glass dome, the kind that the Victorians used to put over wax flowers. It was covering a large leather object on a table on the far side of the room. I was about to ask Eileen what it was when Giles announced that dinner was ready and led us into a little dining-room.

It was as we were eating smoked salmon — definitely wild, not farmed, accompanied by Pouilly Fumé — that the moment I had dreaded arrived.

'Terrible news this, about Una.' Giles squeezed his slice of lemon over his smoked salmon. 'Devastating really.'

'I suppose it's always a danger with old people living alone, a fall like that,' Eileen said. 'It happened in the middle of the night, didn't it? Probably got up to go to the loo and was still half-asleep.'

'I can't believe I'm not going to see her again,' Giles said, shaking his head.

'Did you know her well?' Stephen asked.

'She used to be in and out of the Institute all the time until her arthritis got too much for her. There's a team of ladies from NADFAS — that's the National Association for the Decorative and Fine Arts — who come in to repair the books. She was in charge of them. And then there's the Carwardine collection, you know it's coming to the Institute in memory of her husband? Una was letting us catalogue it in advance. I used to pop round once a week or so. You know, I asked her last time I was round there, or maybe it was the time before, I said, 'Are you sure it's wise living here in this great big house all alone?'' Giles shook his head.

'And what did she say?' Stephen asked.

'Told me to mind my own business. Said that she had no intention of living anywhere else and that when she did leave, it would be feet first.'

I put my fork down. Silence settled over the room. Under the table, Stephen groped for my hand and grasped it.

'Surely there won't be room for all those books in the Institute,' Stephen said. 'What are you going to do with them?'

I gave his hand a squeeze, grateful for this effort to move the conversation on.

'Well. I don't know if I should . . . ' Giles hesitated. He took a swig of wine. 'I don't suppose there's any harm in telling you, though we won't be making it public yet, but Una's also left the Institute a substantial legacy. I'm hoping there will be enough to allow us to take back the premises on St Andrew's Street.' He couldn't conceal the glint in his eye. I felt a surge of dislike. 'We need people to know that we are there. That won't happen while we're stuck in that cul-de-sac, no one goes past unless they're heading for the back entrance to Downing College. There's no footfall.'

'Footfall?' Stephen said.

'It's a term booksellers use,' Eileen said. 'Means passing trade.'

'But do we need passing trade?' I asked.

'I really want to raise the profile of the Institute, pull people in for little exhibitions and so on, increase the membership.' Giles leaned forward eagerly. 'We could have internet access, perhaps even a little café, where the periodical room is now.'

'It's not really the time to be thinking about all that, is it?' Eileen said and I was grateful to her.

That stopped Giles in his tracks. 'Oh, I know,' said he, getting up to clear the plates away. 'It's awful, coming into the legacy in this way. On the other hand it would be sheer hypocrisy to pretend that it isn't going to open up some very exciting possibilities.'

He disappeared into the kitchen.

There was a little silence and then Eileen said, 'I do love the way Giles has done this up.' She waved her hand, taking in the gleaming mahogany table, the silver candlesticks. The dark red walls were scarcely visible for prints framed in bird's-eye maple.

'What are those?' Stephen asked, pointing to some large pictures in primary colours thronged with rearing horses and struggling figures.

'Epinal prints of the Napoleonic wars. Jolly, aren't they? That's Napoleon marching on Moscow and the other one . . . ' She leaned back in her seat for a better look. 'Yes, that's the campaign in Egypt.'

'And those silhouettes?'

'Wellington's lieutenants in the Peninsular War,' said Eileen. 'Dear Giles! If he could be magically transported back to 1815 I feel sure he'd jump at the chance. Don't you think he'd look wonderful in a frock-coat and a top hat?'

I wondered again if they were an item. It was hard to be sure.

'Taking my name in vain?' Giles said, coming in with a casserole dish. His flushed face and the effort of concentration with which he put it on the table made me wonder how much gin he'd put away before Stephen and I arrived. Maybe he'd been knocking it back in the kitchen, too.

With the beef casserole came a couple of bottles of claret. By the end of the second course everyone was squiffy — except for me, I noted dourly. I'd promised Stephen that I would drive.

'Phew,' Stephen said, shaking his head to another helping. 'That was very good, but really . . . '

'Shall we have a little break before the next

course?' Giles asked.

'What is it?'

'Sussex pond pudding. Lots of lemon and suet.'

'A pause would be in order,' Stephen agreed.

'Stephen. You are a good chap,' Giles said, enunciating every word with care, 'and there's something I'd like to show you.' He levered himself up with his hands on the table and got to his feet. 'Follow me everyone.'

Eileen rolled her eyes at me, but she didn't say anything as she got up from the table.

Giles took one of the candlesticks off the table and handed it to Eileen. 'If you could follow at the rear?'

He picked up a second candlestick. We went in single file up the narrow stairs. The flickering light from the candle made our shadows flare and billow on the walls. The sinister effect was dissipated when Giles reached the landing and switched on an electric light. We stood around blinking in the sudden harsh light. Giles blew out the candle and set the candlestick down on the floor. Standing on tiptoe he grasped at a handle in the ceiling. He pulled down a set of folding stairs that led up to a dark cavity above us.

'Better let me go up first,' Giles said. 'I know where the lights are.'

Stephen followed him. I went up next with Eileen behind me. Stephen emerged into the attic and I heard him say 'wow'. As I clambered through the trapdoor, I saw that really no other response was possible. The space covered the whole area of the house. There were no windows, but the floor and the sloping walls of the roof were painted a brilliant white. The space was lit by green-shaded lights that were let down from the ceiling over four large oblong tables. They were covered by landscapes in miniature, little worlds with trees and rivers, the odd farmhouse or barn, thronged with tiny figures.

Giles said, 'I build them up from the contours of the most detailed maps I can find and then I mould them with green and brown Plasticine.' His face shone with enthusiasm.

'Wow,' Stephen said again. He was clearly fascinated.

Giles beamed. He gestured to each table in turn. 'This is the battle of Salamanca. This is Talavera. Those were both during the Peninsular Wars. And that's the Battle of Assaye during the Indian campaign. Wellington probably fought hand-to-hand there.'

'Where do you get the soldiers from?' Stephen asked.

'They come as blanks and I paint them myself.'

'Every sequin hand sewn,' murmured Eileen, who was standing behind me.

It didn't sound as though she had whiled away the long, winter evenings helping Giles to paint toy soldiers. Something sardonic in her tone made me revise my earlier idea about her and Giles.

'And what's this one here?' Stephen asked, pointing to the remaining table.

'This is the one I'm working on now. The big one.'

'You mean . . . ?'

Giles nodded. 'The Battle of Waterloo.'

We stood gazing down at the little figures frozen in their wheeling ranks.

I said, ' 'There was a sound of revelry by night — ' '

Giles finished the quotation: ' 'And Belgium's capital had gathered then, Her beauty and her chivalry, And bright the lamps that shone o'er fair women and brave men.' Byron,' he explained, as Stephen gave him a look of enquiry, 'writing about the Duchess of Richmond's ball on the eve of battle.'

'And Thackeray wrote about its aftermath in *Vanity Fair*,' I said. 'It's possibly the most chilling chapter end in the whole of nineteenth-century fiction. 'Darkness came down on the field and city: and Amelia was praying for George, who was lying on his face, dead, with a bullet through his heart.''

'And there's Stendhal, too, isn't there?' Eileen said. 'Which novel is it?'

'*The Charterhouse of Parma*,' I said. 'The hero is so confused by the smoke and the noise and people running backwards and forwards that he doesn't even realize he's been in the Battle of Waterloo until it's all over.'

Stephen looked up from perusing the table. 'Cass can't help but see everything in literary terms.' It was one of those statements that seems good humoured, but isn't quite. I frowned at him.

Giles said, 'This was one of those great historical events that really caught the literary imagination. And Stendhal's description is just brilliant. That's what real-life battles are like.'

Stephen leaned over the table and his shoulder nudged one of the lights. For a few moments the little figures seemed to tremble and dance in the shifting light.

I gave a little shiver and hairs stood up on my arms.

'Are you OK?' Eileen asked.

'Someone walked over my grave,' I said, hugging myself and rubbing my arms.

Stephen was still absorbed in the battle-scene. 'How do you decide which part to re-enact?' he asked.

'Oh, no,' Giles said. 'I don't re-enact: I reconstruct. You see, it could have worked out quite differently — even Wellington admitted that the Battle of Waterloo was a near-run thing — and that's what I'm interested in.' He leaned over the table. 'Look here. See this farm house? On that side the French cavalry launch a massive attack. On the other the Royal Scots Greys charge forward with the Highlanders hanging on to their stirrups. Conditions were terrible. Big fields of rye-grass and mud everywhere. If Blucher and the Prussian army hadn't arrived in the nick of time, who knows?'

Stephen was intrigued. 'You mean the French might have won the Battle of Waterloo? The whole history of Europe would have been different.'

Giles nodded. 'Exactly so.'

'There's something I don't understand,' Stephen said. 'That's Napoleon over there, isn't it?' He leaned forward and put his finger on one of the little figures.

'That's right,' Giles said.

'So where's Wellington? I can't see him anywhere.'

No one spoke. The silence stretched out. Even Eileen, who had drifted away to one of the other tables, became aware of it, and turned her head.

Giles was blushing.

'Oh, ah, well . . . ' he said. 'Actually, he's here.' He dug about in his trouser pocket and brought out a little figure. He held it up so that we could see a scarlet tunic, a black cocked hat and white pantaloons tucked into boots. I couldn't understand why he was embarrassed.

'I had him on my desk at work, and I hadn't got round to putting him back.'

'He's Giles's mascot!' Eileen said.

Giles grinned. 'I suppose that's it, really. He cheers me up. Gives me moral support on difficult days.'

'I'm surprised that he hasn't been used as a role model for one of those leadership and management courses.' Stephen said. I could see that he was having difficulty in keeping a straight face. So was I.

'Giles is absolutely potty about the Iron Duke,' Eileen said. 'You'll never guess what he's got downstairs. Under a big glass dome.'

'That leather thing? I wondered about that,' I said.

'It's the ultimate piece of Wellingtonian memorabilia. Giles is very proud of it — acquired it at an auction a few weeks ago.'

'It's not — !'

'Yes. It's a Wellington boot! Or rather, it's a boot that once belonged to Wellington. I suppose it's much the same thing.' She giggled.

I knew now who she reminded me of. It was Una. I hadn't made the connection because Una was short with a suggestion of dumpiness, while Eileen was tall with a willowy figure. But they had the same kind of piquant, gamine looks and the same teasing manner that hovered on the edge of malice.

Deep in my handbag, my mobile phone began to ring. It had the usual effect of striking dumb everyone who was present and all eyes were on me as I delved in my bag. I would have switched it off for the evening if it hadn't been for the possibility that Jim might want to contact me. And somehow I felt certain that this was Jim. It seemed to take forever, but at last the phone was in my hand. I unfolded it and put it to my ear.

'Jim Ferguson here. I'm at Dr Carwardine's house. Did she ever show you the books in her bedroom.'

'Yes. Just hang on a moment, will you?' I glanced at the others They were still staring at me. 'I'm terribly sorry. I really have to take this call.'

Giles didn't look pleased, but he nodded and turned back to the Battle of Waterloo. Stephen joined him. Eileen took a step or two away and made a show of examining one of the other battle-scenes.

I turned my back and lowered my voice.

'Do you mean the Henry James first editions?'

'Those are the ones. Can you remember what she had?'

'I think so.'

'Then I need you over here right away. I'll send a car for you.'

'I'm not at home.' I smelt cigarette smoke. I glanced round. Eileen had lit up.

'Where are you?' Jim asked.

'Lensfield Road.'

'Even better.'

I was about to say, 'But I'm at a dinner party.' I realized just in time how fatuous that sounded and closed my mouth.

As if I had in fact spoken, Jim said, 'I'm sorry to disturb your evening, but it's important. Give me the number of the house and my sergeant will be there in five minutes.'

★ ★ ★

A jagged row of gables and clusters of tall chimneys were outlined against a sky glittering with stars. Light from a solitary street lamp filtered through the branches of the trees that shielded the house from the road. I hadn't remembered quite how isolated

Green Gables is. It stands alone near the west end of Brooklands Avenue. On one side, the Botanic Gardens curled round to meet the road in a solid phalanx of dense evergreens. On the other side is the Bowling Green with its dark, squat clubhouse and its big, empty car-park. During the day, and especially during the rush hour, there's a lot of traffic, but at ten o'clock at night the police car was the only one in the broad tree-lined street.

There were butterflies in my stomach as I got out of the car. I'd decided there was no point in Stephen coming — the sergeant had told him that he wouldn't be allowed into the crime-scene — and I regretted now that I hadn't asked him to come and wait in the car.

At first I didn't see Jim. Then he emerged from the porch of the house and made his way towards me, moving gingerly on the icy path.

'Bloody brass monkeys,' he grumbled. 'Thanks for coming, Cassandra.'

He had two flat packets under his arm. I couldn't make out what was in them. They looked like new shirts in their cellophane wrappings.

'What's this all about?' I asked.

'Yesterday I asked Una's cleaner to look round and see if there was anything missing. At first she said not. Then earlier this evening, she rang to say that she had been thinking about it. And the more she'd thought about it, the more she thought that something wasn't right.'

The temperature was still dropping and already my gloved fingers were numb. I was shivering in my thin silk trousers. Jim wasn't even wearing an overcoat, just a leather jacket, but he showed no sign of feeling the cold.

'The bookcase with the Henry James first editions,' he continued. 'She hadn't looked closely at it for a while, but she thinks now that it's not how she remembered it. We'll both have to wear one of these.'

He handed me one of the packets. He ripped the other one open with his teeth and shook out the garment inside. It was a white paper boiler suit. I fumbled with my own packet. He took the packet from me and tore that one open with his teeth, too. He pulled out the suit and tossed it over to me.

'You can put it on over your coat.'

Jim stepped into the suit and shrugged it onto his shoulders. I was still hopping around trying to get my foot in.

'If there's something missing, I need to know right away,' he said. 'That's why I had to drag you away from your friends.' He clasped my arm above the elbow to steady me.

'Good job I decided not to wear my long velvet skirt,' I joked nervously.

He smiled. 'You'd be surprised what people do turn up wearing at the scene of a crime. Had a pathologist turn up in a ball-gown once. Luckily she always keeps a pair of overalls in the boot of her car.'

I knew he was trying to make me feel less nervous and I liked him for it.

'You'll need these too,' he said, handing me a pair of latex gloves.

The headlights of a passing car swept over the house and illuminated us for a moment, making us squint in the glare. In the white paper suit Jim looked as bulky and formless as an astronaut.

We turned towards the house. Even in daylight it was, as Una used frankly to admit, one of the ugliest in Cambridge. The proportions were so odd that you felt like squinting to get it back into true. The style was mostly High Victorian Gothic, but there was the occasional classical touch, a rounded arch here and a pilaster there. The bricks were an unpleasant shade of grey that went badly with the stone quoins that ran like crude stitchwork around the windows and down the corners of the house. The place was bad enough in daylight, but with half the facade in darkness and the rest tinted a sickly orange by the sodium light, it was grotesque.

The Gothic porch had seats on either side and the door was made of oak, strapped and studded with ironwork. Jim must have unlocked the door before I arrived. He pushed it open. A wave of intensely cold, musty air rolled out like an exhalation from the house. It was like going into a church. I drew back. Jim put a hand on my shoulder as if to reassure me. He reached past me to switch on a light and we stepped inside.

'Tell me if anything strikes you as different or strange,' Jim said.

The cavernous double-storey hall went deep into the house. My eyes were drawn immediately to the oak staircase that runs up to a first floor landing and gallery. It was at the bottom of this that Una's body had been found. The way up was barred by orange tape with 'crime scene' printed on it in black. I looked away. Everything else was as I remembered it. Every available piece of wall space was covered with bookshelves, packed solid with books bound in dark colours. The only other furniture was a big, dusty, mahogany table strewn with circulars about double-glazing and car insurance. In the centre was a glass vase of wilting Michaelmas daisies in brackish water. Panelled doors opened off on either side to reception rooms.

I was shivering and it wasn't just from the cold, though in truth the place was as chilly as a mausoleum with a dampness that struck to my bones.

'It's colder in here than it is outside,' I said. 'The heating must have been turned off. The damp — it could damage the books.'

Jim frowned. 'I'll have something done about it. Come on, we'll go up the back way.'

The house was large enough and grand enough to have two staircases, the one for the family and a humbler one for the servants.

We walked across the hall, our footsteps loud on the black-and-white tiles and our breath rising in clouds. My mouth felt dry. I tried not to look up at the landing, but my eyes kept straying in that direction. It was a long way to fall.

'That old lady living here all alone,' Jim said. 'It doesn't seem right, when she could hardly get about.'

When I first met Una I, too, had wondered about that. Una's arthritis made it difficult for her to get upstairs. A stair-lift had been installed, but it only went up to the first floor. There were parts of the huge, rambling house she never visited. But I had soon understood why she couldn't leave. The books meant everything to her. Una was in effect living in a library, and hadn't I always wanted to do that myself?

We made our way up to the first-floor landing. Una's bedroom door had crime scene tape stuck across it. Jim peeled it off and pushed the door open.

'Don't touch anything,' he warned me. 'It's all just as it was.'

I stepped over the threshold and looked around. It was a big room, at the back of the house. The curtains were drawn but I knew it looked out onto a garden dense with shrubs with the Botanic Garden beyond. On the day that Una had brought me in here to show me her Henry James first editions, I'd been struck by the old-fashioned appearance of the room. It must have been furnished in the early days of her marriage, sometime around 1950. The wooden bed-heads, the light oak bedside tables were all of their time: nothing had been replaced.

The bed looked as if someone had just got out of it, the sheets, blankets and a quilt pushed roughly aside. On the bedside table a book was open lying with its spine uppermost and pages splayed. Una hated books to be treated like that. Nothing could have been more eloquent of shock and disruption. I moved closer to see what it was: *The Father Brown Stories* by G. K. Chesterton.

My heart was beating fast and my mouth was dry. The strange sounds on the other end of the telephone that night — the scuffling and the crying out — seemed to echo in my head. I looked around for the phone expecting to see it lying on the floor somewhere.

'Where is it?' I said.

Jim didn't need to ask what I meant. 'The phone's with forensics.'

He was standing close beside me and I could smell something, soap or aftershave, but slightly antiseptic, and elusively familiar.

'Are you all right?' he said gently.

I nodded. 'I think so. Let's do it.'

Jim gestured towards a glass-fronted bookcase. 'Those are the books. The key's in the lock, but the cleaner didn't think there was anything unusual about that.'

'I'll need to take them out.'

'Of course. Let me open it for you.' He turned the key with his fingers on the shaft and the door swung open.

I reached in for a copy of *The Portrait of a Lady*. As soon as I saw the worn binding, I knew something was wrong. The copy Una had shown me had been in pristine condition. My fingers were numb with cold, but I managed to fumble the book open and turned back the title page. The paper was thin and flimsy.

'This isn't a first edition,' I said. '*Portrait of a Lady* was first published in 1878. This edition is 1900.'

'So it's worth — what?'

'Nothing.' I saw the look of surprise on his face. 'Maybe a few quid, no more. It's what booksellers call a good reading copy, but it's not worth much.'

'This isn't the book you saw on the previous occasion?'

'Definitely not. I could swear to that.'

'You'll probably have to.'

He took the book from me and placed it carefully back on the shelf. 'What about this one?' he asked. He handed me *The Spoils of Poynton*. I could tell just by looking at the cover, but I looked inside to be absolutely sure.

'That's not a first edition either.'

Fifteen minutes later we hadn't found a single first edition. Some of the books had simply disappeared. I remembered a collection of short stories containing an inscription from Henry James to Edith Wharton. That had gone, and so had a few others, but most of the books that Una had shown me had been replaced by others worth a fraction of their value.

Jim said, 'What sort of money are we talking about here? What were those books worth?'

I shook my head. 'I couldn't say exactly.'

He waved a hand. 'Aren't you supposed to be an expert?'

'It's their contents that I'm interested in, not their market value. You'll need to ask a dealer. Actually I had dinner tonight with someone who could probably help: Eileen Burnham, she's got a second-hand book shop in New Town. But I doubt if you're looking at more than a few thousand pounds. I wouldn't have thought that was worth killing for.'

'But someone else might and we already know it wasn't you.' He noticed my look of surprise. 'I checked and you were indeed stopped by the traffic police at 7.30 just outside Stretham.'

'Every cloud has a silver lining,' I said dryly.

But Jim wasn't listening. He was gazing at me without seeing me.

'What — ' I began.

He lifted up a hand. 'Wait.'

We stood there in silence. I was conscious of the dark house stretching out all around us, the attics and servants' rooms above, the bedrooms to either side, the reception rooms below and the cold, silent kitchen, and beyond that the stables, which Una and Terence had converted into rooms to house yet more books.

'I thought I heard something,' he said, 'but it must just be the house settling.' He put a hand on my shoulder to steer me towards the door. 'Come on, let's get out of here before we freeze to death.'

I waited by the balustrade and watched Jim put the tape back on the door. Stephen had told me that he had heard on the grapevine that there had been some tragedy in Jim's domestic life, something to do with a baby that went wrong. It must be something serious to change a man like that. I didn't know him well enough to ask. He caught me gazing at him. I blushed and looked quickly away.

Along the landing, the stair-lift was parked at the top of the stairs where Una had alighted from it that last evening. Somehow that said more to me about the finality of death than anything I had seen so far.

Jim joined me. He followed the direction of my gaze. 'It's bad,' he said, 'very bad.'

'You don't get used to it? Dealing with awful things, I mean?'

'Never.' He shook his head. 'Not this kind of thing, anyway. You never get used to it.' As he spoke I saw a flash of the intense energy that had so impressed me when I'd first met him. So it hadn't gone altogether.

'What do you think happened?' I asked,

wanting to know, and yet at the same time, not wanting to know.

'I think he dragged her out of the bedroom and threw her down the stairs. Tried to set it up as an accident.'

I put a hand out to the balustrade. Black spots floated up before my eyes and I felt hot. I closed my eyes.

'Cass?'

I felt the warm weight of Jim's hands on my arms. When I opened my eyes, he was looking into my face.

'I'm sorry,' he said. 'You were very fond of her, weren't you?'

'You said, '*he* threw her down the stairs.''

Jim was staring into my face as though something was puzzling him. 'He? Just a manner of speaking. Though, statistically speaking . . . ' his voice trailed off.

'Yes?'

'You're shivering.'

His hands were still on my shoulders. I had never noticed before what a very pale blue his eyes were. And his lips were unusually well defined for a man. They were parted as though he was about to say something else.

The next moment there was a noise above our heads, a sharp crack as if someone had stood on a creaking board, and the sound had somehow been amplified. The hairs on my arms stood up.

Jim released me. 'What the fuck?'

There was another sound, this time softer, and then another. There was something stealthy about it as if someone were moving quietly around, pausing here and there to touch an object or examine a book.

'There's someone up there!' I said.

Jim frowned and shook his head. 'Can't be. The place is secure.'

'A cat?' I said.

'You stay here. I'll go and look.'

A staircase at the far end of the landing led up to the top floor. Jim disappeared up it, his feet clattering on bare boards. I heard his footsteps over my head as he went from room to room.

After a few minutes I heard his feet on the stairs again. He came towards me, shaking his head.

'No one up there. These changes in temperature make the boards contract and expand. That's all it was.'

I wasn't entirely convinced and I didn't think he was either.

'Come on,' Jim said, without meeting my eye, 'we'd better get you back to that dinner party.'

5

The Dead Secret

That night I dreamed that I was skating across the frozen Fens. I felt the cold on my face. The rhythmic swaying was exhilarating. The ice stretched out as far as the eye could see and in the distance small figures swooped and circled like people in a picture by Breughel. I became aware of a dark figure, a man drawing level with me. He fell into step with me and put his arm around my waist. I reached over to grasp his other hand. We glided along, hip to hip, our hands clasped, in complete accord, moving together across the ice like birds in flight. My companion began to skate faster, we were picking up speed, leaning together into the wind. I felt the first prickling of fear and I was suddenly very cold. Anxious to see who my companion was, I turned my head. The movement was enough to knock us off balance, we went careering across the ice, my companion lost his grip on me, his hand slipped out of mine and I went spinning off into darkness.

I woke up gasping. Gradually my surroundings reasserted themselves. I was lying in bed with Stephen and no wonder I was cold. He had rolled over to the far side of the bed and had taken the duvet with him. When I hauled the duvet back across the bed, Stephen groaned and turned onto his back, but he didn't wake up.

I was wide awake now. The red numbers on the digital clock glowed in the dark. Ten to six. The alarm would go off at seven, and I knew there was not much chance of getting to sleep again. I am a poor sleeper at the best of times and just at the moment I had plenty to keep me awake. I knew that Jim had been my dream companion. It had been his arm round my waist, his hand clasping mine. And what had that been about when we were standing on the landing in Una's house? Lying there in the dark I felt again the pressure of Jim's hands on my arms. Had he really been about to kiss me and had I really been about to let him? The idea was absurd: he was a busy police officer in the middle of a murder investigation and I was a middle-aged married woman whose dear friend had just died. I was letting my imagination run away with me. The situation was enough to make anyone feel a little unhinged, I told myself. The fact that Jim was investigating the death of the woman that I was grieving over was part of his attraction. Nothing sharpens up the libido like the proximity of death and a heightened awareness of one's mortality.

We had hardly exchanged a word after Jim had come down from the attic. He had asked me not to say anything to anyone about the missing first editions, then he thanked me for coming, and his sergeant returned me to Giles's house in Lensfield Road. I hadn't had the presence of mind to ask him what he thought had happened to the books. I pondered that now. It would be a rare burglar that brought along replacements for the things he was going to nick. It looked as if the books had been taken over a period of time. It wouldn't be hard for a thief to dispose of them. There was no shortage of second-hand book dealers in Cambridge, Eileen among them, and no doubt the police would be visiting them all. But wouldn't Una have noticed that her precious books had been stolen and inferior copies left in their place? Just what had been going on at Green Gables?

There was a scuffling sound from the next room followed by a soft thud. I knew what that was: Grace's favourite toy had been thrown out of her cot as the advance guard. Henry was a small hand-knitted octopus that my mother had bought at a charity sale. His body, stuffed with old tights, was an interesting shade of eau-de-Nil. He had a red woollen mouth, Medusa hair made from bits of curly turquoise wool and eight legs that I kept having to sew back on. Grace didn't go anywhere without him. There was a rattling of cot bars as Grace hoisted herself over the edge, a pause while she hunted for Henry, a pattering of feet on bare floorboards and then a warm, compact little body was burrowing under the duvet and snuggling up to me.

Five minutes later we were both asleep.

★ ★ ★

After I'd dropped Grace off at her nursery, I drove to St Etheldreda's. I'd been so upset when Jim broke the news of Una's death to me that I hadn't dealt with any of my paperwork; I hadn't listened to my voice mail; I hadn't even collected my post from my pigeon-hole. There wasn't likely to be anything urgent, but you never knew, and it had been on my conscience over the weekend.

I dropped into my office first and played back my recorded messages. Someone at Sheffield University wanted me to give a paper in their series of research seminars. The finance department had a query about expenses that I'd claimed for a conference. Heffers wanted me to know that the book I'd ordered on Victorian Gothic fiction had arrived. And, oh Lord, my editor enquiring in a voice of steely kindness about the progress of the last two chapters. I'll speak to you very soon, she promised. I had my finger poised to delete when the last message came on.

'Hi there, it's Charles here.'

I didn't recognize his voice and anyway I didn't know anyone called Charles.

'You silly girl,' the voice went on, 'you forgot to leave your home phone number this morning. Not surprising, really, that was quite a night. How about dinner? Give me a ring.' He left a phone number and hung off, leaving me with my finger hovering. Obviously a wrong number, but it was a bit odd all the same, because if he had listened to my recorded message he would have known he'd got the wrong woman. I shrugged and pressed the delete button.

The staff pigeon-holes are just outside the Senior Common Room. I took out the sheaf of messages and letters and I poked my head round the door. I didn't really want to talk to anyone, but I was dying for a cup of coffee. Towards the far end of the room a small group of people were having an informal meeting, heads were bent forward in earnest conversation, diaries were being consulted. Someone from the French department was sitting on a sofa: she gave me a brief, distracted smile and returned to the essays she was marking. No one was likely to bother me. I got myself a cup of coffee and sank with a sigh into one of the shabby over-stuffed chairs.

I leafed through the things I'd taken from my pigeon-hole. Another reminder of books overdue yet again at the University library. An announcement of the next formal dinner. A memo reminding me that a collection was being made for John, the porter, who was about to retire. There was an interview timetable. I was exempt from interviewing while I was on study leave, so I screwed that into a ball and tossed it in the wastepaper basket placed conveniently by the side of my chair. There was something reassuring about all these ordinary everyday communications. All that was left now was a letter that had actually come through the normal post, a rare occurrence these days when so much is transacted by e-mail or phone. The envelope was made of heavy, ivory paper and was addressed to me in a neat, but quavery, italic hand. There was a Cambridge postmark.

As I looked at it, lying there so innocently

in my hand, I felt a tingling that began in my chest and stole up to my face, making my eyes water: I turned the letter over. The envelope was only partly stuck down. I hesitated, unwilling to confirm what I suspected. My fingers were trembling as I opened the flap and eased out the letter inside. It was as I thought. The letter was from Una.

'My dear Cassandra,' I read.

'I've tried to ring you several times and haven't caught you in, but in any case I think this is something best not talked about on the telephone. I know how busy you are with the college and your husband and your little girl, but I would be so grateful if you could find time to come and visit me very soon. I don't know who else I can trust. One way or another I've been a foolish old woman and got into a muddle about things. I've even wondered — am I getting a little senile, imagining things perhaps? I must know if my new suspicions are justified. If so, then I very much fear I've misjudged someone and I would hate that. And there's more: if I'm right, I suspect I'm in danger of losing something very important, something that I've staked a lot on. And staked is the *mot juste*, I realize; it's been akin to gambling, really. I don't want to commit any more to paper, but do you remember that grisly high-table dinner and what we talked about then? I'll tell you more when I see you. I really can't rest until I've got this sorted out, and if anyone can help me do that it will be you, my dear. I'm placing a great responsibility on you, I know that. Cannot write more just now.

With my love,

Una.

PS. Please keep all this under your hat for the time being.'

★ ★ ★

The writing had remained neat up till the end, though the letters had grown larger as if Una was having difficulty controlling the pen. I looked back to the beginning of the letter. The letter had been written on the day of her death. I was touched by the punctilious way that the address and telephone number were written out in full, even though her arthritis must have made that a chore. It was so typical of Una and her reluctance to surrender to old age. 'Academic women can be annoyingly high-minded about what they call 'keeping up appearances', but let me tell you, my dear, it's keeping up appearances that keeps me going. You'll find that too when you get to my age.'

I hadn't noticed the buzz of conversation fading away, but now I realized that the room was almost empty. Only the French lecturer was left and she was still engrossed in her marking.

I got myself another cup of coffee. I read the letter again. I looked at the postmark on the envelope. It had caught the last post on Friday. I tried to work out the timing. The letter had probably arrived at the college on Saturday where it had lain in my pigeonhole all weekend. Or it might be that it had only arrived this morning. It didn't really matter. This letter answered one question, at least in part. I could guess now why she had tried to contact me in those last moments. There was something she had wanted me to know, something that was even more important than summoning help. She had probably known in any case that help would come too late. But what was it that she had been so desperate to tell me? Something to do with the missing first editions? That reference to our conversation at the college dinner was infuriatingly enigmatic. I strained to recollect what we had talked about. All I could remember right now was Smollett and *The Expedition Of Humphrey Clinker*. I somehow didn't think that was it. I could probably retrieve more, but I would need time.

In the meantime Jim would have to know about this. I didn't feel much like ringing him up, but it had to be done. I'd better do that from my office. I was halfway back there when I had an idea. I took a detour to the Reprographics Room and made several photocopies of the letter.

Our principal, Honoria Patrick, has her office in the same corridor. As I came out, I saw that she was standing in the doorway talking to a stocky man who had his back towards me. Honoria is an elegant woman. I always like to see what she's wearing and I had automatically noted the black pencil skirt, the long slate grey jacket and the tailored coral shirt, before I realized that the man was Jim. My heart lurched. I had the copies of the letter in my hand. I knew he wouldn't approve of that bit of private enterprise. They were shaking hands now. I folded the copies and stuffed them in my handbag, just as Jim turned towards me.

★ ★ ★

'This letter explains something I was wondering about,' Jim admitted.

Once again we were sitting in my office, Jim was even wearing the same well-tailored suit, but this time things were subtly

89

different. His eyes kept meeting mine and sliding away. A moment ago he had caught me looking at his left hand. I'd looked away in confusion, but not before I'd seen that he wasn't wearing a wedding ring. Had he been wearing one last time he had been sitting opposite me? I couldn't remember. I was certain though that I'd seen him wearing one on some earlier occasion.

'When we did the house-to-house,' Jim said, 'a woman from the block of flats down the road told us that she saw Una the afternoon before she died. The woman was on a bus, and she saw Una making her way along the pavement. My guess is that she was on the way to the post-box.'

'It wasn't easy for her to get around,' I said.

'No, and it was bitterly cold, getting dark, icy under foot. She was supporting herself with two sticks, the neighbour said. She could have waited until someone could post this for her, but she didn't want to do that.'

'I've been racking my brains about what was worrying her,' I said. 'It must have something to do with the missing first editions, mustn't it?'

'Or maybe it was to do with the fact that she'd decided to leave all her books to St Etheldreda's College.' He spoke so matter-of-factly that at first I didn't catch his meaning and when I did, I thought he had made a mistake.

'The books are going to the Lit and Phil — the Institute,' I told him.

'Una's solicitor had been away on a skiing holiday. I managed to speak briefly to him this morning. He told me that the day before her death Una made a new will. She's left the books and most of the rest of her estate to St Etheldreda's.'

In the silence that followed I heard the distant shrieking and shouting of students larking about in the snow outside.

Jim said, 'Given the value of that house, it amounts to a very substantial legacy. You didn't know?'

I shook my head.

'The will stipulates that the legacy to the college is to be administered by a board of trustees with you as its chair.' His eyes were intent on my face and this time he didn't look away. 'In the first instance the trustees are to be appointed jointly by you and the principal of St Etheldreda's. It's hard to believe she took a step like that without consulting you.'

Now at last I managed to get something out. 'I just — no, really, I'm amazed. I didn't know.'

'When did you last speak to Una?' Jim

asked. He smoothed his hair with the flat of his hand.

I shook my head. 'I hadn't seen her for months. I've already told you that.'

'I didn't ask when you last saw her, but when you last spoke to her.'

I didn't like his tone of voice. 'Same thing in this case.' I was beginning to think more clearly now. 'It must have been a sudden decision. Una had been trying to get in touch. And I was away last week. I took Grace down to my mother's for a few days.'

'Couldn't she have contacted you on your mobile?'

'I don't think she had the number, and she wasn't really up to speed with modern technology anyway.'

Was I imagining it or did I see a flicker of relief on his face?

Another thought struck me. 'She didn't tell Honoria either, did she?'

'Why is it so hot in here?' he asked. He worked his tie loose and undid the top button of his shirt. I saw a tuft of blond hair.

'It's like a hospital', I agreed. I reached out to touch the radiator. It was scalding hot.

'Dr Patrick didn't know about it,' Jim admitted. 'She wants you to speak to her secretary and arrange a time to see her. I told her that I needed to speak to you first.'

The full implications of the news were only just dawning on me. What on earth was Giles going to say?

Jim was looking again at the letter. 'And you don't know anything about these 'new suspicions' that she mentions?' he said. 'That seems to imply the existence of old suspicions.'

'Does Giles know about the new will?'

'Giles?'

'Giles Brayfield. The librarian at the Institute. Does he know?'

There was a muffled thud at the window. Jim started and looked round. A star of melting snow was sliding down the glass.

'It's only a snowball,' I said. 'Students messing about.'

Jim turned back to me. 'I'm going to the Institute to speak to Dr Brayfield later this morning after I've seen Mark Barclay. He's Una's solicitor.' He got to his feet. 'If you think of anything, anything at all, that throws light on this letter — what you talked about at this dinner, for instance — contact me immediately.'

I got to my feet, too. 'Of course I will.' I walked round the table to show him to the door, but he didn't move.

'There's something . . . ' he said, frowning. He seemed to be staring at a point midway between my breasts.

'Yes.' I was close enough to smell that familiar scent.

He raised his eyes and looked into my face. 'The thing is . . . excuse me for mentioning this, Cassandra — '

'Yes?' Pear's soap. That was what it was.

'Your cardigan seems to be on inside-out.'

★ ★ ★

When Jim had gone, I unbuttoned my cardigan and put it on the right way round. He had been amused by my explanation. In fact it was the first time I had seen him really smile. The inside-out cardigan trick was certainly a brilliant idea, but only if you remembered to change it back before you got to work.

I went to the window and pressed my flushed face against the cool glass. Out in the court the snow around the copper beech was all churned up and the students had gone. The sky was a bruised pewter colour and was low overhead. It looked like snow again.

What had I been thinking of? Surely I hadn't believed that Jim was going to make a pass at me right there and then in my office? My face grew hot again. I'd better get a grip on myself. Perhaps this was an early symptom

94

of the menopause. Or was this a mid-life crisis. Who was I kidding? My life at present was one permanent mid-life crisis, but it hadn't manifested itself in this way before.

I went back to my desk and took the copies of Una's letter out of my handbag. I couldn't ignore Una's appeal. The dead can't enforce the obligations that they lay on us, but that makes those obligations all the more binding. I put my hand on the letter and made a silent promise to Una. I would do whatever it took to put things right for her.

First I had to work out what was wrong.

I read the letter again. 'One way or another I've been a foolish old woman and got into a muddle about things. I've even wondered — am I getting a little senile, imagining things perhaps? I must know if my new suspicions are justified. If so, then I very much fear I've misjudged someone and I would hate that.' As Jim had suggested, new suspicions must mean that there were old suspicions, and presumably it was those old suspicions that has caused her to change her will. It seemed likely then that the old suspicions must have been to do with the Institute or someone connected with it.

The telephone broke into my thoughts.

It was Stephen. He sounded weary. 'Could you collect Grace tonight? And do supper.

Something's come up and I'll need to stay late to finish drafting a contract.'

I glanced at my watch. Nearly lunch-time and Honoria would probably want to see me that afternoon. And I'd be well advised to avoid the Institute today: better give Giles a chance to absorb the news.

'Why not? I can't imagine I'm going to get any work done today.' I told him about the letter and the new will.

Stephen let out a long, low whistle. 'Thank your lucky stars that you hadn't got as far as being made a trustee of the Institute. You'd have had a real conflict of interests there. Giles isn't going to like this one little bit, judging by the way he was gloating about it last night.'

It had begun to snow again. Large flakes were drifting slowly down.

'But what if Una thought better of it?' I said. 'What if she died intending to change her will back? Here, listen to this.' I read out the passage that was worrying me. 'She says she had second thoughts. She was worried that she might have got into a muddle and misjudged someone. And if she did and that was why she changed her will, then morally, if not legally, maybe the Institute should get everything after all.'

'The letter isn't really evidence of anything.

It's very vague,' Stephen said. 'And why should Una have made a mistake? St. Etheldreda's is a perfectly appropriate place to receive those books and you're a perfectly proper person to administer the trust.'

It was snowing faster now, the flakes coming down in gusts and flurries.

Up till now, I had been thinking about the impact of the new will on the Institute. But how was it going to effect St Etheldreda's?

'I suppose we have to accept the legacy?' I asked.

'You mean — ?'

'Could we turn it down, if we wanted to?'

'The college is governed by a board of trustees, isn't it? They are legally bound to act in the best interests of the college. And it's hard to see how turning down a legacy of this size could be in your best interests.'

'Even if Giles kicks up a stink?'

I could almost see Stephen shrugging at the other end of the phone. 'The Institute has a governing body, too. If they have any sense, they'll rein him in.'

'I doubt if anyone is going be capable of reining Giles in when he hears about this.'

6

A Minor Accident

As I made my way from the car to the door of the nursery, I struggled to stay upright. Snowflakes hurtled towards me out of the darkness, making me blink as they caught on my eyelashes. The snowstorm had turned into a blizzard. This time I hadn't taken any chances. I'd left plenty of time. I stomped up the steps and rang the bell.

The door was opened by Julia North, who runs the nursery. She's the wife of one of my colleagues at the college and we often chat at college parties. Her eyebrows went up when she saw me.

'What a wonderful hat,' she said.

I was fond of it myself. It's round and black with a fake fur trim and ear flaps. 'I can never decide whether it makes me look like a Cossack or a nun. Or even Scott of the Antarctic.'

'Oh, a Cossack, definitely!' Her voice was high-pitched and over-animated, as though she was addressing a three-year-old. She glanced at her watch. 'You're early actually. I think Miranda's still reading a story to the little ones.'

She opened the door into the toddler room. We looked in. A group of about eight small children were sitting cross-legged on the floor. Facing them sat Miranda, a strikingly attractive young woman with long straight blonde hair and large, mild eyes.

'Goldilocks tried the porridge in the big bowl. It was too hot,' she was saying.

This safe, contained little world with its child-size furniture was reassuring. Yet at the same time its scaled-down tables and chairs and wash-basins gave me a strange, *Alice in Wonderland* sensation as if I'd grown grotesquely large.

Several of the children looked round, including Grace. She was sucking on two fingers. Without taking them out of her mouth, she gave me a huge smile. She turned her attention back to Miranda.

'They'll be a while yet,' Julia said. 'I've got some coffee on in my office, why don't you come and have a cup?'

'I think perhaps I will. Thanks.'

Julia's office was comfortable and functional, with two easy-chairs as well as a desk. The bay window at the back looked out onto a stretch of lawn where the children played in good weather. Today I saw only the reflections of me and Julia set against a swirling pattern of snowflakes.

'Let's shut that out,' Julia said.

She went across and drew a pair of deep red curtains. I sat down in one of the easy-chairs. Julia poured out two cups from a coffee-maker on top of a filing cabinet. She handed one to me and settled herself in the chair opposite.

I took a sip of coffee. It was good: strong and aromatic. I wrapped my hands round the cup and settled back with a sigh.

Julia sighed, too. 'My little luxury, this is.' It was as if she had dropped her professional persona. Her voice had deepened a little and had lost some of its sprightliness.

Julia has two partners, but she is the driving force. She manages the nursery from day to day and cooks lunch for the children. She usually carried all this off with *élan*, but today she looked tired. She must have thought the same about me.

'Difficult day?' she asked, giving me a searching look.

'I couldn't begin to tell you.' And I probably didn't need to. I had spent most of the afternoon discussing the situation with Honoria. If she was right, the news about Una's will would soon be all over the *Cambridge Evening News*. It might even reach the nationals. It was the kind of quirky story that journalists love.

'How about you?'

'Oh, you know.' She waved her hand.

The curtains didn't quite meet. Through the gap I could see snowflakes still turning and tumbling. There's something mesmerizing about falling snow.

When Julia spoke, it was an effort to wrench my attention back to her.

'Actually,' she said, 'I've lured you in here on false pretences. I wanted to have a word with you.'

I pushed myself up in my chair. 'No problem with Grace is there?'

'Oh, no, no, nothing to do with Grace. She's a poppet. She's got a will of her own, but that's no bad thing in my view. No, the thing is — ' She paused, as if trying to think exactly what she wanted to say. I had no idea what was coming, but clearly this wasn't about a trip to the farm at Wimpole Hall or a visit to the museum. 'Look, do you want some more coffee?' she said. 'Can I top you up?'

I shook my head.

She got up and filled her own cup. She took a gulp of coffee and said, 'I'm planning to install CCTV. Most schools have it now. Quite a few nurseries, too.'

'Won't it be very expensive? Is it really worth it for a small place like this?'

'Yes, it's a major outlay. It'll mean a small increase in our fees. That's why I'm sounding you out — and the other parents too.'

'It seems a bit over-the-top somehow. I mean, there's only one entrance and the door's got a glass panel. You don't need a camera to see who's there, do you?'

'It's not just for security. We'd have web cams so that parents could log on and see what their children are doing at any given moment. Don't you think that's a good idea?'

I wasn't sure. On the face of it, there seemed nothing that one could object to. Weren't there often moments during the day when I missed Grace and wondered exactly what she was doing? And yet . . .

Just then the door behind me opened. Grace put her head round it. As soon as she saw me, she shot in my direction like a heat-seeking missile and grabbed me round my knees.

'Ockpuss, Ockpuss,' she shouted and then, even more emphatically. 'Ery!'

'Oh, God. She's lost her octopus,' I said.

'He'll be in the box by the door,' Julia said.

He was. Grace grabbed him and got him in a stranglehold that left her fingers free to go in her mouth.

Trying to fasten Grace into her car seat was like doing battle with the hydra. No sooner was one arm or leg under control than another was flailing about. It was hard to believe that she had only two of each. A piece of advice floated into my mind: 'never coerce your child'. I'd read that in a manual on child-care when I was pregnant and I often pondered it at moments like this.

The wind was blowing up the back of my skirt and big wet snowflakes were melting on the back of the my calves. I gritted my teeth and leaned further into the car.

'No, no!' Grace bawled. Her face went red and her mouth went rectangular, like the slot in a pillar-box.

Encumbered by handbag, gloves, and car-keys, I was at a disadvantage. I thrust the keys and the gloves into my coat pocket and dumped my bag on the roof of the car. I bent again to my task. At last I managed to thrust the buckle of seat-belt into the socket and click it shut. I took a deep breath and straightened up. Before I could stop her Grace leaned over and pushed the red release button. The seat-belt shot back up into its slot. I closed my eyes for a moment to compose myself. When I opened them, Grace had got out of the seat and was clambering through the gap between the front seats. She had left Henry behind on the back seat. I had a flash of inspiration. I snatched Henry up.

'Into that car seat, or the octopus gets it!'

Grace turned round and stared at me. Her mouth fell open. She stretched out an imploring hand. 'Mine, mine, 'Ery mine.'

'You get him back when you're in your car seat. I mean it.'

She pondered her next move. But it was no good. She was beaten and we both knew it. She turned and climbed meekly into the child seat. When I had fastened her seat-belt, I pulled down the central arm rest so that she couldn't reach to unfasten it. I put Henry in her arms. She nuzzled him and gave me a big beaming smile. There were never any hard feelings once the fight was over.

The child-care manual had a point after all, I decided, as I got in the driver's seat and put my key in the ignition. Why resort to physical force when kidnapping and threats are at one's disposal? It's a dirty game, child-rearing.

I drove out of Cambridge, crawled along the dual-carriage, and turned off onto the A10 towards Ely. When I glanced in the rearview mirror, I saw that Grace was fast asleep, tilted over a little in her seat with

Henry tucked in between her head and her shoulder. She had her fingers in her mouth and every time I stopped at a set of traffic lights or a junction I could hear above the sound of the engine the rhythmic sound of her sucking, like the tweeting of little birds.

The roads had been gritted and the snowflakes were smaller now and melted as they hit the windscreen. All the same I went slowly. No one had actually died during the spell of bad weather, but there had been plenty of minor accidents and collisions and I was very conscious of the small life strapped into the seat behind me.

I turned off to the Old Granary with a sigh of relief. As I jolted along the long rutted track, the tall dark shape of Old Granary rose up ahead. We always left the light on in the little hall, but all the other windows were dark.

The security light went on as I pulled up close to the house. I reached over to the passenger seat for my handbag.

It wasn't there.

★　★　★

It was lucky that I at least had my house keys, they were on the same key-ring as my car key. I took Grace into the house and put her in

105

her play-pen with a couple of biscuits and a drinker full of milk. I went back with a torch and I hunted feverishly through the car, brushing aside drifts of tissues, boxes of paper handkerchiefs, Grace's toys. I even looked all round outside the car. I looked again and again and all the time I knew it was no good. I could see myself, full of exasperation with Grace, straightening up and dumping my bag on the roof of the car. I had no memory at all of retrieving it. After I'd strapped Grace in, I had driven off with the handbag still on the roof of the car. In my mind's eye I could see it swaying and sliding this way and that with the movement of the car. The best I could hope for was that it had fallen off when I turned round in the car-park. But there had been snow on the roof of my car. That might have held the bag in place until the car had warmed up enough for the snow to melt, and goodness knew how long that had been.

I went into the house and rang the nursery. The answering-machine told me that no one would be there until 8 a.m the next morning. I tried Stephen, praying that he would still be at his office. He was.

'Really, Cass!' he said, when he'd heard what had happened. 'How could you be so scatter-brained? And I suppose you want me to go over and look for it?'

That was just what I did want, so I bit back the retort that sprang to my lips.

Glumly I prepared scrambled eggs for Grace and got fish cakes out of the freezer for me and Stephen. Grace had finished her supper by the time Stephen rang back.

'Do you want the good news or the bad news?' He sounded weary. 'The good news is that I've found your mobile phone. It was in a snow drift near the junction with Grange Road. But the handbag is nowhere to be seen. I'm coming home now. You'd better start cancelling your credit cards.'

In a way, the credit cards were the least of it. I'd lost all the other things that make up the identity of a middle-aged mother and academic. If the bag had fallen into a glacier instead of a snowdrift and an archaeologist were to disinter it centuries hence, they'd be able to construct the daily life of a middle-aged, middle-class intellectual in considerable detail. There was my personal organizer, containing my diary and my address book. I groaned at the prospect of having to re-assemble all that information. There were half a dozen different library cards, my college staff card, my telephone charge card, membership cards for this and that. There'd be all the tedious effort of replacing them. And then there were things like my make-up case — not much used it was true, but it had a symbolic value — and a small hair-brush that I'd had since I was a teenager, a photo of Grace, my favourite fountain pen, a little World's Classics edition of *Vanity Fair* and, oh no, one of Grace's first shoes.

Tears were rolling down my cheeks as I hunted out the phone numbers for the bank and the credit card companies.

Oh well, look on the bright side. At least Henry wasn't in there.

★ ★ ★

'Do you think we're drinking too much?' I asked.

'Yes. Have another glass.' Stephen reached for the bottle of Rioja.

Food and wine had done wonders for his state of mind; mine, too. We were in the middle of a conversation about the nursery.

'I agree,' he said, 'installing CCTV does seem like using a sledge-hammer to crush a walnut. In a big institution it might make sense but in a small private nursery . . . '

'Exactly. You only have to stand on the stairs with all the doors open and you can see virtually everything. You know, I got the feeling that she wasn't telling me everything. And there's another thing . . . '

'You're not sure that you like the idea of tracking Grace on the internet? Well, neither am I.'

'Really?' I'd assumed that Stephen would be in favour.

'You were expecting me to take the belt-and-braces approach? The more safeguards the better? To be a typical lawyer in fact. Here, do you want what's left of these peas?' I shook my head. 'Look, we've chosen this nursery because it's got an excellent reputation. Grace adores it. Do we really want to watch her every second of the day?'

'You know what? Sometimes that's exactly what I'd like.'

'Shall I tell you something, Cass? A really smart person who was determined to harm a child would find a way of circumventing CCTV. It's not technology you have to rely on, it's people. And to do that you've got to rely on your own judgement.'

'Well, my judgement's telling me there's something a bit off-key about all this.'

'A spot of petty pilfering: that's probably what's bothering Julia. If you're worried, you'll have to tackle her about it. Or I will. And now let's clear up and go to bed.'

Stephen got up and began to stack plates. I drained my glass and got up to put it in the dishwasher.

The floor-length window that looks out over the creek was misted up with condensation. I cleared a space with the palm of my hand and looked out. It had stopped snowing and the world was utterly still under its blanket of snow. When the house was a granary, barges used to moor in the creek underneath it to receive the grain from a chute. The creek is shallower now, partly silted up. It had been frozen over for weeks.

I felt Stephen's hands on my shoulders.

'What is it?' he said.

'I was thinking about Una.'

Stephen put his head next to mine.

I said, 'If only I'd got to the phone sooner that evening.'

'Don't blame yourself for that. You weren't to know what was going on. It was just an unlucky combination of circumstances.'

I turned to face him. 'That's not the point really is it? I hadn't been to see her for months. Oh sure, I was busy: my job, the book, Grace and the chickenpox. Tonight, losing my handbag, that's just typical of the kind of life we lead. Always in a frantic rush, no time for anything. But I *could* have somehow made the time to see Una if I'd felt it was important enough.'

Stephen was silent. He put his arms round my waist and pulled me closer.

'And if I had, then I wouldn't be so clueless about what was happening in the last few weeks of Una's life. Why did she change her will and what did she mean when she wrote to me about being in a muddle? I've got to find out and I don't know where to start.'

'I know most of the solicitors in Cambridge. Who drew up Una's will?'

'I think Jim said, Barclay, somebody Barclay, like the bank.'

'Mark?'

'That's it. Do you know him?'

'We were at law school together and I've had professional dealings with him since then on one or two occasions. If Mark's had a hand in it, the thing will be absolutely water-tight. Look, why don't I give him a ring, explain the situation, sound him out?'

'The other person I could talk to is Giles.'

Stephen pulled back from me so that he could look into my face. He frowned. 'Is that wise under the circumstances?'

'I've got the perfect excuse for being at the Institute. I've got work to do there, remember? I've got my book to write. There are papers that I have to consult. I'll have to bite on the bullet sometime.'

7

The Spoils of Poynton

'How could you do this to me, Cassandra? I can't believe it!' Giles was standing on the steps of the Institute and I was standing in the street below him. When I'd pressed the buzzer, Michelle had told me that she had instructions from Giles not to let me in. She was so embarrassed that she could scarcely get the words out. I had insisted on seeing him. I had waited for five minutes in the cold, then the door had burst open and Giles had appeared on the steps. So far I hadn't been able to get a word in edgeways.

'It's a disaster,' Giles was saying, 'both for the Institute and for me. And I thought you were my friend.'

The *naïveté* of this statement, reminiscent of the playground and childish misery, touched me. 'I *am* your friend, Giles. And I'm so sorry about all this. I had no idea.'

'You've betrayed me. You've gone behind my back.'

'Let's go inside and talk about this. I'm perishing with cold out here.'

The high façade of the laboratories on one side and the library on the other created a canyon through which a bitter wind whistled. My toes were going numb in my boots and my face was tingling.

Giles had come out in his shirtsleeves, but he seemed oblivious of the cold. 'You're not setting foot over the threshold,' he said.

'Oh, come on, Giles you've got to let me in at some point.' I was angry too, now. I hadn't been in the best of moods to start with. A further search outside the nursery that morning had failed to turn up my handbag.

He laughed in a theatrical way. 'Over my dead body.' He lifted his hands to bar the way. One of his hands was clenched as if something was grasped in it.

'I've got to have access to the Geraldine Jewsbury papers,' I said. 'You know I've got a deadline.'

'Not my problem. I have discretion to ban someone from the library if I think fit. And believe me, I do think fit.'

A woman was approaching from the direction of Downing Street. As she skirted round us, she cast us a curious glance.

'You've wrecked everything,' Giles said.

'Now wait a minute. This has nothing to do with me. Una had a perfect right to do what she wanted with her books and her money.'

113

'No, she didn't,' he roared. 'Not after she'd led us to believe that she was leaving those books to us. She couldn't really have meant to disinherit us. It's all your fault — '

I watched in fascination, hardly taking in the sense of what Giles was saying.

He looked so much like Grace having a tantrum: the red face, the creased eyelids, the clenched fists. I suppose there is a two-year-old buried in all of us. It's just closer to the surface in some than in others. Any moment now I expected him to fling himself on the floor and start drumming his heels.

' . . . undue influence!'

I came to myself with a start, hardly able to credit what I had heard. 'I beg your pardon?'

'You heard. You, you,' he cast around for the right words. 'You alienated her affections,' he concluded.

I gave an incredulous snort of laughter. Giles's face turned puce. He came down the steps to stand in front of me. The snow hadn't been cleared away. It lay five or six inches deep and was backed up in drifts along the walls. Giles was wearing ordinary shoes and when he stepped into the street, the snow came up over his ankles and clung to his socks and the bottom of his trousers.

'There's no other way it could have happened,' he said. 'You wormed your way into her affections, played on her vulnerability. You'll laugh on the other side of your face, when I expose you.'

'Now, wait a minute.' My anger was rising again. 'I hadn't seen Una for months before she died. I bitterly regret that, but it's the truth. If I were you, I'd be careful where you repeat those allegations.'

Giles took another step towards me. He was so close that I could see the red veins on his nose. He raised his right hand and I knew that he was about to lose control. I took a step back. He took another step forward. His foot shot off to one side and his arms flailed. The object in his hand shot out and disappeared into a snowdrift at one side of the steps. I thought he was going to fall flat on his backside and I had time to feel a little thrill of ignoble pleasure before he regained his balance. He was breathing heavily.

He said, 'Not a lawyer's wife for nothing, are you, Cassandra? I'm giving you advance warning. I intend to contest the will.'

On that melodramatic note he turned on his heel and went up the steps into the library. The effect was spoilt by the fact that he had to stop to punch the code into the key pad. He stabbed in the numbers with a quivering finger. The door swung open. He went in and slammed it shut behind him.

Oh, well done, Cassandra, you handled that brilliantly. I couldn't believe I had let myself rise to the bait. My heart was hammering away and I felt queasy. A lot of people might sympathize with Giles and feel that he had been led up the garden path, and wasn't that in fact the case? A hollow feeling was developing in the pit of my stomach. It hadn't occurred to me that anyone might seriously think I had anything to do with Una's change of mind. If Giles was going to spread this around, perhaps I really ought to be thinking in terms of slander and libel.

To give myself time to recover, I looked for the object that Giles had dropped. There was a neat little hole in the snow. I thrust my gloved hand down and brought out a small, brightly painted figure. It was the Duke of Wellington. Giles had brought him along for moral support. It was funny in a way, but I knew Giles would hate me laying hands on this token of his vulnerability. I wasn't sure what to do with the little figure. I shook the snow off it and dropped it in my pocket.

I looked up at the windows of the Institute and caught a glimpse of someone looking down. Before I could see who it was they drew their head back. The place had never seemed more inviting. Up there my papers would still be arranged on the table, where I'd left them only last Friday. It felt like weeks ago, but it was only four days. I longed to get back to work on that chapter, to escape into that safe place. For a wild moment I considered waiting until after dark and breaking in. Then reason asserted itself. I would have to wait until I could appeal to the trustees, which would presumably be at their next meeting, whenever that was.

A masculine voice broke into my reverie. 'She might have to buy another little bit of memory.'

I looked round. Two male students were walking past me, heading for Downing College. It was a moment before I understood that the speaker was telling his companion about his girlfriend's computer problems.

There was no point in standing here and risking pneumonia. I turned and picked my way down the road towards Downing Street.

From deep in my briefcase came a trilling sound. I thrust in my hand and brought out my mobile phone. My fingers were numb and I fumbled for a moment or two.

At first, I could hardly hear the voice on the other end.

'You'll have to speak up,' I said.

'I can't,' the voice hissed. 'I daren't.'

'Who is this?'

'I don't want Giles to hear me. I'm supposed to be shelving books.'

I looked back at the library. The figure I'd seen before had reappeared and was standing by one of the windows of the top floor. It was Michelle.

'No, don't look at me!' she said in an agonized whisper.

'Oh, sorry.' I set off slowly down the street, the phone to my ear.

'I want to talk to you. I can get away for lunch at 12.00.'

'Where shall we meet?'

'I can't risk running into Giles.'

'How about the Fitzwilliam Museum. I'll meet you in the Egyptian section.'

★ ★ ★

Anubis is the jackal god of the necropolis and the embalming workshop, the keeper of the gateway between life and death. I was sitting on a bench in front of his display case. Reclining elegantly with his front paws stretched out before him in the posture of a sphinx, he seemed alert and dignified, as though he had fathomed the mystery of death and could no longer be surprised. I almost felt that if I gazed at him long enough I might penetrate some of that mystery myself. The label told me that he was made of painted wood and plaster. There were cracks where his head and neck had been repaired, but that didn't rob him of his enigmatic power. The erect ears and the slender snout were uncannily realistic and so was the hinged tail that hung down over the edge of the glass shelf.

It was quiet in the museum. The white columns and the plasterwork of the ceiling were bathed in a light made brilliant by the snow outside. The windows looked out over the river to Sheep's Green where, often enough, sheep or cows could be seen grazing. It was a strangely bucolic scene for the centre of a city. Every now and then there was the sound of feet echoing on the wooden floor and someone would appear to gaze for a few minutes into the display cases before going away again.

I'd arrived there still agitated, but I felt soothed now by the stillness and the warm.

I had a copy of Una's letter in my briefcase. I got it out and unfolded it and read it through yet again. I almost knew it by heart, but still I had the feeling that I had missed something. She had come tantalizingly close to telling me what the problem

119

was. 'I don't want to commit any more to paper, but do you remember that grisly high-table dinner and what we talked about then?' I had got no further in working out what she meant by that.

I leaned forward, put my elbows on my knees and my head in my hands. I tried again to recall the conversation we'd had. If I could just get past Smollett and Humphrey Clinker . . . I didn't remember things in the way that I used to. My memory was like a huge table that was completely crowded with objects. Every time I pushed something new on to it, something fell off the other side. I remembered what the student had said about buying another little bit of memory. No doubt that would be possible one day. Implanting another memory circuit would be a simple operation done under local anaesthetic, and then goodbye, middle-aged memory loss.

I pressed the tips of my fingers to my forehead and tried to see Una in my mind's eye. What had she been wearing? I saw a velvet tunic, dark, maybe black, with touches of dark blue, a swirl of purple. And then, as if I had pressed the play button on a video, I suddenly heard myself say, 'What a delicious scent you're wearing.'

'*Shocking!* by Schiaperelli,' Una said. 'I've worn it for years.'

And then? And then? I pressed my eyes tight shut.

Yes! Una was telling me that *Shocking!* could be bought only in Paris. And she had stocked up only a few weeks before. Then we were talking about our favourite parts of Paris. I said how much I like the Marais, especially the Place des Vosges and she said — what had she said? I was about to remember something important. It was almost within my grasp. I held my breath and waited for the memory to rise to the surface of my mind.

My mobile phone rang. I sighed as I fished about in my briefcase. The memory had vanished. But I knew that it would return, probably some time when I was least expecting it.

'Cass?' It was Stephen. 'I've spoken to Mark. He's happy to see you. Is two o'clock this afternoon OK?'

I said that it was. After we'd hung up I closed my eyes again and tried to make my mind a blank. There was a waft of air as someone sat down beside me. I opened my eyes. Michelle was looking anxiously at me.

'Are you all right?' she asked.

'More to the point, are *you* all right?'

Her face was wan and there were shadows under her eyes.

She dumped a green Marks and Spencer carrier bag at my feet.

'Here you are.'

'What's this?' I looked inside. There was a black jumper wrapped around something. I pulled the jumper aside and saw a jumble of papers, some typed, some bearing my handwriting. They were my notes for the chapter on twins.

Michelle said, 'I was shelving books when I heard Giles shouting at you outside and saying you couldn't come in. I remembered seeing your papers still there on your desk. I went and got them and hid them. I'm afraid they're in a bit of a muddle. I just stuffed them in the bag.'

I was touched. 'Michelle, this is so sweet of you. It's a terrific help.'

She pushed a wing of blonde hair back behind her ears and bit her lip. Her eyes were filling with tears.

'Hey, what's the matter?' I said gently.

She blurted it out. 'The police — they came to the Institute yesterday. They asked me about Una's books. There are some missing. Some first editions. Really valuable. They think I took them.'

'They think *you* took them?' I couldn't make sense of this.

'I didn't, I didn't!' A solitary tear spilled

over and trickled down her cheek.

'Of course you didn't.' I delved in my bag for a tissue. I pressed it into her hand. 'Now calm down and tell me what this is all about.'

She took a deep breath and said, 'It was because of the cataloguing. But I told them that I never touched the Henry James's. I don't think they believed me.'

Light was dawning. Why hadn't I made the connection before? Giles had mentioned that the collection was being catalogued.

'It was you who was cataloguing Una's books?' I said.

'Every Tuesday afternoon. I'd been going there for nearly a year. It was all in preparation for the books coming to the Institute.'

'Oh dear.'

'I know. It looks bad, doesn't it? But I never even touched those books. I'd never do anything like that. And they've taken my finger-prints!'

'Look, if you were going there every week, they *have* to question you. It doesn't necessarily mean that they think you had anything to do with it.' Even as I said that, I could just imagine how it would look from Jim's point of view. Michelle had gone to the house every week expressly to handle the books. It wasn't likely that there would be many other people with both the knowledge and the opportunity to steal Una's first editions and put worthless ones in their place.

Michelle broke into my chain of thought. 'And they wanted to know where I was when Una died!'

'And what did you say?'

'I wasn't anywhere! I mean, I was at home. In Chesterton. But I don't think I can prove that. My flatmates were out.'

'And they won't be able to prove that you weren't.'

'It's awful, Cassandra. I really liked her,' Michelle said.

Michelle might be better placed than anyone to give me an idea of how Una had been in the last weeks of her life.

'How did she seem the last time you saw her?' I asked.

There was the sound of footsteps. A middle-aged couple came into view and we fell silent. They drifted round the cases, exchanging an occasional comment. As they walked past us, I heard the man say firmly, 'No, it isn't sarcophaguses, it's sarcophagi' and caught a look of amused resignation on the woman's face. She gave me a little smile and raised her eyebrows in a tiny gesture of complicity. The man disappeared into the next gallery and the woman followed him.

Michelle picked up the thread of our

conversation. 'I didn't go last week. I was off work with a cold. But the week before — I don't remember anything being different. We had a cup of tea and a chat, just like always. She wasn't like an old person. You could tell her anything.'

'Did you have any idea she was going to change her will?'

'None at all. Did you?'

I shook my head.

'I couldn't believe it,' Michelle went on. 'I mean, I thought it was all properly settled. Giles certainly thought it was. He was always making a fuss of her, popping round with little presents, sucking up a bit really. That's what Una thought, anyway. She used to give me this little smile, when he wasn't looking.' With a shrewdness that surprised me, she added, 'I think she liked it all the same.'

I was intrigued. 'What sort of little presents?'

'Oh, boxes of Turkish delight, for instance. She liked that. And once — it was her birthday — he brought a bottle of champagne and we all had a glass.'

'Maybe he shouldn't have counted his chickens before they were hatched,' I said dryly.

Michelle looked at her watch. 'I'd better be going.'

We got up and walked in silence to the huge entrance hall. The high-domed ceiling, the two monumental staircases and the heavy black and purple marble gave it the gravitas of a gentlemen's club. The big space was as hushed as a cathedral.

Michelle said, 'I could photocopy those papers for you, the ones you're working on.'

A trick of the acoustics made her voice seem startlingly loud. Michelle clapped her hand to her mouth. The words bounced off the hard surfaces of marble and mosaic and echoed around the staircases before floating up past the statues in niches to be swallowed up by the space under the richly decorated dome. We looked around, but there was no one to be seen except a bored cloakroom attendant who was examining his nails and yawning.

'What would Giles say?' I whispered.

'Well, of course, I wouldn't tell him,' she whispered back.

I was tempted, but only for a moment. I shook my head. 'I can't let you do that. If Giles found out that you'd gone against his express wishes, you'd be in big trouble.'

'I don't care about that. I don't want to stay at the Institute forever. When I've saved up some money, I'm going to travel, and then I want to do my library qualification.'

126

'And for that you'll need a reference from Giles. It really isn't on, Michelle.'

'I just wanted to help.' She pulled up her collar and tugged a pair of gloves out of her pocket.

'You already have.' I patted the bag containing the papers. 'And there's another favour you could do me.' I fumbled in my pocket and brought out the Duke of Wellington. 'Giles dropped this when he was shouting at me in the street. Do you think you could return it? Maybe just pop it back in his office when he isn't looking?'

Michelle nodded and dropped the little figure into her handbag. 'I'll slip out ahead of you.'

She'd only gone a step or two when I remembered that there was something I'd forgotten to ask her.

'Michelle?' My voice echoed in the open space just as Michelle's had done earlier. She turned and looked back at me. 'Yes?'

'That day when I was in a hurry to leave the institute and you wanted to have a word with me. What was that about?'

She looked puzzled and then her face cleared. 'Oh that. I'd kind of forgotten about it. It was funny, though, all the same.' She frowned and tucked a loop of hair back behind an ear. 'It was the weekend before last. I'd been to visit a friend who's a postgrad at Downing. I was going into the town to look for a taxi and when I went past the Institute, I saw that there was a light on in one of the windows high up.'

A crowd of schoolchildren came in from the street, bringing cold air in with them. We stepped under one of the staircases to get out of the way.

'At first, I thought it had been left on by mistake,' Michelle continued. 'But then it kind of flickered, as if someone had moved in front of it. I thought it must be Giles.'

'What time was this?'

'About midnight? I know,' she said, answering the question I hadn't asked, 'but Giles does work very late sometimes.'

'And was it him?' I had to raise my voice to be heard above the excited babble of thirty children being herded through the hall.

'That's just it. On Monday morning he happened to mention that he'd been away for the weekend. And when I thought about it, what would he have been doing up there anyway? It's freezing cold. If he had been there at all, he'd have been working in his office, he's got a little electric heater in there.'

'Did you tell him you thought you'd seen someone?'

She nodded. 'He just laughed and said I'd

got an over-active imagination. That we'd know if someone had broken in and anyway, why would they?' She hesitated, biting her lower lip. 'You know, I've never liked it up there. It's so dark in the winter. I think about those poor little maidservants who used to live in the attics. Cassandra . . . ' Her voice trailed off.

'Yes?' I prompted.

'One of them might have *died* there.'

I didn't want to encourage this line of thought. 'If the Institute's haunted, which I don't believe for a minute,' I said briskly, 'it's much more likely to be the ghost of some demented scholar driven mad by writer's block. It's been a library for a long, long time. It was only a private house for twenty or thirty years.'

'I suppose. And I didn't really actually positively see anyone as such.' She was talking herself out of it now and wanting to be reassured.

'It could have been one of those tiny power-cuts, when the light flickers on and off. Or maybe a bad connection.'

She looked at her watch. 'I've got to get back to the Institute.'

As she turned to go, I said, 'Which room was the light in?'

'It was that one on the far left as you look

up at the building. You know, the one with the travel guides in it.'

I knew all right. That was the room I worked in.

★   ★   ★

I had time for some lunch in the Museum café before my appointment with Mark Barclay at two o'clock. As I drank my soup and ate my sandwich, I brooded over Michelle's story. It had bothered me in a way that I couldn't quite put my finger on. I didn't believe that she had seen a ghost, or anyone else for that matter and yet I knew that I'd feel uncomfortable next time I was working up there in the dusk. At the moment that seemed like a distant prospect. I'd soon be a demented scholar myself, if I didn't find a way of getting back into the Institute.

I tipped a double helping of sugar into my espresso, hoping that it would give me some extra energy. I massaged my aching temples with the tips of my fingers. There was too much going on, too much to sort out. Almost the hardest thing about living through a crisis is that ordinary life runs along in parallel. Work has to be done, meals have to be cooked, knickers have to be washed. I'd already started hunting for my diary to check that I hadn't forgotten anything important, when I remembered that it was in the lost handbag. I clapped a hand to my head. Without my diary, I felt as if I was adrift without a map or compass. I had no idea what I was supposed to be doing. My eye fell on a newspaper on the next table and I could hardly believe it when I saw the date. Only two days to go to Grace's birthday party and not a balloon purchased! She wouldn't actually be two for another few days but for obvious reasons we were having the party on a Saturday. I could start by buying a cake from Fitzbillies on my way to Mark Barclay's office.

The office was a fifteen-minute walk away in one of the old, timber-framed buildings that line Magdalene Street to the north of the city centre. I pulled on my hat, turned the ear-flaps down and went out into the street. It had stopped snowing and the sky was a clear blue that faded into white on the horizon. The sun was dazzling on the snow and there was a Scandinavian intensity to the light. When I sucked the air into my lungs, it was gin-cold and almost as intoxicating. In spite of everything, my spirits rose. I strode off down Trumpington Street towards King's Parade, enjoying the feel of the snow creaking under my boots.

There was something festive about the snow-covered city. There were fewer cars than usual and sounds were muffled. It was as though ordinary life had been suspended. Nearly everyone was on foot. A couple of boys were pulling a girl along the road on a toboggan. Outside Pembroke College there was a row of bicycles each coated in a thick layer of snow. A snowball fight was taking place on the long open space that runs under the intricate Gothic revival screen of King's College. Every ledge and turret of the medieval chapel was outlined in white and the sun striking off the snow made me squint.

When I reached Magdalene Bridge I stopped and leaned on the cast-iron parapet. This was one of the oldest parts of town: one of the original bridges on this site had given Cambridge its name. Every branch and twig of the trees that lined the river was loaded with snow and shimmered in the brilliant light. Below me, snow-covered punts were jammed in the frozen Cam at crazy angles to the bank. I thought of the great freezes of past centuries when everyone turned out onto the ice and you could skate from Cambridge to Ely and beyond. I had a flashback to my skating dream and felt again the pressure of an arm around my waist. I pushed the memory away and hurried on.

When Mark Barclay's secretary ushered me into his first-floor office, Mark was sitting behind a desk in what looked like a kind of Santa's grotto, consisting of shoulder-high stacks of box files, deed boxes and law books bound in brown leather. There was a meandering path to a couple of chairs in front of his desk. Around the room were dark wooden bookshelves, some with books stacked higgledy-piggledy, some empty and dissected by solid lines of dust.

Mark got to his feet and waved a hand. He had hair the colour of toffee, and it was so improbably thick and well-groomed that at first I took it to be a wig. A second glance told me that it wasn't, but I couldn't help glancing at it from time to time to check that it was real.

'Take a seat, Dr James.'

'Cassandra, please.'

'And I'm Mark. Do forgive the mess.'

'Makes me feel quite at home.'

He smiled. 'I finally persuaded my father to retire. I'm in the process of taking over his office. Trying to decide what to keep, what to put into storage.'

I sat down and we looked at each other across a cluttered desk.

There was a reassuring solidity about him. He had the air of an old-fashioned family doctor. What he told me was essentially what I had heard from Jim. There were a few legacies to individuals, such as Una's cleaner, but the bulk of her estate, including the books, had been left to St Etheldreda's College. I told him that Giles was threatening to contest the will.

Mark gave a contemptuous snort. 'Oh no, that cock won't fight. I went over the conditions of the will very carefully indeed with Dr Carwardine. She was quite clear about what she wanted to do and she certainly wasn't senile. In fact her doctor actually witnessed the signing of the will.'

'Giles feels he was led to believe that the books were coming to the Institute, and that he was treated unfairly. Someone from the Institute had actually been cataloguing the books on that understanding.'

Mark shrugged. 'That may have been Dr Carwardine's intention at one time, but her final decision about the disposition of her books is made abundantly clear in this document.' He tapped a folder that lay on the desk in front of him. His big blunt-fingered hands were as well cared for as his hair.

'But there *was* an earlier will?'

He shook his head. 'Doesn't matter. She had a perfect right to change her mind.'

I wanted to ask if he knew why Una had

done that, but I wasn't sure how to put it. There was a silence. Mark leaned back in his chair. He seemed in no hurry to get rid of me. Through the window I could see the tops of trees in one of the courts of Magdalene College courtyards. A crow landed on a branch in a flurry of snow.

Mark seemed to reach a decision. 'Look here, you're going to have to hear about this sooner or later, and it may as well be sooner. I told you that as well as all the books, Dr Carwardine left the bulk of the estate to the college.' He hesitated.

'Yes?' Warning bells were going off in my head.

'Unfortunately, as things stand at present, that amounts to less than seven thousand pounds.'

'Excluding the value of the house, yes?'

'Alas, no. I mean that those are the *total* assets of the estate.'

'But the house alone must be worth half a million or more!'

'Dr Carwardine sold Green Gables around four months ago.'

I stared at him open-mouthed. 'What?'

'She was entitled to go on living there until her death. It was an equity release scheme,' Mark explained, 'or life-time mortgage, as it now tends to be called. This kind of arrangement is fairly common as a way for elderly people to free up capital. Dr Carwardine received a substantial amount of money and the house now reverts to the company with whom she had the mortgage.'

'Was she short of money, then?' That was a miserable thought. I'd always assumed Una was comfortably off.

'That's what I wanted to know. She more or less told me to mind my own business, but she did say, rather tartly, I might add, that she wasn't at the point of throwing chair legs on the fire just yet.'

I couldn't help smiling. I could just hear her saying it.

Mark smiled too. 'She was a game old bird. I shall miss being addressed as 'young man'. I took what she said as an indication that there weren't any pressing financial problems. And indeed I don't see how there could have been. There was her husband's pension, index-linked, so it had kept its value, and she'd inherited some family money.' He spread his hands. 'What more could I say? As long as everything was in order on the legal side — and it was — then it was none of my business.'

'When you said she got a large sum for the house . . . '

Mark hesitated. 'You can probably guess

136

the value of a house of that size in the middle of Cambridge.'

'A large house on Hills Road was on the market for over half a million a month or two ago.'

Mark pressed his lips together. He waved his hand to sketch an upward movement.

'More?' I asked. 'Three-quarters of a million?'

He gave a little nod of the head. 'You're pretty close. The house will probably be converted into luxury flats.'

My head was reeling. 'And there's hardly any of that money left? Where's it gone?'

'I very much want to know the answer to that myself. So do the police. And so will the Inland Revenue.'

I was still working out the implications of this. 'So this means that the college has all the books, but it doesn't have any money to build somewhere to put them?'

Mark nodded. 'I hope that won't be the final position. It depends on what she did with the money. If she put it all on the horses and lost the lot — no, no,' he said, observing the horror on my face, 'I've got no reason to think she did that, but if that was the case — or something like it — then obviously the money's gone for good. Until we know for certain what she did with it, it's impossible to say.'

We sat in silence for a few moments. What I was feeling was totally unexpected. Under the circumstances it would have been in bad taste to get excited about the legacy and anyway I'd persuaded myself that I was pretty much indifferent to it. I'd even complained to myself about how much extra work it was going to let me in for. But as soon I'd heard that the money had all gone, I felt that it was *our* money, the college's money, and I wanted it.

I looked up to see Mark's eyes on me. Perhaps he guessed some of what I was feeling.

'Wills are funny things,' he said. 'I remember when I was an articled clerk, one of the firm's clients left £500 to her gardener. Her children were furious — and mind you, this was a very wealthy woman and they stood to inherit a packet. In their terms it was roughly the equivalent of the fiver we give the postman at Christmas'. He shrugged. 'Money's never just money, is it?'

I'd recovered my equilibrium. 'Maybe Una gave it to Oxfam or the local cats' home and if so, good for her. But I would just like to know — '

'How she managed to get rid of around three quarters of a million pounds in a few months? Me, too. It's hard to imagine. Well, that's not true actually, I can imagine all sorts of things, but nothing that seems at all likely. When you consider that she was pushing ninety — '

' — not to mention almost crippled with arthritis — '

' — it does limit the options. I think we can exclude fast cars and trips to Acapulco and Las Vegas, don't you? But Superintendent Ferguson seems very capable. Hopefully he'll get to the bottom of this.'

'Ah yes,' I said.

The phone buzzed and Mark answered it. 'Fine, ask her to wait just a minute or two, will you?' He hung up and turned to me. 'My three o'clock appointment is here. I don't think there's anything more I can tell you, Cassandra.'

'Thank you for being so frank.'

Mark got up to usher me out.

'You'll let me know — ?' I said.

'As soon as I find out anything. Nice to have met you, Cassandra. Give my best to Stephen.' He opened the door for me.

Something occurred to me. 'The doctor who witnessed Una's will . . . ?'

'That was Dr Jane Pennyfeather. Nice woman.' Mark noticed my look of surprise. 'Do you know her?' he asked.

8

Second Thoughts

Body parts were scattered all over the carpet.

'The head's over here,' Jane said. She held it up by its frizzy blonde hair.

'These cheap toys are always a mistake, aren't they?' I said, picking up a dismembered leg.

'Amazing, isn't it, the mayhem that a handful of over-excited toddlers can create in a couple of hours?'

The guests had departed just a few moments ago and Stephen had taken Grace upstairs to give her a bath and get the jelly out of her hair. I could hear distant shrieks of excitement. Down here a high synthetic voice was singing, 'the wheels on the bus go round and round, round and round, round and round.' No one had switched off the tape after the final game of musical chairs. I picked my way across the floor through drifts of torn and crumpled wrapping paper. 'The babies on the bus go waah, waah, waah — ' I pressed the button on the cassette-player and blissful silence descended.

Jane and I surveyed the room. A Bacchanalian revel appeared to have taken place. There were empty orange juice cartons under the sofa. Cake had been ground into the carpet. One of the curtains was dangling like a limp flag. I recalled that I had seen a little boy swinging on it.

'It won't take long to sort this out,' Jane said, bending down to pick something up off the floor.

I don't see her all that often, but when I do, I remember all over again how much I like her. We had first met after the death of her next-door neighbour, Margaret Joplin, who was my head of department. The train of events that followed brought us together and she was there when I gave birth prematurely right here in the Old Granary. There'd been a bond between us ever since. She was Grace's godmother and I knew that she had also become close to Malcolm, who was Margaret's husband.

'What's this?' Jane asked. She held up a pale blue plastic egg, about the size of her hand.

'Press that red button.'

She did. One end sprang open, the head of a chick popped out, and the egg played the jaunty first bar of 'Old MacDonald had a Farm'.

Jane laughed.

'Hideous, isn't it?' I said. 'Come on, clearing up can wait. I'm going to make a nice pot of Lapsang tea and there's a plate of smoked salmon sandwiches in the fridge. I thought we'd deserve a treat when this was all over. Why don't you put your feet up?'

I brought a tray up to the sitting-room and took a cup of tea and a sandwich up to Stephen. When I came down, Jane had poured out our tea and was lying on the sofa, her eyes closed. She had arrived with the first of the children and I hadn't had a proper look at her until now. I had taken it for granted that she was the same old Jane with the smiley crow's feet and the fair hair, generously salted with white. But I now saw that there was something different about her. Her clothes? That was part of it. She usually dressed rather formally — below the knee skirts, tailored jackets, court shoes, that kind of thing — but today she was wearing a red skirt in felted wool with a band of embroidery around the hem and a beautiful rich blue mohair cardigan. There was something else as well, something more elusive, but before I could put my finger on it, she opened her eyes and smiled at me.

'Are you OK?' I asked.

'Never better.' She patted the sofa beside

her and I sat down next to her.

'You wanted to talk to me about Una,' she said.

It wasn't such a coincidence that Jane had turned out to be her doctor. Cambridge is a very small city and her surgery isn't far from Brooklands Avenue. I'd explained briefly on the phone how it was that the college was concerned with Una's new will and how Una had tried to contact me on the night of her death.

'Did you see a lot of her?' I asked.

'Not a great deal, but I'd got into the way of popping in now and then.' Jane wrapped her hands round her cup of tea and took an appreciative sip. 'There wasn't a lot I could do for her, but I liked to keep an eye on her. And I enjoyed having a bit of a gossip with her. It was just chance really that I ended up witnessing the will. I think she'd been meaning to ask a neighbour, but as I was there . . . ' She shrugged and reached for a sandwich. 'I was happy to do it.'

'And she did understand, didn't she, I mean, she was . . . ' I searched for words that wouldn't seem to cast doubt on Jane's professional judgement.

'In her right mind? Oh, no question of it.'

'So Giles won't be able to contest the will on those grounds?'

Jane snorted. 'Rest easy, Cass. He won't have a leg to stand on if he tries to claim that Una didn't know what she was doing. My God, this was a woman who was still finishing *The Times* crossword every day, boasting in fact about doing it in record time. She was as sharp as a tack and I'd swear to that in court.'

'Giles is accusing me of exerting undue influence.'

Jane laughed out loud. Her cup shook in her hand and she placed it carefully on the coffee-table. 'I'd like to have seen you try. Una was one tough cookie and she knew her own mind. Her lawyer will tell you the same thing, I'm sure.'

'He already has. I just wish I knew why she made the new will, why she changed her mind about leaving the books to the Institute.'

Jane reached for another sandwich. 'I can't help you there. I didn't even know what was in the will.'

It seemed that every path I tried turned out to be a dead end.

Jane said, 'There was something though. Ages ago, it must have been, oh, sometime last spring? I don't know if it had anything to do with this, but it's stuck in my mind because it wasn't like her. That day she really did seem low, she was just sitting there, didn't even have the radio on, and I wondered if her arthritis was bothering her. She told me she'd had a shock. She said, 'You can think you know someone through and through and then . . . ' She seemed about to confide in me, but then she just shrugged and changed the subject.'

'When exactly was this?'

'Let me see now. Oh yes, I know. I'd brought her some daffodils. Must have been March. Look, I don't know what she wanted to tell you, but I bet I know why it was you she wanted to confide in. Una once told me how much you reminded her of her younger self. She knew about what happened at the college when Margaret died. How you wouldn't let things go once you knew something was wrong. She approved of that. 'Nothing is settled until it is settled right', she said. Is that a quotation?'

'Kipling, I think,' I said absently. 'This just makes me feel worse and worse. I should have gone to see her.'

'You weren't to know how things were going to work out. And, Cass,' Jane leaned over and put her hand on my arm, 'try not to feel too bad about her death. Let me tell you something. She didn't just have arthritis, she had cancer, too. She was still just about managing to hang on to her independence. A taxi would come for her once a week and she'd go to the library, do some shopping. But she wouldn't have been mobile for much longer. She was spared that at least.'

'She didn't tell me.'

'I don't think she told anyone. You know what she was like.' She squeezed my arm. 'Come on. Let's have another cup of tea.'

I roused myself. 'I haven't even asked how things are in your neck of the woods.'

'There is some news actually. Malcolm's put his house up for sale.'

So Malcolm had finally decided to move. I'd wondered how long he would go on living in the house where he had been so happy with Margaret. Looking at Jane's face, I saw that there was more to come.

'You two — are you?' I asked. 'I mean — '

'He moved in with me just before Christmas.' The wrinkles around Jane's eyes deepened into a big, beaming smile. 'We decided it was silly to keep two places going when he was spending most of his time at my place. Actually we're thinking of putting my place on the market, too, making a fresh start, maybe somewhere outside Cambridge.'

'It's the best news I've heard for a long time.' Happiness is infectious. I too was grinning all over my face.

Jane's face was glowing. She leaned back

with a sigh of contentment and laced her hands around her stomach. And that was when I knew the answer to what had perplexed me earlier.

Jane was expecting a baby.

★ ★ ★

I mulled over our conversation the next morning as I sat in my office in the college, listlessly pushing paper-clips round my desk. I was really no nearer to finding out what Una had wanted to talk to me about or what had happened to the money and I couldn't think who else to tackle. Neither was I any nearer to getting back to work in the Institute. Professor Greenhalgh, the chair of trustees, was on study leave in India studying Mughal architecture, the lucky devil. The vice-chair, a History lecturer at Robinson college, was in bed with influenza.

I hadn't told Stephen that Jane was pregnant. I couldn't face re-igniting the baby debate until I'd sorted out the thoughts that were churning around in my head. Jane was forty-five, four years older than me. I examined my feelings. Had there been a pang of envy when she told me her news? Well, there was nothing to stop Stephen and I having another bite of the cherry. Of course, wanting to have a baby isn't the same as being able to have one, and Stephen was right, there was no time to lose . . .

When the phone rang, I was miles away. Absently I stretched out a hand for the receiver.

'Cassandra James,' I said.

'Cassie! at last!' It was a deep male voice and there was a caressing cadence to it. The voice was vaguely familiar, but I couldn't put a face or a name to it. 'It's Charles,' he said. 'I've been trying to get hold of you for days. I left a message.'

I remembered now the mysterious voice-mail message that I'd played back on the day that I'd discovered Una's letter.

'I'm sorry, I — do we know each other?'

The voice was surprised and offended. 'Of course we do. We agreed that I'd ring you to fix a time for dinner.'

'I'm sorry. There must be some mistake.'

'You didn't think that the other night. Very far from it.'

Was this some kind of an obscene phone call? 'I'm going to hang up now!' I said.

'No! Please. I'm sorry. I shouldn't have spoken like that.' The voice was contrite. 'But if you didn't want to see me again, I think you might have let me know instead of giving me the run around like this.'

'I don't know who you are or what you're talking about.'

'You're not going to deny that we've slept together!'

I hung up.

A few seconds later the phone rang again.

'You bitch!' he said. 'What about my scarf?'

'If you do try to ring me again, I'll call the police!' I slammed the phone down.

'Cass?' I looked up to see Merfyn standing in my office doorway. 'I did knock,' he said. 'I've got next term's timetable here. Wanted to ask you about Tuesday mornings. What's the matter?'

I told him what had happened. 'He didn't sound like a nutcase. At least not to begin with.'

Merfyn was sitting on the edge of my desk. He was wearing a herringbone tweed suit I hadn't seen before.

'Is that new?' I asked.

'Oxfam's finest, believe it or not. And look,' he turned back one side of the jacket to reveal a scarlet silk lining.

'Oh, very flash.'

'About the phone call: there is another possibility. Maybe there's another Cassandra James. James is a common enough name.'

'But Cassandra isn't and anyway he had got my phone number.'

'It's in the University phone book, isn't it?'

'But why should he think that he knows me . . . ' Something occurred to me. I pressed the start-up button on my computer.

'What are you doing?' Merfyn asked.

'I've just remembered: I *have* come across another Cassandra James. It was when I was searching on the net for reviews of my last book. I'm going to try Google.'

Merfyn moved round the desk to look over my shoulder. 'Why've you got the mouse on the wrong side of the key board?'

'For me that's the right side. I'm left-handed.'

'To think, I've known you all these years and never noticed that.'

To my surprise Google threw up not one, but two possibilities: a paediatrician in Quebec and a geologist in Wellington, New Zealand. Both of them had published research papers that were listed there.

'Well, well,' Merfyn said. 'Could one of them be a visiting fellow, taking the opportunity of being far from home to kick over the traces?'

'How could I find out?'

'I suppose you'd have to ring round the colleges. Or Senate House might have a list. My money's on the medic. They're a notoriously randy lot. I remember when I was a postgrad — '

I never did get to hear that story, because Merfyn was interrupted by the phone ringing.

We both stared at it, transfixed. Merfyn gave me a look of enquiry and stretched out his hand. 'Shall I?'

'No, no.'

I braced myself and picked up the receiver.

But it wasn't Charles. It was Michelle and she sounded as if she was on the verge of tears. She asked if we could meet.

* * *

I opened the door of the Palm House. As I stepped out of the bitter cold, warm, humid air pressed against my face. Pots of scarlet poinsettia and hyacinths in shades of lilac and blue were massed on the shelves just inside, releasing a scent so overpowering that it was almost unpleasant. Ahead stretched a long passage lined with plants that here and there met overhead to make a green tunnel. From it the glasshouses opened out to the right. There wasn't a soul in sight.

I made my way to the orchid room, where I'd arranged to meet Michelle. It was arranged like a conservatory with potted ferns and rattan armchairs. I sank into one of the chairs. The silence was broken only by the soothing murmur of a little fountain. The orchids clustered round me, their Pekinese faces angled towards me as if they were peering into my face. I closed my eyes and pressed my shoulders back, luxuriating in the heat that seemed to penetrate into my bones.

I wasn't much more than a stone's throw from Una's house; it backed onto the Botanical Gardens to the south. Before Una's arthritis had made walking painful, we had sometimes strolled in the gardens and wandered through the Palm House.

Something about the heat, the rattan furniture and the exotic flowers with their fierce little faces threw up a literary connection that I couldn't place. Somerset Maugham maybe? One of those mordant little stories about adulterous tea-planters? I saw in my mind's eye a figure in a baggy forties suit and a Homburg hat. A scene from a film? Yes, it was Humphrey Bogart encountering General Sternwood in the overheated orchid house at the beginning of *The Big Sleep*.

Something clicked into place. My eyes shot open and I sat up as if I'd been stung. I now knew what Una and I had talked about at that college dinner. Through one of those vagaries of the mind that defied rational explanation, the heat and the orchids had unlocked my memory. Classic crime fiction: that was what we had talked about. I could hear Una telling me how much she admired *The Big Sleep*. I was saying that I preferred *The Long Good-Bye*. So what was the significance of that other memory that had surfaced, the one in which Una was talking about the Place des Vosges. Of course, Maigret! At one time Maigret had an apartment there: that was how we had got onto the subject of crime fiction in the first place.

'Cass?' Michelle was standing in the doorway.

I put my thoughts of Una to one side. Now that I'd got hold of this thread, I knew that with time, I'd be able to reconstruct most of the conversation.

Michelle's face was as white as paper and there were shadows under her eyes. Her blonde hair was lank.

'Come and sit down.' I gestured to the other chair.

Michelle perched on the edge of it and put a big canvas briefcase on the tiled floor beside her. Without a word, she pulled a crumpled envelope out of her pocket and took out a letter. She handed it to me.

'What is it?'

'Read it.'

The letter was from Mark Barclay and stripped of its legal verbiage, its message was simple. Una Carwardine had left Michelle ten thousand pounds intending that Michelle should use the money to travel. Mark was instructed to say that it was the deceased's express wish that the money should not be spent on anything sensible. I imagined that he'd enjoyed writing that.

I looked at Michelle. Tears were rolling down her cheeks. She groped in her pocket and brought out a tattered paper handkerchief.

'It's so sweet of her,' Michelle said between gulps. 'She knew that was something I really wanted to do. And she knew that I don't have much money. I hardly earn anything at the Institute. Mum and Dad do their best for me, but I've got three younger brothers, and the eldest has just got a place at Oxford.'

'Una couldn't have done a nicer thing,' I said.

'I had no idea.' She dabbed at her face with the tissue. 'She used to say that she made the most of being young and I should do the same. When she was my age it was the war and she was doing top-secret stuff. She didn't say exactly, but she kind of hinted that there were a lot of men.' Michelle stole a glance at me. 'That she'd slept with, I mean. She told me not to settle down too soon.'

'Excellent advice. Though I don't advise you to leave it as long as I did.'

Michelle gave me a watery smile. She blinked and bit her lip. The tears were welling up again.

I reached over and put my hand on her arm. 'What's up? Why are you so upset?'

'It's the police. I mean it was bad enough about the books, but now — ' She seemed about to break down completely. With a visible effort she got a grip on herself. 'They've questioned me about it. They kept asking me, did I know that Una had planned to leave me some money? They can't really think that I might have killed her!'

'Oh, Michelle!'

I didn't know what to say. There was no point in offering false consolation. The police might well think that was a possibility, even though I couldn't imagine they would entertain it for long. I fell back on platitudes.

'You haven't done anything wrong,' I said firmly. 'Try not to let it get to you. Just go on telling them the truth.'

She calmed down immediately. My authority as her ex-tutor was more effective than what I'd actually said.

I handed her some tissues and she

scrubbed at her face.

'You have told me everything, haven't you?' I said as an afterthought.

She nodded, but straightway I knew that she was holding something back. Put it down to years of watching students tell fibs about lost essays and unobtainable library books. The body language was unmistakable. She hesitated and I thought she was going to tell me what it was, but the moment passed.

'I'll be fine, now, really I will,' she said. 'I mustn't forget this.'

She leaned forward and hauled her canvas bag onto her knees. Out of it she took a thick sheaf of documents.

'This is for you.' She plonked them on my lap. 'I stayed late last night and photocopied the Geraldine Jewsbury papers. Oh, don't worry,' she said, seeing the expression on my face. 'I handled them very carefully. I wore gloves and everything. Gosh, it was exciting. Just like being a spy.' Her *naïveté* was endearing.

'Michelle, I told you not to do this.'

'Oh, don't worry.' Her face was still pink and her cheeks were damp, but there was a glint in her eye. 'I've got all that money now. If Giles does give me the sack, I'll tell him where he can stuff his poxy job.'

9

Stories of the Seen and the Unseen

What could I do? I didn't have the heart to refuse. I justified it by arguing that the danger point was past, Giles hadn't caught her doing the photocopying and it wasn't likely that he would find out. And there was no denying that these photocopies were the answer to a prayer. It was no longer vital that I got Giles's ban overturned.

I took the papers back to my office at St Etheldreda's. After all the turmoil of the last few days, it was a blessed relief to plunge into work and lose myself in it. I came to myself with a start at twenty to six, just in time to collect Grace.

When I rang the bell at the nursery, Julia answered the door. When she saw it was me, her eyebrows went up.

'Stephen collected Grace,' she said. 'I saw him myself. Not ten minutes ago.'

Surely I hadn't made the same mistake all over again?

'It is Monday, isn't it?' I said.

She nodded. 'It did occur to me that you

157

usually collect her today, but I just assumed . . . '

I shook my head to indicate incomprehension. 'I always do Mondays, I don't know what Stephen's thinking of.' Even at the best of times I couldn't claim that our household ran like a piece of well-oiled machinery, but we weren't usually as far out of sync as this.

'As you're here, there's something I want to show you.' Julia led the way into her office.

The furniture had been rearranged to accommodate a bank of television screens showing black-and-white pictures of various rooms in the nursery. In the press of events I'd forgotten all about the CCTV and I was doubly surprised to see it installed so soon.

I gestured towards the screens. 'That was jolly quick.' Now that I had a chance to take a closer look at Julia, I saw that some of the strain had left her face.

'The company rang to say they'd got an unexpected gap in their schedule and could they make a start. They came in last night. There's quite a lot left to do. The front-door camera, for instance, and we won't be online until next week. But at least now I can see just what's going on in the nursery and that should put a stop to — ' she broke off abruptly.

'Put a stop to what exactly?' I asked.

Julia got up and went over to the coffee-maker. 'We'll make sure the system isn't open to abuse. You'll need your own password to log on. Will you have a coffee?'

I shook my head. 'What's happened to make you think that the CCTV is a good idea?'

She bought herself some more time by pouring herself a cup of coffee. When she turned back to me, she had made up her mind. 'OK, it's been on my conscience, Cassandra, that I haven't been entirely frank with you. No, no,' she saw the concern on my face and hastened to reassure me. 'It's nothing to do with the children, at least not directly . . . ' Her voice trailed off.

'But,' I prompted her.

'It's going to sound so funny. We *have* had some petty pilfering, but it wasn't the odd thing going missing that worried me, it was only when things started appearing that I got spooked.'

'Started *appearing?*'

'It's easier to show you. Look at this.' She got up from the desk and went over to the screens. I got up and joined her. 'This one here shows the cloakroom.'

We peered at the grainy picture. There was a row of empty pegs.

'Not all the pegs are allocated to children,'

159

she said. 'There are a few left over at the end. Around, oh, I don't know, three months ago I was doing a last check before I went home and there was a little coat on one of the spare pegs. A nice coat, a red one. I was surprised that someone should have gone home without it, but it does happen. The next day it had gone. But then the day after that, it was there again. I took it into my room and asked around, but I couldn't find out who it belonged to. I put it in the lost property box. And then a few days later, I got in first thing in the morning and it was there on the peg again.'

I felt a chill. The hairs were standing up on my arms.

'I'd had enough,' Julia went on. 'I took it to the Oxfam shop. But that wasn't the end of it.' She frowned. 'You know that box we keep in the cloakroom?'

'I don't think . . . '

'Yes, you do.' She pointed to the screens.

'Oh, that, yes.' It was a box for the stuffed animals and other toys that the children insisted on taking to nursery with them. They were placed in the box to be collected on the way home.

'A couple of months ago, when everyone had gone home, Miranda found a teddybear in there. Brand-new. She'd never seen it before. She left it on my desk. It vanished from there and a few days later it was back in the toy-box. And there've been other things. Wendy found a spare pair of wellington boots, red ones with Paddington Bear on them. They don't seem to belong to anyone either.'

I looked along the row of screens. In one Wendy was swabbing down a floor. The rest showed empty rooms and there was something sinister about the stillness of those grainy black-and-white images. I almost expected a jerky figure to lurch into view at any moment.

Julia said, 'One day I was sitting here doing some paperwork and I suddenly got the urge to check on the children. To go round and actually physically count them.'

I was horrified. 'You thought there might be one missing?'

'No, no, you know what our security's like. That was impossible.'

She hesitated. 'I know it sounds crazy, but I thought there might be one too many. Oh, I didn't do it, of course, I didn't,' she said, seeing the expression on my face, 'but that was when I realized that things were getting out of hand. And I'd been considering CCTV anyway. Like I told you before, more and more places are doing it.' She wrapped her arms round herself. 'Why is it so cold in here?' she said.

'I thought it was just me.'

She put her hand on a radiator. 'The heating's still on. I don't understand this. There's a draft coming from somewhere.'

She looked across the room. The door in the corner was open a crack. It led into the kitchen where the children's lunches were prepared. Julia headed for the door and I followed her.

The kitchen was immaculate. Tea-towels were hanging in straight rows from racks. Stainless steel counters gleamed. The place was like a fridge. The door of the larder was ajar. Julia flung it open and a blast of icy air hit us. We looked past the shelves of rice and pasta. At the far end a sash window was wide open to the night. There was a little pile of snow on the floor.

★　★　★

'Perhaps we should start looking for another nursery place,' I said.

Grace was in bed and Stephen and I were finishing off a bottle of wine in the sitting-room.

'I think you're over-reacting,' Stephen said.

He was stretched out full-length on the

sofa with his head on a cushion. I was lounging nearby in an armchair.

'Over-reacting!'

'That's what I said,' he snapped, 'something wrong with your hearing?'

I sat up with a jerk. 'Hey, no need to take it out on me!'

He didn't say anything for a few moments. Then he sighed. 'I'm sorry. I don't know what's the matter with me.' He ran a hand through his hair. 'You know, I could have sworn it was my day for collecting Grace from nursery. I still can't understand how that could have happened. But, Cass, the thought of trying to find somewhere even half as good . . . '

'I know, I know, I don't fancy tramping around looking at places any more than you do . . . '

' . . . and then maybe having to get Grace onto a waiting list.'

'But if the proprietor is going off her head?'

'Oh, come on.' He raised himself up and stuffed another cushion under his head. 'You said yourself that Miranda and what's-her-name, that cleaner, had found unexplained objects lying around as well.'

'Julia *said* they had found things,' I reminded him.

'She's not likely to lie about something that could be so easily checked.'

'Unless she was losing her grip — '

' — and then she'd be much more likely to think that Miranda and the others were planting things behind her back. You know what? Maybe she *ought* to be thinking along those lines. A disgruntled employee. Someone who's got a grudge against her.'

I frowned. 'Seems a rather round-about way of getting back at someone.'

Stephen shrugged. He reached down to where the bottle of wine stood by the sofa. He poured himself another half-glass and beckoned me over. I let him fill my glass and went to stand by the window. The moon was only half full, but in the garden the covering of snow glowed with its light. Thin clouds were streaming across the sky above Ely cathedral. For a moment it seemed that it was not the clouds but the floodlit towers of the cathedral that were in motion like the masts of a ship at sea.

'Anyway,' Stephen was saying behind me, 'from next week we can go online ourselves and check up on Grace. I vote we leave things for the time being.'

'What about the open window?' I said, turning back to the room.

'A bit of carelessness on someone's part.'

164

'I don't want careless people looking after my child.'

He leaned back on the cushions and closed his eyes as if to indicate that the conversation was over. I sat down on the window-seat and cupped my hands round my glass.

I was so used to Stephen that I rarely looked closely at him. I studied his face now. The lines that ran down from the corners of his mouth were deeper and his hair had more grey than black in it.

He sighed and sat up.

'Have we got any aspirin?'

'Upstairs in the bathroom cabinet. Have you got a headache?'

He nodded. 'I think I'll go to bed.'

He hauled himself off the sofa.

I was about to say something conciliatory, maybe even go to bed early too — God knows, I was tired enough — when the telephone rang. Stephen was walking past it and picked it up on the second ring. Something in his face changed as he listened to the voice on the other end.

'It's Jim. For you.' He held out the phone.

When I took it, he turned and left the room. As I put the phone to my ear, I heard his footsteps retreating up the wooden stairs to our bedroom.

'Ah. So you *are* there.'

'Yes, I'm here.' My mouth had gone dry.

'There's been an attempt to break into Green Gables. The crime scene people set up an alarm and it was triggered this evening.'

'Did you catch them?' I said breathlessly.

'No. They had too much time to get away once the alarm had gone off.'

There was a little pause, long enough for me to start putting two and two together.

'Why have you rung me?' I asked.

'I've been ringing round everyone who has any connection with the case,' he said.

'You're ringing to check that I'm at home?' I asked incredulously. 'You really believed it might have been me?'

'Well, now I know that it wasn't, don't I?'

I put the phone down without saying good-bye.

10

Dr Jekyll and Mr Hyde

I knew it was stupid to be so angry and upset, but I couldn't help feeling mortified. I lay awake seething. I told myself that of course Jim had to check up. It didn't necessarily mean that he thought it might have been me. I tried to think rationally about the situation. Jim had said he had rung other people connected with the case: Giles, presumably, and Michelle. I wondered who else was in the frame. And why would someone want to break into Una's house anyway? If it was the murderer, they couldn't hope to destroy any forensic evidence when the police had already gone over the place with a fine-tooth comb. And if it wasn't the murderer, who was it? Just a common-or-garden burglar who had realized that there was no one living in the house? What was there to steal except for books? Maybe it was the same person who had stolen the Henry James first editions? I tossed and turned. Stephen was restless too. I dropped off several times only to be woken up when he kicked me or flung an arm over me.

At six o'clock I woke with a start. My throat was dry and there was a hollow feeling around my temples. My subconscious must have been working overtime, because I woke up with a decision already made. I would go and see Eileen Burnham. OK, so Jim had told me not to mention the missing first editions to anyone, but so what? After our exchange the previous evening, I didn't feel very co-operative. Anyway, I could probably pump Eileen without letting anything slip about Una's missing books.

After I'd dropped Grace off at nursery, I drove to New Town and found a parking meter just off Trumpington Road. There was a bitter wind that tugged at me like a demanding child and somehow found its way inside my clothes. Someone once told me that the winds that blow across the Fens sweep down across Europe from the frozen steppes of the Urals and I can well believe it. I was shaking with cold when I arrived at Burnham Books.

It was one of the times when Eileen was in the shop. I could see her through the window, sitting at a desk and talking into the telephone. As I went in, almost blown through the doorway by the force of the wind, Eileen smiled at me and raised a hand in a gesture that meant she wouldn't be long.

'Yes,' she said into the phone, 'the shop is open weekday mornings, or I could post it to you.'

I looked around. My immediate impression was of warmth and light and perfume, somehow reminding me of the Palm House in the Botanic Gardens. The pale carpet was thick under my feet. There were books, but not a huge number, some arranged on beech shelves and some in display cases. The scent came from a huge spray of lilies in a vase in the window: a few books on botanical themes had been scattered artfully around it. The place was more like an expensive clothes shop than a second-hand book shop.

'Fine . . . Fine . . . yes, see you soon, glad to be of assistance. Bye then.' Eileen hung up.

'Simply ghastly,' she said to me in a quite different voice. She tapped the cover of the book in front of her.

It looked as if it dated from the 1970s. The soft focus photograph in unconvincing colours showing a naked man and woman lying entwined in a meadow.

Eileen opened the book and read aloud from the blurb. ''All great artists have studied the nude, but life models aren't always available . . . '' She wrinkled her nose in amused distaste. 'It's basically soft porn masquerading as a book for artists. Someone actually asked me to track down a copy.'

'It *is* rather tacky,' I agreed.

She grinned at me. 'Oh, well, collectors come in all sizes and shapes. Luckily for me. For every book, there's a buyer, that's the bookseller's mantra. It's just a question of bringing the two together. Talking of which, Cassandra, can I interest you in a very nice copy of Geraldine Jewsbury's *The Half-Sisters*?'

I was momentarily side-tracked. 'I've been wanting a copy of that for ages. How much?'

'£75.'

'A first edition?'

'Alas, no. You'd expect to pay a lot more for that.'

'How much more?'

'Hard to say. You could be heading up towards a thousand. Maybe more.'

I forced my attention back to the matter in hand. 'What would be the going rate for a first edition of Henry James's *Portrait of a Lady*?'

There was a silence.

'*Portrait of a Lady*,' Eileen said thoughtfully. 'There were only seven hundred and fifty copies of the first issue of the first UK edition. They don't very often come on the market. You could be looking at as much as

170

£7,000. Depends on the condition.'

'Are the earlier novels worth more?'

'Tends to be the case.'

'*Daisy Miller*?'

Eileen shrugged. '£3000?'

'And the later stuff? *The Spoils of Poynton*, for example?'

'Oh, a lot less. Two hundred quid would get you something decent.' Eileen's face was sombre. 'This is about Una Carwardine's books, isn't it? The police have already asked me about them.' She came to a decision. 'I don't see why I shouldn't tell you. The Henry James first editions that Una owned? Well, those books weren't stolen.'

I stared at her. 'But I saw for myself — '

'Yes, yes, they're gone all right. Una sold them. How do I know? She sold them to me.'

'And the books that are there now?'

'I supplied those as reading copies. I suppose you want to know the whole story?'

'You bet.'

'I think we'd better go through to the back.'

She opened a drawer in the desk and took out a sign that read 'Please ring bell.' She hung it on the door.

'Follow me,' she said.

The back room was a small kitchen with linoleum on the floor and a yellow Formica table with matching chairs. It was chilly, and when Eileen bent down and switched on the two-bar electric heater, there was a smell of burning dust.

'I don't tend to use this room very much,' she said. 'I do most of my paperwork in the flat upstairs. Want some coffee?'

'No thanks.'

'Mind if I have a ciggie?' She brought out a packet of Balkan Sobranies.

'Go ahead. Haven't seen a packet of those for years.'

'I didn't used to like them very much. That's why I started smoking them. I thought it would make it easier to cut down.'

'And did it?'

'Nope, just got used to them. Take a seat, why don't you?'

She lit a cigarette, took a deep drag and let the smoke curl slowly out of her mouth. 'It all started about a year ago. Una rang me one day. She'd been interested in first edition crime and sensation fiction for years and she'd bought the odd thing from me. There was something she wanted that was coming up for sale at Sotheby's. She asked me to go and bid for it on her behalf. No big surprise there, I do that sometimes for my customers. On commission, of course.'

I felt a sneeze coming on and only just

managed to get a tissue out of my bag before it arrived.

'What was it that she wanted?' I asked, wiping my nose.

'Mrs Henry Wood's *East Lynne*. A first edition. You don't see them very often and it went for £16,500.'

'What!' It came out as a yelp.

'It *is* an unusually high price for a Victorian novel,' Eileen admitted, 'but it's extremely rare. And this was also an association copy.'

'Meaning?'

'In this case that it had belonged to Wilkie Collins.' She looked at me with a pitying expression. 'You don't really know much about the trade, do you?'

'Why don't you enlighten me?'

'OK,' she said. 'A crash course. To put it crudely, at one end of the market there's your bog-standard first edition, plain and unadorned. There might be dozens, even hundreds, or thousands of those. All depends. Then there's the signed edition with just the author's signature. Obviously there'll be fewer of those and that'll bump up the price.' She took another drag on her cigarette. 'And then we move onto association copies of various kinds, like the one I've just mentioned from Wilkie Collins's library. There'll only be one of those. Actual value will depend on the intrinsic interest. For example, a copy of *A Tale of Two Cities* inscribed by Dickens to George Eliot came on the market a while ago. Something like that is very, very desirable to a collector and you're looking at the high end of the market. And right at the top is the presentation copy: that's where there's a printed dedication *and* the book is signed to the person it's dedicated to.'

'I see,' I said slowly. 'And that was the kind of thing Una liked?'

Eileen shrugged. 'When it came up. She bought plenty of stuff without association. And not just nineteenth-century stuff either. I remember I found her a very nice copy of *Hercule Poirot's Christmas*. She enjoyed the thrill of the chase. You know, for some collectors that's all that matters. They're not really interested in the book itself. I'm not saying that was the case with Una. She did love them as physical objects, but she relished the excitement too.'

Eileen mashed out her cigarette in a saucer.

I remembered what Una had said in her letter: 'akin to gambling, really.' That made sense now.

'So why did she sell the Henry James first editions?'

'Sorry. Didn't I say? She was running short of cash. She sold some books in order to buy others. It wasn't just Henry James that went. There was a very nice first edition of Darwin's *Voyage of the Beagle*. I managed to get £56,000 for it.'

'*Lady Audley's Secret:* was that the most expensive thing she bought?'

Eileen shook her head. 'As far as I know, the single most expensive item was a copy of *The Hound of the Baskervilles*. She paid £75,000 for that.'

I stared at her in disbelief. '£75,000!'

'With dust jacket,' she said, as if that explained everything. 'That makes it very, very rare. Just a few copies in existence.'

I was beginning to understand why Una had needed to sell the house. 'How much do you think she spent in all?'

Eileen considered. 'Well, I've started to make a list for the police, so I'll have more idea when I've finished that. But I'd say somewhere in the region of a hundred thousand or so, on top of the money she got from cashing in books from the collection.'

That left an awful lot of money unaccounted for.

'Was she buying things right up until the end?' I asked.

'I don't know. She did a lot of her own bidding by telephone. I bought the odd thing for her, but really I was more of a consultant.

I let her know when things were coming on the market, what she could expect to pay, that kind of thing. And anyway I was out of action for about three weeks before Una died. Kidney stones it was. I was in hospital for ages getting over the op and the infection.'

Just then the doorbell rang.

Eileen and I looked at each other.

The door into the shop was ajar. By leaning back in her chair Eileen could see who had rung the bell. She turned back to me with an expression that combined concern and amusement.

'It's Giles,' she said.

* * *

'He owned up to being on the same errand,' I told Merfyn. 'He wanted to find out what had happened to Una's books. And to do him justice I think he was genuinely concerned about Michelle being under suspicion.'

'And he actually apologized to you?' Merfyn was sitting in one of the armchairs in my office, long tweed-clad legs stretched out in front of him. He had dropped in to confer with me about appointing an external examiner.

'Well, sort of. You see, I took the bull by the horns. I asked him if he didn't think he was being a little petty-minded. I said, 'What would the Duke of Wellington have done?''

Merfyn spluttered with laughter. 'You said *what?*'

I didn't reply immediately. My nose was tickling and the next moment a volcanic sneeze threw me back in my chair.

'Coming down with a cold,' I explained. 'The thing is that Giles is a great admirer of the Iron Duke. But I think he was having second thoughts anyway. He said that perhaps he had over-reacted and that he shouldn't have accused me of exerting undue influence. And he shouldn't have banned me from the library either. But he did warn me that he is still going to recommend to the trustees that they contest the will on the grounds that the earlier will represented Una's true intentions. Can't blame him for trying, I suppose.'

'Really, Cassandra, you are being maddeningly high-minded about all this,' Merfyn said.

'I can afford to be. I've spoken to Una's doctor and he hasn't a hope in hell of succeeding. And I don't think the trustees will back him up. But he was pinning all his hopes on that legacy — God knows, the Institute could do with the money — and he isn't ready to let it go. And there's something else, something Giles doesn't know.' I hesitated. How much should I tell Merfyn? 'You'll have to keep this to yourself for now,' I warned him. 'Though I don't suppose it's going to remain a secret for very long.'

'Cross my heart,' Merfyn said with the earnestness of a little boy. It was one of the endearing things about him: he'd reached fifty without ever quite losing that wide-eyed enthusiasm.

I told him about the sale of the house and the missing money.

Merfyn gave a long, low whistle. 'So the legacy may yet turn out to be a white elephant. We'll have all those books and no money to build somewhere to put them.'

'I've found out what happened to some of the money,' I said. I explained what Una had been doing.

Merfyn slowly sat upright. An enormous smile spread across his face. 'You don't mean to tell me that Una was selling off Terence's first editions of Henry James so that she could buy *crime* fiction?'

I was slightly nettled. 'I yield to no one in my admiration for *Portrait of a Lady*, but these days most people would agree that novels like *East Lynne* and *Lady Audley's Secret* are also worth studying.'

'You'd have to have known Terence to

appreciate the joke. He was an unreconstructed scholar of the old school, dead against any form of popular culture. Not that he didn't have a point. You only need to spend an evening in front of the TV to see that we're going to hell in a handcart. But he did take that point of view to extremes. For him Henry James was the *non plus ultra*.' Merfyn kissed his fingers. 'Fiction had been going downhill ever since.'

'What about Graham Greene? Evelyn Waugh?'

'Mere vulgar upstarts.'

'You're exaggerating. What about all those sensation novels that he and Una collected?'

'That part of the collection was Una's work. It was one area where they really didn't see eye to eye. He was very sniffy about it. And he really did worship Henry James. Talking of books, is that something that you've just acquired?' He pointed to my desk where there was a book in a paper bag with an elegant design showing the façade of Burnham Books. 'May I?' he asked.

I nodded. I still wasn't quite sure how Eileen had got me to part with £75. I'd never paid so much for a book in my life.

'So it's odd then, isn't it, that she chose those particular books to sell off?'

'I wonder . . . ' Merfyn said as he turned

the pages of *The Half-Sisters*. 'You know, I really didn't care for Terence Carwardine. You remember what Danny Kaye said about the Himalayas? 'Loved her, hated him.' Well, it was like that. Celia and I were invited round for dinner a few times and we went because we liked Una. But Terence seemed to me to be a bitter and disappointed man.'

I was incredulous. 'Oh, come on, Merfyn. What did he have to be disappointed about? He had a career that most people would give their right arm for. Master of a Cambridge college, chairing important committees, general editor of this series and that.'

Merfyn held up a hand. 'No, hear me out. I'm not denying that as a young man he was very talented. He had a good idea and he wrote a ground-breaking book about it. But that was about it. My guess is that intellectually he had run out of steam years ago. He knew that and it was eating him up.'

I considered this. Was Terence Carwardine one of those people who peak so early that the rest of their career is inevitably a disappointment?

'You only had to be in his presence for ten minutes to feel it,' Merfyn went on. 'He couldn't rest until he'd made you feel small.'

I was remembering something myself now. 'Didn't I once hear that there was some trouble with a student?'

Merfyn nodded. 'He got a reputation for being a bit of a bully. A Ph.D. student — more than one, I think — asked to be transferred to another supervisor. Of course, he was in pretty poor health by then. That could have accounted for some of it.'

I pondered what Merfyn had said. Success is relative. I'd once taught a mature student who had been thrilled to scrape a pass on his first year course. He'd left school at fourteen and even that level of academic achievement had been beyond his wildest dreams. Other students had ambitions that even a first-class honours degree couldn't satisfy. All the same . . .

'I never had any inkling of this from Una,' I told Merfyn.

My nose was running in earnest. I dabbed at it with a tissue.

'Look at it from her point of view,' Merfyn said. 'She simply couldn't afford not to see him in the best possible light. They didn't have children, so her whole life had been given over to supporting him. She never owned up to doing more than bits of research for him, reading proofs, compiling the index, but I'd be surprised if there wasn't a lot more to it than that. She'd have got a lot further on her own merits if she hadn't been shackled to him.'

Merfyn tended to exaggerate, I knew that, but still, the picture he painted was a plausible one. In my experience there is almost no limit to what people can ignore in a marriage. In fact it could be argued that a certain selective blindness is essential for the perpetuation of the human race.

But Merfyn's theory didn't account for everything.

'That doesn't explain why she flogged the Henry James,' I pointed out. 'Far from it.'

'I was getting to that.' There was a hint of reproof in his voice. 'Suppose that all those years, she goes along with it, colluding with the myth of his greatness, bolstering him up. And she goes on doing it after he's dead. She intends to devote the rest of her life to creating a suitable memorial to the dear departed. I bet part of the Institute would have been named after him. And then something happens . . . ' He spread out both hands in an expansive gesture.

'What kind of something?'

He shrugged. 'I don't know. Maybe she found he'd been plagiarizing someone else's work. Whatever it is, the scales drop from her eyes, and she realizes that Terence Carward-ine is not the man she'd thought he was.' The Welsh sing-song in Merfyn's voice grew more pronounced as he got excited. He leaned forward eagerly. 'It makes her mad to think that she put him first all these years! Sod that for a game of soldiers! What better revenge than to dispose of the books that were his pride and joy and use the money to buy some of the fiction that he despised.'

What had Una said to Jane? *You can think you know people through and through and then* . . .

'I bet the old bugger is turning in his grave,' Merfyn added. He didn't sound displeased at the idea.

'If you're right, it could explain Una's new will. Maybe in the end she decided that — '

But I didn't finish what I was saying, because at that moment I realized that Merfyn wasn't listening to me. There were raised voices outside my office. Merfyn got to his feet and I followed him to the door. Out in the corridor a big, broad-shouldered man was arguing with John, one of the porters, and was shaking off the restraining hand that John had laid on his arm.

'I've got to insist that you leave the premises immediately,' John was saying. His face was set and unhappy. Porters aren't security guards or bouncers. John was overweight and nearing retirement.

'I'm not leaving until I see her,' the intruder said. I was sure I'd never seen this man before, but his voice was oddly familiar.

The threat of violence seemed to thicken the air, making it hard to move, or even to breathe. I wanted to step back, but I forced myself to stand my ground. For a moment the man reminded me of Stephen, but it was a superficial resemblance based on his dress — pin-striped suit, white shirt, and sober tie — and the floppy dark hair, threaded with silver, that he was pushing back from his forehead as he spoke. His face was coarser than Stephen's, fleshier, with thicker lips. He was one of those men who seem to take up more space than their size warrants and he was radiating anger like a furnace gives off heat.

Merfyn and I spoke at once:

'What's going on here?'

'Do you need some help, John?'

The man turned to look at us. His eyes travelled over me and then dismissed me. He saw the name in the slot on my door and his eyes narrowed.

'So this is her office. I'm not leaving until I've spoken to Cassandra James.'

Merfyn and I exchanged glances. The man strode past me and pushed the door open with such force that it bounced back from the wall. He scanned the room.

'Where is she?' he demanded.

Merfyn took a step forward and stretched out an arm to make a barrier between me and the angry stranger.

By now I had recognized the voice. 'You're Charles, aren't you?'

He had been gazing around the room as if there might still be someone in there, crouching under the desk perhaps or squeezed into a cupboard. Now he spun on his heel and stared at me. He frowned.

'Yes?'

'I'm Cassandra James,' I said. 'You've made a mistake.'

'No,' he said, shaking his head, but I could tell that he wasn't sure of himself any longer. He looked at Merfyn.

Merfyn said, 'She's right. This *is* Cassandra. I'm afraid someone's been giving you the run around, old chap.' He spoke gently but firmly, like someone trying to calm an over-excited child.

'No,' Charles said, but he spoke without heat. Now that the anger had left his face it seemed to have sagged a little. He looked tired and middle-aged.

John had dropped back, relieved no doubt to let me and Merfyn take over. Now he asserted himself again.

'I want you to leave right away, sir,' he said.

'It's all right, John, I want to get to the

bottom of this,' I said.

He made a show of looking doubtful. 'If you're sure . . . '

'Quite sure.'

'Well then, I'd better get back to the lodge.' We watched as John made his way down the corridor, his relief evident in every contour. By tacit consent none of us spoke until he was out of ear-shot.

Charles cleared his throat. 'I must apologize, I really must. And what I said on the phone, too.' His face was red. 'I suppose that was you, as well, wasn't it?'

I nodded.

'God, I'm sorry,' he said. 'You did sound so much like her. I really am so sorry. Look, I think I'd better — ' He gestured in the direction that John had taken. Now that he had realized his mistake, he couldn't wait to get away.

'Oh no, you don't,' said Merfyn. 'You don't get off that lightly.'

Charles glanced at his watch in a transparent attempt to excuse himself. 'I really must . . . '

'You owe me an explanation,' I said. 'Come into my office.'

Charles hesitated and then made a gesture of capitulation. 'All right, who knows, maybe you'll be able to shed some light on this.'

He was an accountant working for a firm that had offices on Regent Street. He had gone for a drink after work with colleagues and they'd ended up making a night of it. A woman who was alone in the bar got attached to the group and she had showed a flattering interest in him. One thing had led to another and they had spent the night together.

'First time since my marriage broke up,' he said, looking down and fiddling with a gold cufflink. 'I don't usually go in for one-night stands. Just got carried away, thought it was the beginning of something.'

'She said her name was Cassandra James?' I prompted.

He nodded. 'She took my scarf. A cashmere one. I lent it to her when we came out of the pub. My daughter gave me that for Christmas and I was damned if I was going to let her hang onto it. That was another reason why I was so keen to track her down.'

'She said that she worked here?'

He hesitated. 'She wrote her number on a bit of paper, but when I woke up the next morning, she'd gone and I couldn't find the piece of paper. I thought I remembered something about St Etheldreda's, but I'm not sure how I knew that. And I'm not even sure what exactly she said her job was.'

Merfyn and I looked at each other.

'What did this woman look like?' Merfyn asked Charles.

'Did she look like me?' I wanted to know.

Charles glanced up at me and looked away again. 'Sort of. A bit. Her hair was lighter and not as short as yours. And she was younger.'

'How much younger?' I asked.

He shrugged. 'Sorry. I'm rotten at guessing ages. And it was dark in the bar and then, well, I was pretty drunk to tell you the truth.'

'What colour were her eyes?' Merfyn asked.

'Um, blue? Maybe?'

'Did she have an accent of any kind?' I asked.

'Not really. When I rang up the college and got you, well, I did think it was her, though the funny thing is that now that I can see you as well as hear you, you don't sound *that* much like her.'

Merfyn rolled his eyes in exasperation. 'Didn't she have *any* distinguishing features?'

Charles pursed his lips and shook his head. 'Not really, I mean, she wasn't anything out of the way in looks.' He brightened. 'Oh, yes, there was one thing. She had a birthmark, quite a large one.'

'Where?' I asked.

'On her left breast.'

'Wonderful,' Merfyn said, 'all Cassandra has to do is round up all the forty-something women with short brown hair in Cambridge and ask them to strip to the waist. Then she'll know who's been impersonating her.'

The telephone rang. As I got up to answer it, I said, 'If she *is* impersonating me. Do we really have any evidence?'

But all that went out of my head as soon as I heard the voice on the other end of the line.

It was Stephen's secretary ringing to tell me that he had been taken ill at the office and she didn't think he was fit to drive home.

11

When It Was Dark

Chickenpox can be terribly debilitating in adults. The spots on Stephen's chest explained a lot of his behaviour over the last few days: his absent-mindedness, his lethargy, and his bad temper. I wasn't sure that it explained everything, but there wasn't much opportunity to reflect on that or on anything else over the next few days. I had disappeared into a domestic black hole. Simple survival was all I aimed for.

By the following day Stephen was covered with painful, itchy spots from head to foot. His head ached so badly that he couldn't read or even listen to the radio. He was feverish and I was, too, because by then my cold was in full bloom. My eyes watered and my nose dripped. On the next day, Thursday, I got up, drove Grace to the nursery, came home and got back into bed. By now Stephen was sleeping in the spare room on the ground floor. Now and then I emerged to stagger downstairs and heat up a can of soup, swallow some paracetamol, or dab calamine lotion on Stephen's spots. By the afternoon my temperature was even higher than his. I couldn't stand up without feeling giddy. My mother left work early and drove up from London to collect Grace from nursery. She stayed over until the weekend. By that time my temperature was normal. My ears still crackled with catarrh and my head felt as if it was full of glue, but I was more or less functional.

On Saturday morning my mother took Grace out and a luxurious silence settled over the house. If there is one thing more exhausting than looking after a sick child, it is looking after a riotously healthy one, when you are sick yourself.

I made some tea and took a tray into the little ground-floor bedroom.

Stephen was propped up on the pillows, reading an old orange Penguin paperback of Cherry Apsley-Gerard's *The Worst Journey in the World*, the story of Scott's ill-fated Antarctic expedition. Bill Bailey, who clearly thought we had stayed at home expressly to provide him with company and somewhere warm to sleep, was stretched out beside him on the gold and red duvet cover. He opened his eyes the merest slit and flexed his paws in greeting.

Stephen looked up briefly. 'I've just got to

the part where they have to shoot the ponies and feed them to the huskies,' he informed me.

'There's always someone who's worse off than you are.' I sat down in the armchair and put the tray on the bed. 'Any more spots this morning?'

'No, and the old ones are drying up.'

The single bed took up half the space, and the rest was filled by a bedside table, the single chair I was sitting in and makeshift bookcases of bricks and planks. This was an annexe for the over-flow from my study and classic crime and adventure fiction — Agatha Christie, Josephine Tey, Ngaio Marsh and John Buchan — rubbed shoulders with battered relics of my childhood, such as *Alice in Wonderland* and the Famous Five.

I sat back and closed my eyes for a few moments while the tea brewed.

'Cass?'

'Mmm?' I opened my eyes.

Stephen had closed his book and was looking at me. 'You know the doctor said I shouldn't go back to work for at least a week? I'm thinking about going down to Devon and convalescing at Martha's.'

Stephen's sister Martha and her husband run a farm in Devon, close to where Stephen was brought up.

I poured out the tea.

'How would you get down there?' I asked. 'You're not well enough to drive. I suppose I could take you at a pinch . . . but then there's Grace to think of, too.'

'Two things. Firstly, I can get someone to drive me down. There's Frank, the chap we use at the office to drive us to Heathrow. I imagine he would be glad of the money. And the other thing: Grace could come too.'

I stared at him, the teapot still in my hand. 'But — '

'Do think about it, Cass. You know Martha would love to have her. She wouldn't see it as a chore. It's the kind of thing she takes in her stride.'

Unlike me, I thought. Martha and I couldn't have been more different. It seemed no effort at all for her to turn out huge meals for her strapping husband and teenage sons, not to mention the lambs and kittens and chicks that regularly took up residence in her kitchen.

Stephen interpreted the expression on my face correctly. 'You have other strengths,' he pointed out. 'Martha is my sister and she is a wonderful wife and mother and I love her dearly, but I wouldn't care to be married to a woman who never reads anything except women's magazines and the *Livestock Gazette*.'

'Nice of you to say so.' I put his tea on the bedside table. 'But it wouldn't be much of a rest for you, would it, with Grace around?'

'I could stay in one of their holiday cottages. Grace could be with me at night and she could toddle around with Martha during the day.'

'What if it's not convenient for her?'

'It is. I spoke to her on the phone this morning, while you were out getting the paper.'

'So you've already arranged it all!'

'No, no, of course not, but do think about it, love. Your mother's got to go back to London tomorrow, hasn't she? So you could come with us and stay for a night or two. Settle Grace in, have a bit of a rest. You're still not well yourself.'

Stephen lay back with an air of fatigue and closed his eyes. He was almost as pale as the pillows he was propped up against and the pockmarks on his face hadn't completely healed yet. Bill Bailey was gazing at us, disturbed by something in the tone of our voices. I put up a hand and ruffled his luxurious belly fur. He purred and his eyes narrowed to liquid green slits.

I turned over Stephen's proposition in my mind. Perhaps there was something to be said for it. At least he would get a proper rest if he was well away from the office. I'd get a rest, too, if I was here on my own. And I was so far behind with my writing schedule . . . Could I really afford to turn down a chance to start catching up? On the other hand, to be parted from Grace . . .

'How long did you have in mind?' I asked.

'No more than a week at the most,' Stephen said, without opening his eyes. 'You know, some time apart might do us both good.'

I was startled. 'How do you mean?'

'Well, all this business about having another baby. I know I've been putting pressure on you. Maybe we both need time to mull it over.'

'Oh, well, yes, maybe . . . ' I rubbed my face. There was an ache that seemed to spread out from the roots of my teeth into my left cheek bone. I brought my cup of tea up to my face and inhaled the steam.

'I wonder if they're any closer to finding out who killed Una,' Stephen said. 'Funny that Jim hasn't been in touch with you. Or has he?'

'I haven't spoken to him for days. Not since that evening he rang here, in fact.' I deliberately met Stephen's eyes. He looked thoughtfully into mine.

'You know,' he said, 'I get the impression

that you don't think as highly of Jim as you did.'

'I think he's a very able police officer.'

'Oh, quite.'

There was a silence. I pressed my cup of tea against my aching cheek.

Stephen said, 'Why don't you move into the flat while I'm away? You can walk into the Institute from there and I'd feel easier if you weren't doing this drive every day.'

'Aren't you forgetting something? No pets allowed.' I pointed to Bill Bailey. He yawned and stretched out a languid paw.

'I suppose I could always take him to Devon.'

'He'd hate that and there'd be ructions with the farm cats. No, he'd better stay here. And I'd better stay with him.'

Stephen put his empty cup on the bedside table. 'That's settled then. I'll phone Frank and see when he can take us.'

★ ★ ★

Frank drove us to Devon on Sunday. I spent Monday reading and sleeping and working my way through Martha's enormous meals. Grace toddled round helping to feed the chickens and doing little jobs that were invented for her. She couldn't stay away from the tiny premature lamb that had a bed in the slow oven of the Aga and was fed with a bottle. Stephen slept a lot and by the time I left to go back on Tuesday, the colour was coming back into his face. I felt better, too: I was still croaky but the ache in my sinuses had gone.

I spent the train journey from Exeter to Paddington rereading Elizabeth Gaskell's *Wives and Daughters* and making notes for my chapter on stepsisters. The world outside receded as I followed Molly Gibson along muddy country lanes, eavesdropping on her thoughts as she fretted over her father's remarriage and her acquisition of a fascinating and flirtatious new sister. It was not until I had crossed London on the tube and caught a train from King's Cross to Cambridge that my thoughts turned reluctantly to the present. I stared out at the gently rolling countryside and wondered how the investigation into Una's death was going. I couldn't bring myself to ring Jim and in any case he probably wouldn't tell me anything. I told myself it wasn't surprising that Jim hadn't been in touch. He was working round the clock to break a murder case. After Royston the fields got flatter, more Fen-like. The air was a sumptuous blue that was deepening imperceptibly into night. Mist drifted in across snow-covered fields, luminous in the twilight. The question of the missing money nagged at me. According to my calculations around half a million was unaccounted for. I was still pondering that when the train drew up at Cambridge station.

I intended to have a quick meal there and then drive home. My car was at the college, where I had left it so that I could drive Stephen home in his own car on the day that he had been taken ill. As my taxi crawled through the Cambridge rush-hour, I saw with a sinking heart that the mist was thickening into fog. On the Madingley Road we hit a bank of it and the driver slowed to a crawl. I revised my plans. I'd better set off soon, before the weather got worse.

When I'd paid off the driver, I hesitated outside the main entrance. Should I go left and head round the building to the carpark or should I turn right into the college to collect my mail and check my messages? I needed a pee. That was what decided me, along with the barely acknowledged hope that there might be a message from Jim.

There was the usual bumf in my pigeon-hole, though not too much of it. I guessed that Merfyn had filtered out the things he could deal with.

On dark winter days there's something

about the dead, even light in college corridors and the echo of solitary footsteps that makes the spirits sink. You'd scarcely credit how few people are around at 6.30; the students are in the dining-room and most of the tutors have gone home. As I headed for my office, I promised myself a treat when I got home: scrambled eggs on toast and a large gin and tonic. I'd watch TV, or read that novel I'd been saving up. It was literally years since I'd had an evening with no interruptions.

The first few messages on my voicemail came as no surprise. My editor was disappointed not to have received anything from me yet: if my book was to go into the next catalogue, they'd need everything by the end of February. Sheffield University wondered if I had got their previous message asking me to give a paper in their series of research seminars. They needed to finalize their arrangements for the next semester. The finance department wanted to know why I hadn't answered their query about expenses for that conference in Edinburgh. It was a relief when the next message was from Eileen, telling me that she had just acquired a nice little library of sensation fiction; she'd be pricing some of the volumes at less than £20. Was I interested? Even if I wasn't, how about lunch sometime?

The last message was from Jim. When I heard his voice, my heart did a curtsy.

'Just to let you know,' he said, 'there are one or two promising lines of inquiry. If there are any important developments, I'll be in touch.'

That was it: no hello or goodbye and not much news either, but it was better than nothing. The warmth that spread through me told me how much I'd minded not knowing what was going on. As I listened to the message again, I gazed out into the courtyard. The fog curled and billowed, slowly expanding to reach into the corners of the courtyard, like milk poured into a bowl of water. Even as I watched, the lights on the far side of the court faded away and the lamp by the copper beech became a watery yellow star that marked the limit of my vision. Time to head for home. I hoped I hadn't already left it too late.

From my office, the quickest way to the car-park is through the large court and then the smaller one to a corridor that leads to a side-door. As I let myself out, I shivered and pulled the flaps of my hat down over my ears. The lanterns on top of their cast-iron posts gave off a weak yellow light that scarcely reached the pavement. The fog was in constant gentle movement, teasing the eye. It was like sitting in a stationary train when the train next to you pulls out: the effect was disorientating. I stumbled more than once as I picked my way across the uneven flagstones.

I had almost reached the copper beech when I heard a sound. It was distorted and muffled by the fog, and I couldn't tell what it was or where it came from. A door shutting perhaps? I looked around, but the fog had closed in behind me. Both sides of the courtyard had disappeared. I could see only two or three feet ahead of me as I picked my way to the archway into the second court. I glanced back again. The banks of fog had drifted apart to form a ragged tunnel. Was someone standing under the beech tree? Before I could be sure, the fog had shifted again and the tunnel had closed up. 'Night and silence! Who is there?' The words spoken by Puck in *A Midsummer Night's Dream* came into my head. It was ridiculous to feel nervous — if anyone was there, it had to be a student or another member of staff — but my heart was beating fast. I pushed on, not looking back, my ears straining for the sound of footsteps behind me. It seemed to take forever to get to the other side. I opened the door and stepped over the threshold into light and warmth. There was a murmur of voices. I saw a couple of young women walking along, deep in conversation. I followed them down the corridor and when I reached the end, I looked back to see if anyone had followed me in. There was no one.

The car-park was lit by floodlights and the fog was a little thinner here. I'd parked the car close to the building and I saw it straightaway. All the same I couldn't quite shake off a sense of unease and I was pleased to see one of the porters doing his rounds.

The car was covered with a patina of ice and inside it was like a deep freeze. I switched the engine on and turned the heater on full blast. I got out again to clear the windscreen. The ice was so solid that I bent the scraper. I cleared an area the size of a dinner-plate and gave up. Easier to wait for the heater to do its work. I switched on the radio and caught the end of the weather forecast. Temperatures were set to rise and a thaw was in prospect. It couldn't come soon enough for me.

When the side windows were clear too, I put the car into gear, and crawled across the car-park in first.

As I edged out onto the Madingley Road, I saw a figure in a woolly hat and scarf and voluminous coat standing at the bus stop. It took me a moment to realize that it was Wendy.

I stopped and wound down the car window.

'Hi there.' My voice so husky that I sounded like Marlene Dietrich.

Wendy had been looking the other way. She turned with a startled expression.

'Can I give you a lift?' I asked.

She muttered something that I didn't hear. 'Sorry?'

'Oh no, it's really kind, I'm fine, honestly.'

'Where do you live?'

'Arbury. I don't want to take you out of your way.'

'It isn't — or hardly at all.' I reached over and opened the door. 'Hop in.'

She hesitated and I thought she was about to refuse. Then she stepped towards the car. She seemed to be hung about with more bags and scarves than she could manage She clambered in, catching her shopping bag on the door. Her coat settled over the gear stick. When I moved it, she blushed and muttered an apology.

I pulled away from the kerb and crept off down the road, my eyes glued to the rear lights of the car ahead of me. She didn't speak and I was happy to concentrate on the road ahead. It was only when we were in a queue for the traffic lights at Magdalene Street, that the silence struck me as awkward. I cast around for something to say.

'You're not at the nursery tonight?' I said,

glancing sideways at her.

'No, it's my evening class, but it finished early. The weather . . . people were worrying about getting home . . . '

'Are you still planning to do an Open University course?'

Her face brightened. 'Yes, I'm going to start next year.'

A large piece of ice slid off the roof and down the windscreen. I switched the wipers on. There was a crunching sound and fragments of ice spun off to left and right.

'Dr Carwardine used to work at the college, didn't she?' Wendy said.

Her voice was soft and this seemed such a *non sequitur* that I wasn't sure I'd heard her properly over the sound of the engine.

'Una? Una Carwardine?' I asked.

Wendy nodded. 'I cleaned for her. Once a week.'

'You did?' I looked at Wendy. Her face was pale and her nose seemed more pointed than I remembered, but that might have been the light from the streetlamp. 'Then it must have been you who — '

'Yes, I found her. I wasn't even expecting her to be at home. I thought she was still away on holiday.'

'It must have been a terrible shock.'

'Oh it was.' Wendy twisted her hands on

the handle of her bag. She raised a hand to her mouth and I saw that her nails were bitten to the quick. When she saw me looking, she put her hand back in her lap. 'I was that fond of her,' she said. 'And then when the solicitor wrote to me about the will, you could have knocked me down with a feather. Ten thousand pounds, she'd left me.'

You could have knocked me down with a feather, too.

'That's wonderful,' I said.

'It was ever such a surprise. And the solicitor said that she wanted me to spend it on my education. She put that in the will.'

The driver behind me sounded his horn. I hadn't noticed that the traffic was moving. Hastily I put the car in gear.

I said, 'She must have known how much you wanted to do your Open University course.'

'We got talking one day over a cup of coffee and she came right out and asked me. Wendy, she said, have you ever wanted anything so badly that you'd be prepared to give up almost anything for it. And I told her, I've always longed to go to university, but you know, I left school when I was sixteen and then I got married, and it didn't work out and there's my little girl . . . '

'How old is she?'

'She's two.'

Wendy went on speaking almost in a undertone, more as if she was talking to herself than to me.

'Fancy Dr Carwardine remembering . . . I just can't get over it . . . '

I made sympathetic noises, but I was only half-listening. What Una had said seemed to imply that she had spent that half a million on just one thing. What could she have wanted so desperately? A book? But could one spend half a million on a book?

We'd reached the top of the queue now. The light changed and I pulled away.

As Wendy directed me through a maze of streets I managed to ask a few tactful questions, before I got too hoarse to speak. It was clear to me that Wendy had no idea why Una had changed her will and that she only knew about the second will as far as it concerned her.

We drew up outside a long four-storey block of flats built of brick and lit by security lights. The fog had begun to disperse and I saw balconies crowded with household junk. Snow coated the scrappy rose-bushes in the flower-beds. A doctor's surgery occupied part of the ground floor and the notice on the door told its own story: *no drugs or money on these premises which are alarmed*. This part of Cambridge was a world away from the city of the colleges and the commons. Some of the people who serviced that privileged world — the shop assistants, the waiters, the cooks and the cleaners — lived out here in the hinterland.

I didn't drive off until I had seen Wendy safely inside.

* * *

As soon as I pushed open the door of the Old Granary, I knew something was wrong. The sound of a key in the lock usually brings Bill Bailey running, but today there was no mew of welcome, no paws padding down the stairs. I dumped my bag in the hall and stood there listening. The silence fizzed in my ears. I went into the kitchen and looked at Bill Bailey's food bowl. I frowned when I saw how much food was left. Bill Bailey wasn't young and wild. He was middle-aged, like me, and long hunting trips were confined to warm weather. I went round the house, calling his name and checking that he hadn't been accidentally shut in a room or even a cupboard. The house was empty. I remembered that once he'd gone missing and it had been a couple of days before we discovered that he'd got trapped in one of the outhouses. I got a torch

207

and went to check.

During my drive home a wind had got up and the fog had begun to disperse. Only a few streaks remained on the snow-covered fields. Any moment I expected Bill Bailey to come running and wind himself round my legs, but he was nowhere to be seen. Puzzled and uneasy, I went back indoors.

I unpacked the food Martha had given me: a dozen free-range eggs, a home-made loaf of bread and some cold chicken and ham. I switched on the radio for company and got out a pan to scramble some eggs. It was as if I had stepped back into the old life when I had lived here alone. I had a curious feeling of lightness, as if I'd taken off a corset and was expanding into the air around me.

I ate the eggs, washed up and poured myself a modest glass of Black Bush Irish whiskey. I went up to the study to sit on the window-seat. A huge yellow moon, almost at the full, hung low in the sky. The towers of Ely cathedral, chalk-white in the floodlights, seemed to float in mid-air. I raised my glass to Una's memory. Ten thousand pounds: that was a lot to someone on a cleaner's wages — close to a year's wages was my guess. A price couldn't be put on the hope for the future that Una had given Wendy.

I went to my desk and switched on my

computer. I logged onto the Internet and typed in the address of a website for tracking down second-hand books that I often used for my own modest purchases. I sat with my fingers on the keys, wondering where to start. More or less at random I typed 'Jane Austen' into the author box, and *Pride and Prejudice* into the title box and asked for the books to be listed in the order of the highest price. It took a while for the reply to come. When it did, I found that the most you could spend was £50,000 for a first edition, described as 'very fine' by a dealer in Connecticut. What might be rarer than a first edition of *Pride and Prejudice?* I typed in a request for a first edition of *Gulliver's Travels*. A dealer in York was offering one for £14,000. I typed in *Paradise Lost*. That was so rare that there wasn't a first edition for sale. The most expensive item was a private press copy published in 1905 and going for £12,500.

I was starting from the wrong end. I ought to have begun by thinking about the type of book Una was likely to have bought. I went to Google and requested a list of dealers specializing in nineteenth and twentieth-century first editions. One of the things that came up was a website offering searches for rare books. I typed in Wilkie Collins and *Moonstone*. I was offered a 'very fine' first edition for £4,000. I typed in Agatha Christie and scrolled down the list that appeared. *The Mysterious Affair at Styles* was priced at £6,000. A crisp, clean copy of *Hercule Poirot's Christmas* could be mine for £4,000 and a slightly battered copy of *The Secret of Chimneys* was a snip at £750. I've always fancied collecting golden age crime fiction, but have never got further than the bookshelves of ancient green Penguins in the spare room. With these prices I wasn't likely to. And yet . . . these were such paltry sums when set against Una's buying power. Maybe it wasn't a single item, but a collection that she had acquired. I thought back to my conversation with Una at the college dinner and another part of it popped into my head. We'd talked about G. K. Chesterton, comparing favourite Father Brown stories. And I remembered that there had been a volume by her bed. Was there some kind of a clue there?

My mobile phone rang and I fished it out of my handbag.

'Cass?' It was Stephen.

I opened my mouth and nothing came out. And I mean nothing. I sat there opening and closing my mouth like a fish.

'Cass? Cass?' Stephen said. 'Are you there?'

With a massive effort I managed to clear

my throat enough to whisper into the phone. 'Voice gone.'

'Oh, Lord. You'd better not talk more than you have to. But what's going on? The land-line's been engaged for ages.'

'Internet,' I croaked. 'Sorry. Grace?'

'She's absolutely fine. Fast asleep. But have you heard the weather forecast?'

'Uh, uh,' I said, meaning no.

'They're predicting a thaw starting tonight and it could be a rapid one. You do realize what that could mean? The ground's been frozen solid for weeks. There won't be anywhere for the water to go. There'll be floods. You'd better go over to the flat.'

'Cat,' I hissed.

'Oh, for goodness sake, smuggle him in if you have to.'

'No, no,' I gave the words as much emphasis as I could muster. 'Not turned up.'

'Then go without him. You could be stranded out there. And if your voice goes completely you can't even ring for help. It's not safe.'

'Uh, uh.'

'You're in thrall to that bloody cat,' Stephen said.

It was too much effort to answer that.

'You weren't here during the 1978 floods. I was. The whole bloody city was under water and villages were cut off for days. You know someone even died?'

'Mmm,' I managed.

'I can see you're not going to listen to reason. I've got a bad feeling about this. I'll ring you in the morning.' With that he hung up.

I leaned back in my chair and rubbed my eyes. I hadn't realized how tired I was. I was spinning my wheels anyway. What I really needed to do was follow the money. No doubt there were reference works containing lists of books sold at auction and what they had fetched. They would tell me what half a million pounds could buy. I'd try the Lit and Phil or the University library in the morning.

My anxiety about Billy revived. The glass of whiskey was sitting forgotten by the computer. I drained it and went to open the front door. It didn't seem as cold as it had earlier. The wind had got up and was sweeping the snow into shallow drifts. The night was full of noises: the rustling of the reeds in the waterway under the house, the thrashing of the laurel bush by the front door. Forgetting about my voice, I tried to shout, but all that came out was a croak. There was a chance though that he would see the light from the open door and come galloping across the fields. I waited, but he didn't appear. I couldn't leave without Bill Bailey. I'd had him since he was a kitten. He'd seen me through the break-up of a marriage, and he had been my faithful companion during the years before I'd met Stephen.

Still fretting, I climbed the two flights of stairs to my bedroom. When I pushed the door open there was a mad jangling noise. I switched the light on and saw Grace's musical egg rolling across the floor. It wobbled to a halt. The yellow chick stared up at me. Hand clasped to my heart, I waited for my pulse-rate to settle. Once in bed I lay awake, dead tired but unable to sleep. The wind was sending cold drafts in through the crevices around the window frames. The house was creaking like a ship at sea.

I kept almost dropping off and then waking again with a jolt. Once I was sure I heard Grace calling for me and I'd hoisted myself up on my elbows before I remembered that she was in Devon. At last I fell asleep. It must have been around five o'clock that I woke up, instantly alert, my heart pounding, certain again that I had heard a baby crying. A great bulging wobbling eye was staring down at me. It was a few seconds that I understood that I was looking at the moon, distorted by the old glass in my bedroom window.

I got out of bed and put on a cardigan.

The wind had swept the snow into ridges so that the huge fields looked like a frozen sea. The moonlight was so brilliant that you could have read a newspaper by it. All that flatness, all those straight lines, that's not natural, I thought, and realized that it *wasn't* natural. No landscape could be more artificial. The Fens were once known as the drowned lands. They were drained in the seventeenth century, but the sea is always waiting to take them back. Every now and then *Cambridge Evening News* runs a commemorative feature on the great flood of 1947, the worst in living memory. There had been a long period of heavy frost followed by freak rainfall and high tides. The river Ouse breached its banks just below St Ives, whole villages were submerged under two metres of water, and cattle were stranded on pockets of high ground. The grainy black and white photos show huge expanses of grey water, with here and there a few chimney pots and tree-tops poking out. I remembered those now as I stared out over the frozen landscapes. They said it couldn't happen again. The Denver sluice had been refurbished in the 1980s, and the pumping stations were powered by electricity . . .

I heard the cry again, thin and high like the wail of a baby. But this time, I didn't think of

Grace. I ran downstairs, switching on the lights as I went. I opened the front door. The light from the hall revealed a trail of bloody paw-prints that led back into the night.

There was a plaintive mewing and I looked down to see Bill Bailey huddled on the doorstep.

12

The Story of the Treasure Seekers

There was a smell of singed fur. The vet put down something that looked like a miniature soldering iron.

She stroked Bill Bailey's head. 'All done. You are a good boy, aren't you?' He pushed his face against her hand.

'He'll be fine now,' she said. 'Don't let him walk around on it today — though shouldn't think he'll want to, poor old boy — and keep him indoors for a few days. It looks as if you could do with staying indoors too. You can keep each other company.'

I nodded mutely. My voice had completely gone and I hadn't been able to ring the vet. I'd just gone to the surgery and waited for her to show up. Bill Bailey had broken a claw on one of his front paws. It happened now and then, the vet said. He'd probably caught it as he jumped up into a tree and his weight had pulled the claw away. He'd managed to drag himself home, but he hadn't been able to get through the cat flap. She gave him a local anaesthetic so that she could remove the nail-bed and cauterize the wound.

I took Bill Bailey back to the Old Granary and packed a suitcase. I'd already spent a couple of hours moving books and everything else I could carry from the ground floor up to the first floor. The thaw hadn't come yet, but I could sense a change in the air. The sky was overcast again, though whether the clouds heralded snow or rain, it was hard to say, but in any case I couldn't face another night there on my own. If Bill Bailey had to be confined to quarters it might as well be at the flat. The difficulty would be smuggling him in, but I had a stroke of luck there. Mr Walenski, the gimlet-eyed caretaker who lived on the premises, was driving out of the car-park as I drove in. I didn't see a soul as I sneaked up the stairs with the cat carrier. By lunch-time Bill Bailey was curled up fast asleep in his basket in the bathroom, the warmest place in the flat, and I was poking about in the kitchen looking for something to eat. There was nothing at all in the fridge, but there were tins of baked beans and a tin of ravioli in the cupboard, and in the little freezer a loaf of sliced bread and one or two frozen meals. I ate baked beans on toast in the kitchen. I made myself some coffee — coffee-beans are the one thing Stephen always has in stock — and took it into the sitting room while I decided what to do next.

The flat is on the top floor of one of those thirties blocks and faces south over the river. There are many different Cambridges and this particular one is close to my heart. It's bounded on the north by Chesterton High Street and to the south by Newmarket Road. Elizabeth Way bridges the river and forms a natural boundary to the west and to the east is Stourbridge Common, for centuries the site of one of the largest and most disreputable fairs in Europe, thought to be the inspiration for Vanity Fair in John Bunyan's *Pilgrim's Progress*. The fair was abolished by the Secretary of State in 1934, but the area still has something a little louche about it. On summer evenings the river is busy with swans, with single scullers skimming across the water and with the rowing crews tracked by hectoring coaches on bicycles. Barges with cats and flowers in pots are moored along the banks and form a little community all of their own. Horses and cattle stray across the common.

Today weeping willows drooped leafless over the water and the tall chimney of the old steam pumping station on the other bank rose stark against a sombre sky. The barges had gone to their winter moorings. The river was iced over and was pocked with star-burst cracks where children had chucked stones on it. A black-and-white collie jumped onto it and skittered around before its anxious owner managed to summon it back.

I sat back in my chair and closed my eyes for a few moments, breathing in a smell that mingled dusty books with a faint whiff of Cussons Imperial Leather soap. It was so redolent of Stephen that it gave me a little pang of longing. I ought to let him know where I was. I tested my voice. All that came out was a creaking sound and I could feel the strain in my vocal chords. There wasn't much point in seeing a doctor. This had happened to me before — voice loss is an occupational hazard for teachers — and the only thing that helps is steam inhalation and lots of fluid. It would probably be a good idea to have a few hours' sleep, but I was too wired up for that. I really ought to go to the Institute and get on with the book — I didn't dare think how far behind schedule I was — but I wasn't going to do that either. Or at least, not yet: I promised myself that I'd spend a couple of hours there later in the afternoon.

Right now there was some research that I wanted to pursue anonymously, without Giles — or even Michelle — looking over my shoulder. The University library was the place.

I got out my laptop, plugged the modem into the phone line and e-mailed Martha, telling her that I was at the flat. As an after-thought, I sent Stephen a text message. He probably wouldn't see it for days. For someone who makes his living out of patent law, he's surprisingly resistant to modern technology.

I looked in on Bill Bailey and made sure that everything he needed was next to his basket. He was fast asleep and didn't stir.

I let myself out of the flat and set off on foot for the library.

★ ★ ★

I pushed a note across the counter to the man on duty in the Rare Books department. He made an alarmed face and raised his hands in mock surrender. Just my luck to get a joker. I gave him a look of wry resignation. He grinned and read the note. Underneath what I'd written, he scribbled a line or two and turned the piece of paper round so that I could read it: *Book Auction Records* and *American Book Prices Record.*

I took the pen. *In the reading room?* I wrote.

He nodded.

Thanks, I mouthed.

You're welcome, he mouthed back.

I picked up my piece of paper and departed.

Book Auction Records and *American Book Prices Record* are published annually, so there are several shelves of them. I began with the most recent. The entries are listed under author. I ran my finger down the pages, stopping to make a note of anything that had fetched more than £150,000. A Shakespeare first folio for $5.6 million . . . £140,000 for a first edition of Moore's *Utopia* . . . £230,000 for a twelfth-century French manuscript of the book of Genesis . . . $675,000 for a work by Copernicus . . . $2,000,000 for an Archimedes palimpsest. Half a million pounds wasn't out of the question, it seemed, for something sufficiently old or rare. After half an hour I realized that I wasn't finding anything later than Shakespeare.

I jotted down some of the big hitters from the nineteenth century, but hardly any of them commanded figures over £50,000. I checked on G. K. Chesterton, but nothing had gone for more than a few hundred pounds. The £75,000 that Una had paid for *The Hound of the Baskervilles* seemed pretty much the top of the range for the type of fiction that she was interested in. Even an inscribed first edition of *David Copperfield* fetched only £65,000. *Only £65,000!* It was a fantastic sum. I shook my head. I couldn't believe I was thinking in these terms. Exactly the same words in the same order could be purchased for around a fiver in any book shop. I understood why Una had sounded half ashamed in her letter to me.

I pushed on, running my finger down page after page, my mind a blur of first editions and variants and dollar signs. And then, in the volume of *American Book Prices Record* for 1998, I found something: a copy of Lewis Carroll's *Alice's Adventures in Wonderland* sold for 1.4 million dollars. *Exceedingly rare,* ran the blurb, *one of twenty-three remaining from its first suppressed print run.* It was obvious really. Rarity *and* a whiff of scandal: that was the winning combination. If something like that had come on the market over the last month or two, it would be too recent to be listed in *Book Auction Records.* To find out I would need to contact all the major auction house. Since I couldn't speak, I'd have to e-mail them and it might take days for them to reply — if they replied at all.

I sighed and looked at my watch. Half past three. There didn't seem any point in going on. I put the notebook in my bag and reshelved the books, and headed for the ladies loo by the stairs down to the issue hall. I swore under my breath when I saw the sign that said 'temporarily closed.' To get to another ladies loo, I had to double round almost to the back of the library and go up a couple of flights of stairs. To understand what happened next you have to know something about the layout of the library. The reading room is in the centre of the library with a smaller periodicals room that opens behind it. On the landing outside the second-floor ladies loo is a narrow floor-length window that looks down into the periodicals room. Most people who use the periodicals room probably aren't aware of it. I'd never noticed myself until the first time I came up here. It's like being in a minstrel's gallery. I always stop and glance down, drawn by the fascination of seeing without being seen.

My eye was caught by the outline of a familiar figure halfway down the long narrow room. It was Giles. He was consulting the library assistant at the central desk. There was a woman beside him and even before she turned her head, and the gleaming curtain of hair fell back from her face, I felt a little shock of recognition. It was Eileen. Instinctively I took a step sideways so that I was out of sight. I looked round the corner of the window. The assistant went to fetch something for them. Eileen and Giles had their heads close together, engaged in earnest conversation. Of course the protocol of the library meant that they had to speak in low voices, and yet they had the unmistakable air of conspirators. At one point Eileen even glanced round as if to make sure that no one was overhearing them. The assistant came back and handed Giles a book. At this distance I couldn't make out what it was. Giles went to a table further down the room and Eileen followed him. They settled down together and Giles began to turn over the pages of the book.

I continued into the ladies, my mind full of questions. It's not uncommon for people who don't work or study at the university to have a reader's ticket. As librarian of the Institute, Giles would naturally have one, and Eileen's professional interest in rare books had no doubt made her eligible too. It was even possible that she was a graduate of the university. And there could be any number of reasons why Giles and Eileen would consult something in the library together. Why then did I feel an absolute conviction that they were on the same errand as I was? I wondered whether they'd seen me as they went through the reading room on their way to the periodicals room. I'd been tucked away down at the end, with other people sitting between me and the entrance, so it wasn't likely that they'd have spotted me. Unless of course they'd wanted to consult *Book Auction Records* and *American Book Prices Record*. They could easily have seen me and sneaked away without my noticing.

I stared at myself gloomily in the mirror. My hair was sticking out at all angles. I must been thrusting my hands in and out of it. I don't even know I'm doing that half the time. Lipstick rapidly applied that morning was now smudged. I had a wild-eyed look and no wonder. My head was buzzing. Where could I go to think and be quiet? I remembered my resolution to go to the Institute. I'd do that later, but right now I needed a place where I could be certain no one would bother me or even think of looking for me.

★ ★ ★

Alan ran his fingers through my hair.

'You should come and see me more often,' he said.

His eyes met mine in the mirror. I shrugged in what I hoped was a disarming way.

'Oh, I know, I know. Busy, busy, busy, but all the same . . . ' He pursed his lips. It's interesting, isn't it, that even hairdressers who aren't gay often have a camp manner?

'With hair this short,' Alan continued, 'you really ought to have it cut every six weeks.'

I nodded.

'Lucky I had a cancellation.'

Alan is young enough to have spiky hair, dyed blonde, and a small diamond stud in his nose. He is that rare and restful thing: a silent hairdresser. Once the preliminaries are over, there's no chat about where you are going on holiday or whether you are going out this evening. On the rare occasions when he spoke, it was invariably about hair.

As Alan turned my head from side to side, I wondered if my intuition about Giles and Eileen was way off the mark. Because to guess that Una had spent a great deal of money on something, they would have to know that the money was missing, and how could they know that? Could Jim have told Giles about the missing money? Why would Jim do that? Could he have been trying to startle Giles into some kind of admission? Or maybe . . .

Alan broke into my thoughts and what he said was almost as surprising as the fact that he had spoken at all.

'You've got an admirer.'

I arranged my face to express interest and curiosity.

'They say imitation is the sincerest form of flattery, don't they?' he went on. 'Someone came in yesterday wanting a haircut just like yours. Mentioned you by name.'

I raised my eyebrows in enquiry.

'Hang on a moment.' Alan moved round to my side to trim my fringe. 'Close your eyes, please.' Neither of us spoke as the cool steel slid along my forehead. Falling hair tickled my nose.

'We're nearly done.' Alan handed me a tissue so that I could dust my face. 'Just let me tidy up the back. Yes, Jason did her hair. I had to explain what you usually have. I think she had her hair coloured too.' Something seemed to strike him. 'She asked for an auburn rinse. You've got some red in your hair, haven't you? Of course, yours is natural.'

He took hold of my hair on either side and gently pulled it straight to check that the lengths matched. His eyes met mine in the mirror.

'Who was it?' I mouthed.

'You want to know who it was? I didn't get her name and Jason's not in today. But I can have a look in the book, when we're done.'

He worked on in silence, but this time it was far from restful. He held up a hand mirror to the back of my head and I duly

227

admired the effect, but my heart wasn't in it, and he could tell.

'Come on,' he said.

I followed him to the desk.

He leaned over it and turned the appointment book round. He flipped back a page and ran his finger down a column.

'It must have been his ten o'clock appointment. Yes, this must be it.' He frowned. 'That's funny. She's got the same surname as you. Look, it's James. Elizabeth James.'

I stared at the appointment book.

'Is something wrong?' Alan asked.

I took a pencil and wrote in the margin, *Elizabeth is my middle name. I don't think this is her real name. I need to know who she really is.*

'We always ask for a phone number, in case we have to cancel for some reason. It should be on the computer. We could try ringing it?'

I nodded.

'Gemma,' he said to the receptionist, 'call up Elizabeth James, would you?'

Gemma had been looking on with interest. She nodded and tapped at the computer keyboard with long frosted fingernails.

Alan and I waited in silence.

'Got it,' Gemma said. 'Shall I dial it for you?'

Alan looked at me. I nodded.

'What shall I say if someone answers?' Gemma asked.

'Pretend they've left their gloves here,' Alan said.

But that didn't turn out to be necessary. Because as soon as Gemma had keyed in the number, there was a ringing sound from my briefcase.

My admirer had given them the number of my mobile phone.

13

The Turn of the Screw

It was dark when I left the hairdresser's and small, wet snowflakes were falling. The wind was cold on the back of my newly shorn neck. I got out my fur hat and put it on, pulling the flaps down over my ears. I set off for the Institute, scuffing up the snow as I walked along. Charles had said that the woman using my name had short hair, but not as short as mine. Well, she'd put that right now. This wasn't a paediatrician in Quebec or a geologist in Wellington, who just happened to have the same name as me. This was someone who wanted to *be* me.

Alan and Gemma had been infuriatingly vague when I had pressed them for a description. All Alan remembered was her hair, and all Gemma remembered was that she had paid in cash, of course. How did she come to have the number of my mobile phone? A image came into my head. In the Fitzwilliam Museum there's a little watercolour by Rossetti called *How They Met Themselves*. It shows a pair of lovers in a forest coming face to face with their mirror images. To meet one's *doppelgänger* is an omen of death and there is horror in the faces of the doomed couple as they gaze at their sinister counterparts. I took a couple of deep breaths and got a grip on myself. I don't believe in the supernatural and anyway the idea of a *doppelgänger* that picked up men in bars and went to the hairdresser's was absurd. Or was it? Maybe that's exactly how the post-modern *doppelgänger* would behave. I could see this forming the subject of a learned paper at some time or other.

By now I'd reached the entrance to the Institute. I rang the bell.

Static crackled on the intercom. Then I heard a laconic American voice. It was MaryAnne, Giles's other assistant. She's married to an Englishman who works at the Observatory and has been at the Institute for years. 'Who is that?' she asked.

I turned my face towards the CCTV camera so that she could get a good look at me. A few seconds passed before she buzzed me in. When I reached the top of the stairs she was standing waiting for me.

'I didn't see you go out.' She sounded puzzled.

I stared at her. I had no idea what she meant.

'I don't understand it.' She said. 'The thing is, I buzzed you in, about half an hour ago.'

I pointed to my throat to indicate that I'd lost my voice and led her over to the issue desk.

It wasn't me, I wrote on a piece of scrap paper.

MaryAnne read it over my shoulder. When I turned to look at her, there was a strange expression on her face.

'I was sure it was you. The hat, no one else has got one like that, and she had a coat like yours and a library card.'

I shook my head. *Haven't been in all day*, I wrote.

'Then who's upstairs sitting in your seat and working at your desk?' she asked. 'I saw her just a few minutes ago, when I went up to shelve a book.'

'What!' I'd forgotten I couldn't speak. It came out as a wheeze. I felt a surge of absolute fury and my first impulse was to get up there and see who the hell it was.

MaryAnne put her hand on my arm. Her face was troubled. 'There's something wrong, isn't there? Shall I come up with you?'

I was about to nod my head, but then I remembered the lay-out of the building. There were two ways down from the gallery. The main one was via the spiral staircase but it was also possible to come down via a narrow set of servant's stairs and emerge just inside the main entrance. If MaryAnne stayed here she could cover both exits.

I explained in dumb show and headed for the spiral staircase. The Institute is quiet at this time of day and the gallery was deserted. I ran along to the staircase that leads up to my room. Before I stepped out of sight, I glanced down. MaryAnne nodded as if to say, I'm at my post. As I looked up the stairs I could tell that the desk-light was on in my room. It is impossible to go silently up uncarpeted wooden stairs and it was probably my attempt to be stealthy that alerted her. When I emerged into the room it was empty, except for Florence who was curled up asleep in the circle of light from the desk-lamp. The sense of sudden departure was almost tangible. I could almost see her, bending over the books, pretending to study them, pretending to be me. It was as if she had left a faint outline in the air.

The door that leads back into the extension was ajar. My heart was racing as I crossed the room and stood at the threshold. There were no lights on. Seven-foot high stacks stretched back into the gloom. Darkness pressed down on the glass roof overhead. I couldn't help remembering those M. R. James ghost stories where sinister things happen among the book stacks. I summoned up a mental map of the Institute. There are only three doors into the extension, one from this room, one from a corresponding room on the first floor and one between Giles's office and the issue desk. I could still flush her out into the issue hall, where she would be cut off by MaryAnne.

I walked down the central aisle pulling at the light cords as I went. The fluorescent bulbs pinged and flickered into life behind me. My footsteps reverberated on the iron-grided floor. It struck me that the booming noise could mask other footsteps. I stopped halfway down the aisle and stood stock-still. The vibrations faded away until all I could hear was my own rapid breathing. I held my breath and listened. It was silent, but this was a listening silence. There was someone nearby, someone who was also holding their breath and waiting.

Through a gap in the books I caught a glimpse of something glimmering in the darkness of the next aisle, the pale binding of a book, perhaps. I moved my head a fraction and it was gone. I moved my head back and saw that it was the light reflected from the glossy surface of an eye-ball. I gasped. Someone was standing there in the dark, so close that I could have reached out and touched them if it hadn't been for the stack between us. The eye disappeared and there was a crash and a yelp. I knew what must have happened. She had tripped over one of the wooden stands that are used to reach the top shelf. The next instant feet were clattering down the aisle. The sound ricocheted around the ceilings and floor, making it hard to tell which way she had gone. I ran back the way I had come, guessing that she would head for the front of the building. But she'd gone the other way. When I looked back down the lighted aisle, I saw her silhouetted against the far end. I hared back. When I reached the end she had disappeared.

Off to the right there was an area of light and a swinging door. The sign next to it gave me a jolt: fire escape. I'd forgotten there was one. I rarely penetrated this deeply into the Institute. I pushed through the door and found myself on a concrete floor. Galvanized steel staircases lit by subdued wall lights led up and down. I heard distant footsteps below. I ran down clearing the steps two at a time. I swung round a corner, then another, and then a terrible jarring cacophony began. The sound bounced off the walls and made my ears ring. A blast of cold air came up the stairs. I flung myself round the last corner. Ahead of me stretched a long, narrow passage, ending in an open door. I stumbled out of it and found myself on a pavement with rain on my face.

It was as if I had stepped through a magic door and found myself in a different world. I was surrounded by hurrying people. A woman with her head down and an umbrella slanted against the driving sleet bumped into me and muttered an apology. A bus passed by. And then I understood. I was in St Andrew's Street. When the Institute sold off the street front premises, it must have kept this narrow passage as a fire escape.

I looked around, not wanting to admit defeat. My *doppelgänger* was nowhere in sight. She could have dodged into a shop or jumped on a bus or simply lost herself in the crowd.

I don't know how long I stood there with the rain soaking into my clothes, while behind me the alarm pealed on and on.

★ ★ ★

'It's funny that you're left-handed, Cass,' Merfyn said.

I was eating chicken cacciatore with him and his wife Celia in the kitchen of their house just off Hills Road near Homerton College. Bill Bailey was eating Whiskas in the

236

conservatory. After the debacle at the Institute I had got a taxi to the college. Through a combination of gestures and writing things down I had managed to tell Merfyn what had happened. He'd insisted that Bill Bailey and I come and stay the night.

'You know what that means?' Merfyn went on. 'You probably had a twin in the womb. There's this theory that left-handed people begin as twins, but very early on in the pregnancy, one foetus is absorbed by the other.'

Still unable to speak, I had to be satisfied with a grimace.

'Merfyn! Really!' Celia said.

She's the sort of woman I think of as quintessentially English, tall and slim with untidy hair and that fine skin that wrinkles early, especially around the eyes. I picture her in a country house with several dogs at her heels, brogues on her long gentlewoman's feet, and a trug containing a pair of secateurs over her arm. Actually she's a high-flying civil servant who commutes to London every day.

Merfyn took a swig of wine. 'No, but don't you think it's fascinating? You know, I almost envy you, Cass, having your own real life *doppelgänger*. The literary precedents are so distinguished, particularly in the nineteenth century. Stevenson's *Doctor Jekyll and Mr*

Hyde of course — '

'Merfyn!' Celia glanced at me to gauge my reaction. I gave a resigned shrug. It was no more than I'd been thinking myself. And Merfyn had actually written a very well-received book on the supernatural in nineteenth and twentieth-century fiction.

'And there's that short story by Conrad, 'The Secret Sharer',' Merfyn continued. 'Some of the best stuff is earlier in the century: Edgar Allan Poe's 'William Wilson'. And then there's *Confessions of a Justified Sinner* by James Hogg, to my mind a strong contender for the most terrifying story of the century. It's never clear whether the sinister double is an hallucination or the devil in disguise. You're actually writing a chapter on twins in your book, aren't you, so it's funny — '

'Enough!' Celia said. 'Cass has been spooked enough already! Get your head out of the clouds. This is serious. We don't know how this might be tied up with Una's death and the missing money. You're seeing the police in the morning, Cass?'

I hope so, I mouthed. I'd sent Jim a text message simply saying I'd lost my voice and I needed to see him. I was waiting for a reply.

I mopped up the last delicious mouthful of chicken and onion and celery. Merfyn divided the remains of the bottle between the three of us. 'I'll open another one,' he said. He got up and stacked the dinner plates. 'Just fruit and cheese and biscuits for afters.'

I reached for the pad and pen that Celia had placed by my plate and wrote a brief summary of how far I'd got in working out what Una had done with the money.

Merfyn came back from the sink where he'd been washing grapes and read my account over Celia's shoulder.

Celia said, 'Half a million spent on a book. If you're right about that, it doesn't surprise me all that much. It fits in with my feeling about Una.'

'And that is?' Merfyn asked.

'That she was a risk-taker. Someone who could hold her nerve and wasn't afraid to go for broke. I wouldn't have cared to play poker with her, I'll tell you that much.' She reached out and took a grape. 'And the last minute change of mind about her will? What was that about?'

'Maybe we'll never know for sure,' Merfyn said. 'It's so tantalizing. Una was this close,' He paused in laying out the cheese on a board and held up his hand with his thumb and forefinger almost touching, '*this* close,' he repeated, 'to telling Cass everything: what she did with the money, why she changed the will, even who was about to murder her.' He hesitated. 'I do wonder — '

'No!' Celia said.

I had to be satisfied with shaking my head vigorously and waving my hands in denial.

'Oh, I know you both thought it was a load of hooey that time when I was going to seances.'

Celia and I nodded in unison and exchanged looks of resignation. This had happened when Merfyn was doing research on his book, and although it hadn't turned out badly in the end, Merfyn had promised Celia that he wouldn't go to any more.

'Before we resort to the supernatural, let's see what we can discover by the light of our own unaided intellects,' Celia said dryly. 'The murder, we'll have to leave to the police. But as for the missing half million, there, I believe, we can make some headway.'

Merfyn cut a slice of cheese and arranged it on a cracker. 'It seems to me that Cass has already made considerable headway.'

'She's done very well,' Celia admitted in a manner that I found faintly patronizing. She took a stick of celery. 'But if you don't mind my saying so, Cass, you've gone about it in a typically academic way, all that combing through records, when really all you need to do . . . ' She paused and gave her attention to cutting a slice of Wensleydale of exactly the right size.

Merfyn looked at Celia, the loaded cracker poised in mid-air.

'Yes?' he said. 'Go on. All you need to do? You've got our attention.'

'All you need to do,' Celia continued calmly as she snapped her stick of celery, 'is ask the right person.'

Merfyn snorted and the cheese fell off the biscuit. 'Is that all?'

'That's all.'

Merfyn scooped up the cheese. He shook his head.

'You civil service mandarins,' he said through a mouthful of cheese. He turned to me. 'When Celia says to one, go, he goeth. To another she says come, and he cometh. A thousand minions do her bidding day and night.' He turned back to Celia. 'Under those circumstances, it's easy enough to track down the appropriate expert.'

'Oh really?'

I could see that she was nettled. She's something high up in the Home Office. Merfyn had once told me that she was Grade Five, and I'd gathered that was pretty impressive.

'Yes, really. In fact I could ring round the auction houses myself in the morning. No problem.'

'What time is it?' She squinted at her watch. I realized that she was rather drunk, too. 'Quarter past nine,' she announced. 'OK, before midnight — long before, most likely — I'll have a plausible answer to Cassandra's question. Care to bet on it?'

'By midnight? You're on.'

She looked from me and then at Merfyn again. 'On condition that you both give me your full co-operation.'

I nodded.

Merfyn hesitated. 'What's the stake?'

'Dinner at Twenty-Two?' This was one of the best restaurants in town.

Merfyn was visited by a doubt. 'You don't *already* know the right person to ask, do you?'

Celia shook her head. 'Absolutely not. Now, do either of you have any connection, however remote, with a dealer in rare books or even with anyone who might know such a person?'

Merfyn said. 'I do know one or two dealers, but not very well. I certainly don't have their home numbers.'

I wrote 'Eileen, but . . . ' on my pad and showed it to Merfyn and Celia.

'Best not,' said Merfyn. 'We don't know the extent of her involvement.'

Celia nodded. 'Think again, both of you.'

Merfyn frowned. 'I got talking to someone

at a party. She said that her son worked for Sotheby's. Or was it Christie's Or even Bonhams?'

'Which department?'

'Ceramics. I think. I can't remember the name of the woman. Or even which party it was. Might have been at Margery's.'

'Let's pinpoint the time of year. What were you drinking? Mulled wine, punch, Pimms?'

Merfyn was gazing with unfocused eyes in an effort of concentration. 'White wine,' he said. 'And we were eating a mushroom risotto. A very good one.'

'I remember that risotto. It wasn't Margery's. It was Tom and Rosie's. I can't remember the woman's name either. I was at the other end of the table.' Celia stood up. 'I'll make the phone calls from the study.'

She poured herself a glass of wine and took it with her.

'I thought that would do it,' Merfyn said with satisfaction. 'Celia's so absurdly competitive. She never can resist a challenge.'

The look I gave him said, *You did that on purpose?*

Merfyn winked at me, He got to his feet and grabbed the wine bottle. 'We'll go and watch the show, shall we?'

★   ★   ★

243

One expects flamboyant people to be untidy, but Merfyn's study was extraordinarily neat. There were piles of book stacked up here and there, but everything was squared off with geometrical precision. Celia was sitting at the desk with an address book in front of her and the phone to her ear.

Merfyn perched on the edge of the desk. I moved a pile of books off a chair so that I could sit down.

Celia doodled on the message pad as she waited for an answer. It became evident that she wasn't going to get one. Frowning, she hung up.

'Fallen at the first hurdle?' Merlyn enquired pleasantly.

Celia ignored him. She tapped the table with her pencil while she considered her next move. She came to a decision and leafed through the address book.

She punched in a number and this time the phone was answered.

'Miriam?' she said, 'How are you? Yes, yes, I'm fine, Merfyn too, and the girls, yes. I'm ringing to ask you: do you remember that dinner party last summer at Tom and Rosie's? Merfyn got talking to a woman whose son works at Sotheby's or Christie's, and I was wondering — oh, Penelope Holmes, that's marvellous and do you have — wonderful.'

She scribbled something down on the pad. 'Yes, we must get together very soon.'

She rang the number she'd been given and again we heard one side of the conversation. It was masterly. I always enjoy seeing a professional at work. Nothing was said that wasn't strictly true, but somehow Celia had managed to convey the impression that a light-hearted after-dinner game was in progress and that she wanted to speak to Penelope's son in order to settle a bet. Penelope gave Celia her son's mobile phone number. The phone call ended on a note of high good humour and the extension of an invitation to a drinks party in February.

'I didn't know we were having a drinks party,' Merfyn said as Celia hung up.

'We are now,' Celia said as she tapped in the new number.

Celia caught the son at a restaurant in Mayfair. He didn't have a home phone number for anyone in the book and manuscript department, but he had an ex-colleague who now worked for a dealer in rare books on East 46th Street in New York. She might still be at her desk.

'Of course!' Celia said when she'd hung up. 'Why didn't I think of that? It's only just after five on the East coast. I could have contacted one of the big New York auction houses straight off.'

She dialled International Enquiries and then the number that they gave her. While she was doing that, Merfyn went to the kitchen and got the bottle of wine. She raised a hand to show me that her fingers were crossed as she waited for the phone to be picked up at the other end.

I was sitting on the edge of my chair. Just as I was giving up hope, the phone was answered and Celia said, 'I wonder if I could speak to Caroline Webster . . . oh, good, thanks.'

She covered the receiver with her hand and hissed, 'They're checking if she's still in the building. Cass, you'd better listen in. There's an extension in the hall.'

By pulling the flex to its limit, I arranged things so that Celia and I were in sight of each other.

Celia dropped her story about the bet and gave a brief account of the situation, though she didn't actually mention Una or the Institute or the college by name.

Caroline's voice was light and pleasant. 'Something nineteenth century and around half a million sterling,' she said, 'maybe more, so we're talking up to around a million dollars. Does it have to be nineteenth century? There's big money in twentieth century manuscripts these days. An early draft for a chapter of *Ulysses* might go for a million bucks.'

Celia looked at me and I shook my head.

'Let's stick with the nineteenth century,' Celia said. 'And there's likely to be a connection with crime fiction or sensation fiction.'

'I wonder . . . maybe Edgar Allan Poe? Some of the first editions of his early works are just incredibly rare. He published them himself in tiny editions and they were just pamphlets really. Very few have survived.'

Celia looked at me. I shook my head to indicate uncertainty. I'd assumed that it was a British writer. Why hadn't I thought of someone like Poe, and more to the point, why hadn't Merfyn? American literature was one of his specialities.

Caroline was still talking. 'A copy of the 1827 *Tamerlane and Other Poems* fetched $150,000 dollars around ten years ago. No way of knowing what it would go for now. A first edition of *The Prose Romances of Edgar Allan Poe* was sold in New York for $230,000 last year and it wasn't even in very good condition. I've got the sales catalogue here somewhere.' There was the sound of papers being shuffled. 'Yes, this is it: Now just let me

. . . yes, here we are. Published Philadelphia, 1843. Octavo, original wraps, spine lacking, rear wrap detached, repaired tear to blank lower margin of front wrap, some foxing. It's described as 'the recently discovered 15th copy.' As a dealer you'd be lucky to come across something like that once in a lifetime. Though, as a matter of fact — '

'Just let me write that down,' Celia said, repeating the titles out loud. 'What were you about to say?'

Merfyn was about to pour wine into his glass. He paused with the bottle in mid air.

Caroline said, 'I don't know if I should . . . it was just a rumour. A story was going around a few mouths ago that there were two newly discovered copies about to come on the market. And that there was something very, very special about one of them.'

'In what way?' Celia asked.

Merfyn poured out the wine.

Caroline lowered her voice. 'An inscription.'

'And that would bump up the value?'

'And how! The exact amount would depend on the nature of the inscription. I couldn't put a price on it. I've heard nothing more, so I'd more or less decided there wasn't anything in it, but now I'm wondering . . .'

'Thanks. You've been very helpful.'

'My pleasure. If you do turn up something, and there's any question of it coming on market — '

'I'll ask the principals to bear you in mind.'

Celia hung up. She looked at her pad and she read back the titles, '*Tamerlane and Other Poems . . . The Prose Romances*. They don't sound like the kind of thing that Una — '

She was interrupted by Merfyn spluttering.

We looked at him. His face was bright red and it bore an odd expression.

'Do you have something to contribute, Merfyn?' Celia enquired with steely kindness.

Merfyn put his head in his hands. 'I can't believe I didn't think of it before. I could kick myself.'

'What are you talking about?'

'You haven't a clue, have you? You did not think to ask,' he said, enunciating each word with exaggerated precision, 'you did not think to ask her the titles of the stories in *The Prose Romances of Edgar Allan Poe*.'

'Well, what are they?' Celia demanded.

'There are in fact only two. One is 'The Man That was Used Up' and the other . . . ' he paused for effect.

'And the other?'

'It's only the story that laid the foundations

of modern crime fiction as we know it,' Merfyn said, his voice getting higher and higher like that of a ranting Welsh preacher. 'Only the story in which Poe introduced Auguste Dupin, the granddaddy of all fictional detectives. Only the story without which there would have been no Sherlock Holmes, no Father Brown, no Hercule Poirot.' He lowered his voice and shook his head. 'The collector's item to die for. Are you with me?'

'"The Murders in the Rue Morgue,"' Celia said.

I nodded my head. That had to be what Una spent the money on. I felt it in my bones. If there was a Holy Grail of crime fiction this must be it. It was the first detective story ever written.

14

The Two Destinies

Opening that third bottle of wine had been a mistake, a big mistake. I realized that as soon as I opened my eyes. I was fine as long as I didn't move a muscle. But I only had to tilt my head the tiniest fraction to feel as if something had come loose inside my skull and was rolling around inside. Very slowly I eased myself up onto one elbow. I switched on the bedside lamp.

Bill Bailey was asleep on the end of the bed. On the bedside table someone had placed a large glass of water and three white tablets. There were a couple of books, too. I squinted at the titles: a biography of Edgar Allan Poe and the other was Poe's *Tales of Mystery and Imagination*. There was a note as well, *Cass, decided to let you sleep. Celia at work; I've gone into college. Make yourself at home, eggs, etc. in fridge. Love, Merfyn. PS. Thought you might need the aspirin.* I sucked up some of the water and swallowed the tablets gratefully and looked at my watch. Nine o'clock! I hadn't had this much sleep since before Grace was born. I cleared my throat experimentally and said, 'testing, testing'. I had a voice again, a croaky one, it was true, but I could at least communicate. I checked my mobile phone. The battery was low, the little sign was flashing at me, but there was enough left for me to read Jim's message. *Police Station 12.30*

If we were right about where the money had gone, then the question remained: where was the book now, if something so insubstantial as this little pamphlet could be called a book? The most hopeful scenario was that it was somewhere in Una's house, hidden among the thousands of books. It would be quite a job searching for it, but it would eventually come to light. If not — I shook my head and a stabbing pain shot up my neck and did a circuit of my head. I'd forgotten about the hangover.

I dragged myself out of bed and splashed cold water on my face. I felt queasy and at the same time ravenously hungry. Food usually helps. Over two scalding cups of tea and a plate of scrambled eggs, I thought about what had happened in the Institute. In the light of day the *doppelgänger* was less threatening. And after all she'd run away from me, hadn't she? I decided to go back to the Institute and reclaim my space. Maybe in her panic she had even left a clue. I hadn't really looked properly the night before. It was only a five-minute walk to the police station from there. I packed up my things, inveigled Bill Bailey into the cat carrier and let myself out of the house.

As soon as I opened the door, I knew that something was different. The silence of the snow-bound world had been broken. Melting snow was dripping off the eaves and somewhere water was trickling in a drain. Even as I stood on the doorstep, a block of snow slid down the roof and landed with a flump on the lawn.

The thaw had begun.

I drove to Stephen's flat and I took Bill Bailey up first. I had no sooner shut the door in order to go back down and get my bag, than Mr Walenski appeared as if from nowhere. I gave a guilty start. I wasn't sure if he had seen me on the stairs with the cat carrier. Apparently not. He wanted to reassure me that should there be a flood, he was fully prepared with sandbags and was ready to go into action at a moment's notice.

'I was here in 1978 when we had to evacuate people by boat,' he said with a glint in his eye. Mr Walenski is Polish. He settled here after the war and is past retirement age.

I expect the residents' association is too scared of him to suggest pensioning him off.

'Gosh, that must have been exciting,' I murmured, backing off towards the stairs and praying that Bill Bailey wouldn't start mewing inside the flat.

I managed to escape, but I was still feeling flustered as I tramped into town through a mixture of slush and snow. I'd almost got to the Institute before I remembered that I'd intended to phone Stephen and there wasn't enough power left in my mobile phone. I turned the corner into Downing Place and saw a police car parked outside the Institute. A little knot of people was clustered round the entrance. My heart skipped a beat and I stopped in my tracks.

Someone touched my sleeve. I turned to see MaryAnne.

'What's happened?' I said.

'Don't know,' she said, frowning. 'I've just got here. I've been to the dentist.'

She broke into a trot, slipping and sliding on the half-melted snow. I picked my way after her.

The uniformed policeman at the door was telling people to go away.

An elderly man was saying, 'But officer, I've got important work to do.'

'I'm sorry, sir, there's no possibility of your

using the library today. You may as well go home.'

'What's happened?' MaryAnne asked.

'You'll hear about it in due course, madam.'

'But I work here. What's going on?' She was gripping my arm so tight that it hurt.

'What's your name?'

'Mary Anne Segal.'

'The Superintendent might need to speak to you.' He stood aside and opened the door. 'If you could just wait here, inside the door.'

She was still holding my arm and I moved with her. 'Cassandra James is one of the trustees,' she explained. I didn't contradict her.

The policeman hesitated and seemed about to protest, but he stood aside and let us in.

I looked up the shallow staircase. The inner door into the library was partly open. A subdued and purposeful hubbub was audible. I could see the top half of a woman sitting on an upright chair, her head down as though she was feeling faint. Jim Ferguson appeared, wearing a white paper boiler suit with the hood pushed back off his head. His face was haggard. My heart seemed to turn slowly over in my chest. Jim squatted down on his haunches to be on the same level as the woman and put his hand on her shoulder.

255

She lifted up a face as white as Jim's suit. It was Michelle and I could tell that she had been crying. He leaned close to murmur something to her. She looked past him. When she saw me, she made a noise midway between a cry and a gulp, as if someone had punched her hard in the stomach. She got to her feet and pointed at me. Jim looked round and his mouth fell open. There was something absurd about their consternation. They were like actors in some overblown melodrama. I felt irritated and at the same time very frightened.

I moved forward. Jim got to his feet.

Then Michelle was running through the door and down the stairs and the next moment I received her into my arms. She clung to me and buried her face in my shoulder.

I met Jim's eyes over Michelle's head. Some of the strain had left his face.

'What's going on?' I said.

He ran both hands over his head. 'There's a body upstairs. Michelle identified it as yours.'

* * *

'The face is so badly bruised that I wasn't sure at first,' Jim said. 'But the hair is exactly like yours. She's wearing a coat like yours. There's a handbag lying next to her. It contains various forms of identification bearing your name. And when you couldn't be contacted at your office or at home . . . '

'I should have let you know — I've moved into Stephen's flat.'

'And you weren't answering your mobile.' He scrutinized my face as if he'd hadn't really looked at it properly before.

We were at a table in a small room that leads off the reading room. A detective constable had produced some tea from somewhere. Someone had taken Michelle home.

'Where is she — I mean, where did Michelle — ?' I asked. My voice came out as a croak.

'In the extension. On the top floor. In the, let me see . . . ' he flicked through a notebook, 'In the Typography section. It's not much used, apparently, but Michelle went up there to shelve a book, and when she turned on the light, she saw the body.'

'Oh God!'

Jim's eyes were on my face. 'You think you know who it is?'

'Yes, I mean, no.' I told him about the previous day.

'I need you to look at the body, Cassandra,'

he said. 'I'm sorry,' he added, seeing the expression on my face. 'I know this has been a shock.'

'Of course, if you think I must . . . '

'You'll have to put on a protective suit. We don't want you contaminating the crime scene.'

When I'd been kitted out, we went through the issue hall to the spiral staircase. Jim gestured for me to go up first. I went up and waited at the top for him. We went along the gallery and up the stairs through the room where my books were still laid out on the table. My stomach was churning. The world of Victorian sisterhood seemed unreal and remote and infinitely desirable.

I pointed to the desk. 'She'd been sitting there. I think I just missed her.'

'Who's been sitting in my chair?' Jim murmured.

His words seemed to open a door in my mind. I can't explain it, but as soon as he said those words, I knew who my double was. There was no time to reflect on this revelation or even to absorb the shock, because Jim was ushering me into the extension and down a flight of stairs to the floor below. Down at the end of one of the aisles I could see a dazzling light and white-suited figures.

Jim gestured for me to go first. What happened next remains in my mind as a jumble of sensations: the sound of the iron grid of the floor vibrating under our feet; the pressure of Jim's hand in the small of my back — was that to reassure me or to keep me moving forward? As we approached the body, the people surrounding it fell back, seemed to disappear. There was nothing in the world except me and Jim and the huddled shape on the floor. I stopped. Jim urged me on. My feet moved reluctantly forward. Under the arc lights every detail seemed to stand out. It was like a film set. The body was lying face down. I saw a cap of sleek brown hair with red highlights and the curve of a cheek, dark with dried blood. I looked away.

'Do you know who this is?' Jim said.

'I think so . . . ' My voice was a husky whisper.

'Make sure. I know it's hard, but look again.'

I forced myself to look back. My eyes slid away again. One of her arms was flung out. The fingers of the hand were gently curled. Yes, I knew that hand with the fingernails, bitten to the quick. But there was still a surprise left in store. Hardly able to believe my eyes, I bent forward and stretched out my own hand.

'No,' said Jim. His hand closed firmly around my wrist. 'Don't touch her. Do you recognize this woman?'

'It's Wendy. Wendy Shale.'

'Dr Carwardine's cleaner?' He frowned.

I nodded. 'And there's something else: I can't understand it. She's wearing my ring, the ring that Stephen gave me for our anniversary.'

★ ★ ★

I had been so certain that the ring was somewhere in the Old Granary and that Grace had hidden it that its unexpected appearance had an almost supernatural quality. I found myself again and again returning to the puzzle of how it came to be on Wendy's finger. It's odd, the way the mind works when you're in shock. Classic displacement, of course; as long as I was wondering about that, I didn't have to think about the greater mystery of how Wendy came to be lying dead on the floor of the library. My thoughts could swerve round that face with its bloody and battered features. And there was something else, a dark shape somewhere on the margin of my mind, that I didn't want to have to examine, not yet, not while I could be pondering over the lost ring.

'Can you identify this as yours?' Jim said. He pushed a large transparent evidence bag containing a brown leather shoulder-bag across the table.

We were back where we had been before and there was more tea. I wondered vaguely how many cups of tea and coffee got drunk in the course of a murder investigation. It seemed that nothing could happen without one.

I nodded. 'I left it on the roof of my car. I suppose Wendy found it in the car-park when she left work.'

'When she left work?'

I realized that Jim didn't know about Wendy's job at the nursery. I explained about that. 'It's clear enough what must have happened,' I concluded, 'but I don't know how she got hold of the ring.'

'Was there a set of house keys in the handbag?'

'No, no, there wasn't.' And in any case I knew there was something wrong with that idea. What was it? My brain seemed to have slowed down. Yes. It was before I lost my handbag that I realized that my ring had gone missing.

'Was that on a day that you'd been to the nursery? Could the ring have slipped off your finger? Perhaps when you took a pair of gloves off.'

I saw myself standing in the hall at the nursery, water dripping from my coat. I saw myself going into the cloakroom. Of course that was it.

'I must have taken it off to wash my hands.'

Had I washed my hands? Yes. I didn't remember taking the ring off, but there was no other explanation.

There was a knock on the door. A man put his head round it and said, 'They're moving her now, Guv. I don't know if you want to . . . ?'

Jim nodded. He stood up. 'I'll be back shortly, Cassandra.' He went out, taking my handbag in its evidence bag with him.

I was left alone with my thoughts. For the hundredth time I saw in my mind's eye that outstretched hand bearing my ring. I knew I'd never be able to wear it again. I found myself straining to hear what was going on outside, but there was nothing. It occurred to me that it would be difficult to manoeuvre a body down the spiral staircase. They would be taking Wendy down the servants' staircase.

Time passed. I noticed the cup of tea and took a sip. It was lukewarm and heavily sugared. I got up and went over to the window. There was an ambulance in the street and I was just in time to see the doors being closed. It drove slowly off. Jim was on the pavement deep in conversation with one of his officers. As I watched, he gave a final nod and turned to come back into the Institute.

A minute or so later the door to the reading room opened and Jim came back in. He looked at me with concern.

'You're very pale,' he said. 'Are you OK?'

I bit my lip, trying not to cry. 'Poor Wendy. It's so awful. Why would anyone do that? And what's going to happen to her child?'

'There's a child?'

I nodded. 'She mentioned a little girl. She said she was a single parent.' That affected me in a way that Wendy's death hadn't. Perhaps the shock was beginning to wear off. Tears welled in my eyes.

'We'll make sure the child's taken care of.' Jim pulled a handkerchief out of his pocket and passed it to me. 'It's a bit crumpled, but it's clean.'

He didn't look too good himself. There were broken veins in the whites of his eyes and the skin around them was pink. The light glinted off a patch of stubble that he must have missed shaving.

He said, 'I am puzzled about what Wendy Shale was doing in the library.'

I didn't quite follow him. 'Well, but she was pretending to be me.'

'Yes, yes, I understand what she was doing when you chased her out of the library, but how did her body come to be there this morning?'

My mind was still working sluggishly. 'I suppose Michelle let her in, thinking she was me, like MaryAnne did last night.'

'We'll know more after the PM, but the pathologist says she's been dead for at least eight or nine hours.'

'But that means . . . ' I struggled to work it out.

'She'd been there since the early hours of the morning,' he said. 'Probably somewhere between midnight and two o'clock.'

'I just don't see how that's possible. I mean how did she get back into the Institute?'

'Maybe she never left it.'

'She must have done. She let off the alarm.'

'Did you actually see her in the street?'

'Well, no,' I admitted. 'I assumed she'd managed to lose herself in the crowd.'

'Setting off the alarm could have been a ruse. She could have doubled back into the book stacks. It wouldn't have been difficult to hide until after closing time. The place is a labyrinth.'

'But why would she want to stay in the library after it had closed?'

'Why would she want to steal your

handbag and dress up like you? We're not talking about someone who was behaving rationally here. And anyway, she did get back into the library somehow and . . . '

Met her killer there, the words hung unspoken in the air.

'You're no fool, Cassandra,' Jim went on. 'It must have occurred to you: Wendy was passing herself off as you in a place that you frequented. Maybe she wasn't the intended victim.'

It hadn't occurred to me, but only because I hadn't let it. Now it was out in the open. The dark shape I had so far managed to keep at bay had assumed a definite form.

'The dog it was that died,' I heard myself saying.

'Sorry?'

'Seeing one's double, one's *dopplegänger*, is supposed to be a portent of death. Well, it was — '

Jim finished the sentence for me. 'But in this case it was the *doppelgänger* that died. Is it common knowledge that you're living in Stephen's flat?'

'No. It was a spur-of-the-moment thing. Merfyn — that's one of my colleagues — and his wife, they know, but I haven't told anyone else.'

'Let's keep it that way.'

15

The Secret Sharer

'What was that?' I asked. There seemed to be some interference on the line.

Stephen raised his voice. 'You said you were OK! How *can* you be OK? You've just had to identify the dead body of someone who was masquerading as you!'

I found myself playing devil's advocate. 'The resemblance mostly came down to clothes and a haircut. Once someone got a good look at Wendy's face, they'd realize it wasn't me.'

'What does Jim say about this?'

'He says I should be careful.' In fact he had told me to put the chain on the door and had given me strict instructions not to allow anyone, anyone at all, into the flat. He had advised me to put on the answering machine and screen my calls. I had taken this to heart. Fortunately the woman who had lived there before Stephen had been obsessed with security. There were locks and bolts everywhere, including the windows, even though the flat was on the third floor. I was sitting in the bedroom with the door bolted. Bill Bailey was asleep on the bed beside me.

'I should just think he does!' Stephen said.

'It doesn't make any sense. Why would anyone want to kill me?'

'This must have something to do with Una, mustn't it? It's too much of a coincidence. There must be a connection. Perhaps whoever killed her was afraid that you were on their track.'

'But I'm not!'

'You can't deny you've been poking about.'

There was a book that belonged to me on one of the bedside tables: Trollope's *The Last Chronicle of Barset*. I began to fiddle with it, turning it this way and that, aligning it with the edge of the table.

'Well, yes, but — but I wasn't trying to find out who killed Una. The police are much better equipped to do that. I just wanted to know what it was she wanted to tell me and to find out what happened to the money.' Bill Bailey yawned and stretched. I ran my hand in and out of his soft belly fur. I was floundering here. Maybe in some corner of my mind I *had* hoped that what I discovered would throw light on Una's murder.

Stephen wasn't going to let me off the hook.

'They're probably all tied up together.

Once you pull out one thread, the whole thing will unravel. You asked me why someone would want to kill you — '

I couldn't hear his voice over the racket on the line.

'Speak up!' I shouted.

'No need to yell!' Stephen said. 'Why would they want to kill this other woman, this Wendy?'

'I don't know, but the very fact that she had this other life and was pretending to be me shows that there was a lot that I didn't know about her.'

For a few moments I heard only the throb of static. 'I really don't like this,' he said.

'You don't say!'

'I ought to come back.'

'But are you well enough?'

I got up and walked to the window, taking the phone with me. The world outside had changed from white to piebald. In the wilderness next-door, patches of mud had emerged from the snow and the trees were no longer pure filigrees of white. It had begun to rain, a fine drizzle no more than a haze in the air.

Stephen said, 'The truth is I feel awful. I go wobbly if I stand up for more than a few minutes. Even if I could get Martha to drive me to the station — '

'No, no, you mustn't. One of us should be with Grace and you couldn't possibly travel with her.' Just speaking Grace's name made me yearn for her. 'Look, maybe I could come to you.'

'You shouldn't be driving when you've had a shock like that. And another thing: have you heard the weather forecast?'

I rubbed my forehead. 'Can't remember when I last heard the news.' The collie dog and its owner came into view on the other side of the river.

'They've predicted torrential rain sweeping up the country from the south-west. It's already reached us. Can't you hear it?'

'I just thought it was a bad line.'

'That's rain drumming on the roof of the holiday cottage. I don't want you driving into this.'

'The Fens will be OK, won't they? I mean, it's not like the old days, there are drainage pumps.' The collie lolloped to the edge of the river, hoping to have another game on the ice. But the ice had gone and it seemed to me that the water was higher.

'Yes, but driven by electricity. It only needs one or two powerlines to be brought down . . . '

I felt a flicker of panic. It was one thing to be alone by choice, but to feel that I might not be able to reach Stephen even if I wanted to was another matter.

Stephen said again, 'God, Cass, I really don't like this.'

I got a grip on myself. 'I could hardly be safer, short of moving into the police station. This place is like Fort Knox. And hardly anyone knows I'm here. I'll ring you every day.'

'Twice a day. At least. And remember to keep that bloody mobile charged.'

It wasn't until I'd put the phone down that I realized that I too felt pretty awful. My temples were throbbing and my mouth was dry. I pressed my hot forehead against the cool glass. The man and the dog had gone and there was no one in sight. A breeze was ruffling the surface of the water. Something flickered over to the left at the edge of my vision. I turned my head and saw a fox, standing motionless just beyond the boundary of the lawn, dark muzzle lifted as if he was sniffing the wind. He seemed to have registered my movement as I had registered his. He turned his head and looked up. Had the bitter cold driven him in from the frozen countryside? I felt a moment of connection with him, a sense of fellow-feeling. Then, so quickly that he seemed there one moment, and gone the next, he vanished into the bushes.

The sight of him had taken me out of myself, given me a sense of a world elsewhere. I looked at my watch: it was half-past two. I assessed my condition: I was bone-weary and still hungover. I wanted to sleep, but first I knew I should eat. I went into the kitchen, took a loaf of sliced bread out of the freezer, prised off two slices with a sharp knife and put them in the toaster. I opened a tin of baked beans. Once the food was on the plate in front of me, I felt ravenous. I wolfed it down, then I poured myself a large Scotch and took it into the bedroom. I felt about under the pillows. As I'd guessed, there was an old T-shirt of Stephen's under there. I drew the dark red curtains, stripped and put on the T-shirt, and got into bed with *The Last Chronicle of Barset*.

It must have been the after effect of shock. I didn't read a word or even take a sip of the Scotch. With the suddenness of a candle being extinguished, I fell into a dreamless sleep.

★ ★ ★

When I woke up, it was dark and the illuminated dial of the clock said half past seven. Was it evening or morning? My head was heavy with sleep and I didn't know why I was in Stephen's flat. All I knew was that something had woken me up. The sound came again. A scratching noise. I rolled over in bed and fumbled for the switch of the bedside light.

Bill Bailey was sitting by the bedroom door. He looked imploringly at me. Either he was hungry or he needed his litter-tray. It all came back to me now: Bill Bailey's broken claw, the flight from the Old Granary, Wendy's death.

I got out of bed and unbolted the bedroom door. Bill Bailey slid round it and disappeared into the kitchen. On the back of the bedroom door hung Stephen's dressing-gown, an ancient garment of dark green woollen plaid with a rip in one sleeve. I put it on and was enveloped by the scent of Cussons Imperial Leather soap. The sleeves flopped down over my wrists. I rolled them up and went into the kitchen. Bill Bailey was squatting on the litter-tray gazing straight ahead with unfocused eyes.

The digital clock on the automatic oven told me that it was evening. Incredibly it was still the day that I had seen Wendy lying dead between the book stacks. I slumped into a chair and ran my hands through my hair. I knew I still hadn't absorbed the full dimensions of this. It was, in a way, worse than Una's death, this brutal cutting short of the life of a woman who was still young. And what would happen to her daughter? I couldn't think about that now.

I put the kettle on and looked round for something to eat. It was either tinned ravioli or a supermarket chicken tikka masala. I needed something more like a real meal. I rang the Italian restaurant on Milton road and ordered a pizza, some coleslaw, and some garlic bread. After I had hung up the flat seemed unnaturally quiet. It was strange being here without Stephen and yet it was comforting, too, as though there was part of him here. The heavy mahogany furniture and the faded red and blue rugs had come from the North Devon vicarage where he had spent his boyhood. The sitting-room was the kind of place where you imagined yourself toasting crumpets by the gas fire and we had indeed done that in the early days.

I switched on the TV. There was a choice of a gardening programme, a makeover-your-wardrobe programme, a soap that I never watched, or a re-run of Inspector Morse. I left Inspector Morse on for company and padded off to the bedroom to get dressed. I rummaged around in my bag for a clean pair of knickers. My hand touched a book, two books. I pulled them out and when I saw the titles my hand shot up to my mouth: *Tales of Mystery and Imagination* and the biography of Edgar Allan Poe. I sat down on the bed with the biography in my hand. It seemed incredible, but the truth was that I had forgotten all about 'The Murders in the Rue Morgue'. The shock of Wendy's death had simply blasted it out of my head.

I was still sitting staring at the book, when the telephone rang. I went to the sitting-room door and waited for the answering machine to pick up the call.

It was Jim.

'Cassandra, are you there?'

I grabbed the phone. 'Yes?'

'I'm at Wendy's flat,' Jim said. 'I need to talk. I'll be round in half an hour.'

On the television screen Inspector Morse was strolling across a shaved lawn in the courtyard of an Oxford college. Sergeant Lewis was hurrying towards him.

'There's something I want to tell you,' I said.

Behind me in the hall the doorbell rang.

'Was that the doorbell?' Jim said. 'Go and see who it is.'

I peered through the distorting lens of the fish-eye. Two figures with massively enlarged heads were standing outside. I recognized one of the waiters from the Italian restaurant bearing a big square box.

'Hang on a minute,' I called and went back to the phone. 'It's the pizza delivery man.'

'I'll see you soon.'

'Wait. I want to know — Wendy's child — '

But it was too late. He'd hung up.

★   ★   ★

I already knew something about the short and turbulent life of Edgar Allan Poe, the poverty, the alcoholism, the estrangement from one friend after another, ending at last with the collapse in a gutter in Baltimore and death at the age of forty. While I was eating my pizza, I leafed through the biography of Poe, until I reached the period around the publication of 'The Murders in the Rue Morgue'. Poe had married his fourteen year old cousin, Virginia, in 1836. By 1843 she was desperately ill with tuberculosis. I skimmed the pages, absorbing some of the details of their short marriage. In the year *The Prose Romances of Edgar Allan Poe* was published, Poe was desperately poor. As his young wife lay dying in the winter of 1846–47, he tried to keep her warm her by wrapping her in his old army greatcoat. Their large tortoiseshell cat lay on her chest. According to an eye-witness account, 'The coat and the cat were the sufferer's only means of warmth, except as her husband held her hands, and her mother her feet.' In no way did *The Prose Romances* represent a turn in their fortunes. Precious few were sold and it was priced at only twelve and a half cents. If my suspicions were correct, one of them was now worth somewhere approaching half a million pounds. I was still brooding over this when the doorbell rang.

I let Jim in. His hair was wet and water was trickling down his face. He ran his hand over his head and flicked the rain off his fingers.

'It's pissing it down,' he said, wiping his feet vigorously on the mat. He shrugged off the leather jacket he'd been wearing over his suit and I hung it on the back of the door.

He took his briefcase into the sitting-room.

'I want you to see these,' he said, sitting down on the sofa by the coffee-table.

I sat next to him and was conscious of the smell of damp wool. Jim moved my plate with its crust of pizza to one side, took an envelope from the briefcase and slid some photographs out onto the coffee-table.

'Don't touch them,' he said.

He fanned them out so that I could see them all. There was a photograph of me getting out of my car at the nursery and another, looking as if it were taken on the same day, of me walking up the steps of the nursery with Grace in my arms. There was one of Stephen standing on the pavement outside his office talking to someone I didn't recognize. There was a photograph of me walking out of the main entrance of the college. I stared at them open-mouthed. It was uncanny, as though I'd been allowed a glimpse into the past.

'You had no idea she'd taken these,' Jim said. It was more of a statement than a question.

I shook my head. 'Now I know how it feels to be stalked by the paparazzi. These must go back months.'

'We've spoken to the neighbours,' Jim said. 'Wendy used to live with her mother, a selfish, domineering type, had Wendy completely under her thumb.'

'What about the child?'

'No child. There's never been one. It was just part of the fantasy life.'

It was a relief that there was no one left to be motherless, but I felt deprived of something. That little girl had become real to me and now she had simply vanished into thin air. It triggered off a longing for Grace.

'Mrs Shale died about eighteen months ago,' Jim went on. 'That was probably when Wendy started to lose her grip.'

'It was soon after that she took my course.'

'These are just a few of the photos. There are hundreds at her flat. We found them pinned up everywhere.'

'That one,' I said, pointing to a photograph of the Old Granary with Bill Bailey sitting on the doorstep, 'it must have been taken last summer. There are leaves on the trees. She didn't have a car. To get that picture she must have caught the train or bus to Ely and walked across the fields. How did she know we wouldn't be at home?'

'She probably rang first. Have you had many phone calls when you've picked up and there's been no one there?'

'That did happen a few times. I didn't think anything of it. Actually, it happened on the night Una died. That was why I couldn't dial 1471.'

I wanted to ask whether Una's death and Wendy's were connected and if so, how, but I didn't think I would get an answer. I guessed Jim was feeding me only the information that he wanted me to have. I looked sideways at him. He was gazing at the left-over pizza with a hungry expression.

'When did you last eat?'

'What? Oh, I had a sandwich earlier.'

'You must eat. There's more pizza in the kitchen,' I said. 'I can heat it up for you.'

'No, no, really.'

'It'll only go to waste if you don't have it.' I stood up.

'Well, OK, I mean, thanks. But don't bother to heat it up. It'll be fine as it is.'

He followed me into the kitchen and propped himself against the wall. He watched while I slid a piece of pizza out onto a plate.

He said, 'Those photos satisfied Wendy for a while, allowed her to live your life by proxy. But the time came when it wasn't enough to be on the outside looking in. Perhaps it was finding the handbag that tipped her over the edge.'

'Sometimes you see an item in the newspaper about someone who's gone around pretending to be aristocratic and has run up huge debts funding a lavish life style. I can understand that in a way. I mean why *shouldn't* they be aristocratic? It's just an accident of birth and the people who really are, haven't done anything to deserve it.' I spooned coleslaw onto the plate.

'But that's not true of you, is it? Your job, your academic qualifications: you worked hard for those,' said Jim. 'She could have done the same.'

I wasn't so sure. She had been a mediocre student, as far as I could remember and wasn't that the point, that I couldn't really remember? Wendy had been unexceptional in every way. I saw her sitting at my desk in the Institute, pretending to be a serious academic. Had her own life had been so empty, that she'd been driven to occupy someone else's?

I put a fork on the plate and handed it to Jim.

'I think someone else wants feeding.' Jim gestured to the doorway.

I turned to see Bill Bailey. He was sitting with his tail neatly curled round his paws He was far too polite to make a fuss, but his eyes implored me.

'Poor Wendy,' I said, reaching for a tin of cat food and Bill Bailey limped over.

'No, no, not poor Wendy!' Jim said with a vehemence that surprised me. 'She wanted to have something — to be something — without having to work for it.'

'But she was obviously off her head,' I protested, as I hunted in a drawer for the tin-opener.

'Yeah, yeah, but it's just an extreme form of what I see every day. And don't underestimate the seriousness of what she did. She stole your identity, Cassandra. No knowing where it could have ended.' He hesitated. 'It's a funny thing. According to the neighbours there's never been a child in Wendy's flat, but we found some children's belongings.'

'What kind of things?' I asked as I fitted the opener to the tin.

'This and that. A coat, a pair of little wellingtons.'

I paused with the tin half open. 'Red wellingtons?'

Jim looked at me keenly. 'I think they were. What's the matter?'

I told him about what had been going on at the nursery.

Jim looked grim. 'Who knows how long she would have been satisfied with an imaginary child.'

A cold finger touched my heart. 'You think Grace could have been in danger?'

'No telling with someone as seriously disturbed as Wendy.'

'But why me? That's what I can't understand.'

There was a discreet miaow. I'd forgotten all about Bill Bailey. I prised back the lid of the tin and squatted down to fork food into his bowl.

'Oh come on,' Jim said. 'You were everything she wanted to be. Attractive, intelligent: to her you were glamorous. You can see it from the way she photographed you. You were the star in her own private picture show.'

'Glamorous? Me?' I snorted in disbelief.

'You really can't see it, can you?'

It wasn't so much the words as the change in his tone that alerted me. I looked up, our eyes met, and it was as if a current had been switched on. I understood that far from imagining the sexual charge between us I'd completely underestimated its force. My stomach lurched as if I was going down in an elevator and the blood rushed to my face. Jim was frozen with his fork halfway to his open mouth, like one of the figures in Wendy's photographs.

Bill Bailey miaowed again and pushed his head against my leg. Jim put his fork on his plate.

'I'd better — ' I said.

' — feed him. Yes.'

I busied myself with the cat and tried to think of a neutral topic of conversation. My mind was a blank. The silence stretched out.

Jim cleared his throat, and said, 'In the morning I want you to come to the station to formally identify your handbag and its contents.'

'Oh, fine, yes.'

There was another silence and then Jim said, 'On the phone earlier you said there was something you wanted to tell me?'

'Oh yes,' I said, feeling that my relief at this change of subject was all too obvious. I told him about the *Prose Romances*.

Jim listened without commenting, his face giving nothing away. When I'd finished he pursed his lips and nodded.

'Why do I get the feeling that this doesn't altogether come as a surprise?' I said.

'We've been coming at it from the other side. The money from the sale of the house was in an account that we only discovered a few days ago. There's not much of it left. We've traced a payment of nearly half a million pounds to a dealer in rare books in Chicago. Our colleagues in the US have agreed to interview him for us. And when I tell you that he specializes in nineteenth and twentieth-century first editions . . . '

He put his plate on the table. 'I'm going to ring the States.'

'And after that?' Only later did it occur to me that I had spoken as though I had an unquestionable right to an answer.

'I'm going to the house.' He was taking his coat off the back of the door.

'You mean to Una's?'

He nodded.

'You're going to look for it?' I said.

He shrugged his coat on. 'I've already requested that someone from the Met's Fine

Art Squad be seconded to us. They'll be here in a couple of days, but I can't wait until then. I'll get my sergeant to meet me over there.'

'Can I come too?' I heard myself saying.

16

Ships That Pass in the Night

Jim's sergeant emerged from the porch with an umbrella and a flashlight and met us halfway as we ran to the house through pelting rain. In the porch we put on paper suits, jostling each other in the narrow space and muttering apologies.

Jim switched off the alarm and swung open the door into the hall. He stood back to let me go in first.

I already had my foot on the threshold when I had a moment of feeling that I couldn't go into the house. My sense of foreboding was so strong that it was all I could do not to turn and push my way out past the two men behind me. I forced myself to stand my ground. Don't they say that there is a primitive part of our brain that is unchanged since the days when we crept out of the sea into the swamps? Something's not right here, it was telling me, and the hairs were standing up on my arms.

'Cassandra?' Jim said. I took a deep breath,

the bad moment passed, and I stepped into the hall.

Jim followed me. He looked at me curiously.

'Are you all right?' he asked.

'I think so, but . . . ' I managed to locate one element of my malaise. 'Is it just me, or is it very hot in here?'

The mausoleum chill of our earlier visit had been replaced by a steamy heat and there was a disgusting smell, redolent of decay. The stairs were still taped off and everything was much as it had been before. But the dust was deeper on the hall table and the Michaelmas daisies had collapsed into a rotting mess in their vase. That was where the smell was coming from.

Jim made an irritated sound in his throat. 'When I told them to switch the heating on, I didn't mean them to turn it into a bloody hothouse.'

'This could do more harm to the books than not having any heat at all,' I said, momentarily distracted from our quest.

'I know,' Jim rubbed his face with a weary hand. 'People just don't think. Dave, do something about this, will you?' he said to his sergeant.

Dave nodded and scurried off.

Already I was sweating under my layers of

winter clothes and paper.

Jim and I had hardly exchanged a word on the drive across Cambridge. On my part I knew I was on sufferance and didn't want to say anything to make him change his mind. I was only on board because I said I knew what *The Prose Romances of Edgar Allan Poe* looked like. And I did. Well, more or less, and I *am* an expert on nineteenth-century fiction. In any case we could hardly hear each other speak over the thrumming of the rain on the roof and the hectic tattoo of the windscreen wipers. Visibility was terrible and sheets of water lay across the roads.

Now Jim said, 'For now, we'll work on the assumption that the book is here somewhere. Dr Carwardine could have put it in a safety deposit box somewhere but there aren't any keys that haven't been accounted for. Of course there's a third possibility.'

Dave gave the thumbs up as he came across the hall. 'I've turned the thermostat down,' he said.

Jim nodded, 'Let's get started then.'

'What was the third possibility?' I asked.

'What? Oh, yes. That it was stolen on the night of the murder.'

I was aghast. 'You don't really think that?'

'Probably not. I think that's what the

prowler was after, in which case it'll still be here.'

My heart sank. I hadn't fully faced the fact that we had found our way out of one maze only to discover that we were at the entrance of another. It was pointless knowing that Una had bought the *Prose Romances* if it could never be recovered.

I looked around. Down here every wall was lined with books and it was the same on the landing. And beyond that there was room after room all crammed with books. 'You realize that it's just a pamphlet,' I said despairingly. 'It's so thin that it could actually be concealed inside another book. It could be anywhere.'

'Let's narrow it down. This was Dr Carwardine's most cherished possession. I'm guessing she would have wanted to have it somewhere where she could easily get her hands on it and movement was painful. So we can scrub the second floor. There's no stair-lift and judging by the dust, no-one's been up there for months. My guess is that she hid it somewhere on the first floor. We'll start with the bedroom and work out.'

Every book had to be taken off the shelf and opened. If I'd been on my own I would have been tempted to stop and read a page or two here and there, but working with Dave meant that I had to keep up a steady pace. We soon got into a routine. Dave would hand me a book. I would check it and put it on the floor until the whole shelf was cleared. Then we would replace the books and move on to the next shelf where I would hand Dave the books. Jim worked close by, looking under rugs and seat cushions and behind pictures. It's surprising how dirty old books can be. Soon our gloved hands were filthy and the dust was making me sneeze. It was a mind-numbing activity and yet it required total concentration. As I clambered up library steps to reach high shelves and crouched down, knee joints cracking, to reach the lower ones, I revised my view of library work as a sedentary occupation. After ten minutes, I was sweating as if I was in a sauna.

I went back down to the porch and took off my sweater so that I was wearing only a t-shirt and jeans under my paper suit. Five minutes later Dave wiped the sweat off his face and went down-stairs to follow suit.

We found the occasional item inserted in the pages: a postcard of the Arc de Triomphe sent to Una in the fifties, a French metro ticket, even a tarnished silver paper knife, which someone had used to cut the pages and had left in as a book mark. Once Dave gave a cry of discovery. Sandwiched between two volumes of a novel was a thin booklet. My heart skipped a beat, but a quick look at the uneven typography and crude wood-cut on the cover told me that it was an early nineteenth-century chapbook, and nothing to do with Poe.

We worked on in silence. Jim moved next door to the bathroom. Dave and I went on bending and stretching and opening and closing books as though we were working on a production line. Now and then I felt a brief return of my earlier unease and found myself listening intently, without knowing what I expected to hear. There was never anything except the rain pelting against the windows and the creaking of floorboards. The rhythm of the work and the heat induced a state of lethargy. It was an effort to keep going and my eyes kept slipping out of focus.

It was quarter to twelve when I replaced the last book on the last shelf in Una's bedroom. I straightened up, flexed my shoulders and rubbed my aching back. The search had taken us an hour and a half, yet apart from the kitchen and the bathroom the bedroom was probably the least book-populated room in the house.

The same thing must have occurred to Dave, because he said, 'I've been trying to work out how many books there are in the house. It can only be approximate, of course, based on the average number of books on a shelf, some shelves being much longer than others . . . '

I caught myself thinking that he resembled a large white rabbit. It was partly the white hooded jump-suit, also the paleness of his eyebrows and eyelashes and the large front teeth. All he needed was a pair of big floppy ears . . . I gave myself a mental shake and tuned in again to what he was saying.

' . . . There could be as many as thirteen and a half thousand left to do. At a rate of five seconds a book, that would take ninety-three and three quarters hours. With the two of us working eight hours a day that would be, oh, let's call it six days, shall we?'

'Cassandra?' Jim had appeared in the doorway. 'Are you OK?'

'I think I'm getting a bit light-headed. It's still so hot in here.' My throat was hoarse from the dust.

'We'd better have a break,' Jim said.

'I've got a bottle of mineral water in my car,' Dave offered. 'And a flask of coffee and some biscuits.'

'Good man.'

'I'll go and get them, shall I?'

He went along the gallery and disappeared down the back stairs. A moment later we saw him cross the hall. Jim and I remained together by the banister. We were like people standing at the rail of an ocean liner. The rain beating against the windows contributed to the sensation of being afloat, drifting together through the night.

Jim sighed. 'At times like this I wish I hadn't given up smoking.'

'Me, too. How long's it been?'

'Five years ago. New Year resolution. And you?'

'The same, funnily enough. You never really stop wanting one, do you?'

'You never do.'

As if by mutual agreement that we needed a few moments of solitude, we moved away from each other. Jim turned away from the banister and took a few steps backwards and forwards, swinging his arms to ease the tension in his shoulders.

I strolled down the gallery, my eye caught now and then by the title of one of the books that lined the wall from floor to ceiling. I thought of Dave's estimate. The company who had done the deal with Una would want the house cleared as soon as the police had finished with it as the scene of a crime. How on earth were we going to move all these books to St Etheldreda's and where were we going to put them? By now I had reached the foot of the narrow staircase up to the second floor. Jim was at the other end of the landing. Down in the hall Dave appeared with a bottle of water under one arm and a thermos flask under the other.

And that was when it happened.

Directly above my head there was a sharp crack like a car back-firing. Dave stopped dead in his tracks. Jim turned and looked at me, his head cocked for the next sound. When it came, it was like nothing I had ever heard before. The image that sprang to mind was of ice floes crashing and grinding together. The whole house quivered as if it were alive and in pain. There was a thud on the ceiling above us, then another, and another. There was an awful groaning noise. Vibrations were coming up through the soles of my feet. I looked up the stairs to the second floor. Something amorphous and monstrous was emerging from the dark and moving towards me. I couldn't make sense of what I was seeing.

The next instant something thudded into my shoulder and sent me staggering. There was an arm round my waist. I was half-towed, half-dragged along the landing. We reached the servants' staircase. Jim stepped into the doorway and yanked me in beside him. He braced his arm against one door jamb and pressed me against the other.

I looked back. A dense dark cloud of dust billowed out onto the landing and engulfed the place where I had been standing. It slowly expanded into the hall, unfolding like a mushroom cloud. Dave, still clasping the bottle and the thermos flask, was backing away. His eyes and mouth were stretched open like a frightened man in a cartoon. There was a muffled rumbling that grew louder, gathering momentum, like an avalanche. The dark cloud now contained hard-edged tumbling objects. It was as if an enormous wheelbarrow of books and bricks had been tipped down the stairs. More followed, and yet more, until books were banked up to the full height of the balustrade. There was a splintering sound as it gave way and a cascade of books and bricks descended with a crash into the hall.

That marked a climax and the rumbling slowly died away.

Jim and I continued to stand squeezed together in the doorway.

There was one last vibration, like the aftershock of an earthquake. A book that was precariously balanced on the landing slithered over the edge and landed with a thud on the pile below.

Silence descended. Particles of dust drifted up into the vault of the hall.

'I can see the headlines now. *The Body in the Library. Cambridge Don Killed by Falling Books.*' I poured out the Scotch with a trembling hand. It was two o'clock in the morning and Jim had driven me back to Stephen's flat. I was still in a state verging on hysteria, not knowing whether I wanted to laugh or cry.

'If you hadn't acted so quickly . . . ' I said, handing Jim a glass.

'Oh, you'd have got out of the way in time,' he said.

He spoke calmly, but I knew he was more shaken than he wanted to admit. He sat down on the sofa.

I took the armchair opposite. 'I'm not so sure. I was frozen to the spot.'

When the dust had settled, we made our way cautiously out of Green Gables and Jim had called the fire brigade. It was a gable wall collapsing into the house that had released the deluge of books.

'How did you know what was happening?' I asked.

I took a gulp from my glass. More Scotch went down than I'd intended. There was a star-burst of warmth in my chest and my head swam.

'I didn't know,' Jim said. 'Ridiculous as it sounds, my first thought was that it was an earthquake and that a doorway was the safest place to be.' He rubbed his head. A little cloud of plaster-dust rose up. All three of us had looked as if we'd been dipped in talcum powder. My eyes felt sore and gritty. The paper suits had protected our clothes from the worse, but particles of dust had still worked their way inside.

'The weight of all those books was just too much for that old house,' Jim said.

'If it had happened when Una was living alone there . . .'

'Probably it wouldn't have done. You said the place was kept at a more or less constant heat.'

'Yes, of course,' I rubbed my forehead. 'I'm not thinking straight.'

'The gable wall must have been bulging for some time.'

'You know, I love books and I think of them as benign things — after all, I make my living from them, but *en masse* like that . . . the noise was deafening. My ears are still ringing.'

'Water got in between the cracks — '

'It was like 'The Fall of the House of Usher'. When the narrator first arrives, the crack is scarcely visible. Then at the end it widens and zig-zags down the building. That description — how does it go?' *Tales of Mystery and Imagination* was lying on the coffee-table. I picked it up and leafed through it.

'It was because the heating had been switched off that the gable wall froze so solidly, and then a sudden thaw and the heating being on so high . . . '

' "I saw the mighty walls rushing asunder — there was a long tumultuous shouting sound like the voice of a thousand waters — and the deep and dark tarn at my feet closed sullenly and silently over the fragments of the House of Usher." '

Jim was staring at me. 'What are you talking about, Cass?'

'It's a short story by Edgar Allan Poe.'

'What?'

'Oh, never mind. Look, about *The Prose Romances*. We're scuppered, aren't we?'

He sighed. 'For now. We'll have to get the structural engineers in tomorrow and the house will have to be shored up somehow. God knows when we'll be allowed back in there. But no one else will be able to get in either.'

'What are you going to do now?'

'Now? I'll go home and better grab a few hours sleep.'

'Where do you live?'

'Near Over.'

'I know. Out past Longstanton.' It was a village eight or nine miles north-east of Cambridge.

'I've dossed down in my office once or twice, but I haven't been home for a couple of days and last thing I need at the moment is burst pipes.'

Alcohol and exhaustion, not to mention the shock of nearly being swept away by an avalanche of books, loosened my tongue.

'What about your wife?' I blurted out.

He looked up with an expression that I couldn't read. Surprise maybe, but something else, too. 'Didn't you know? Didn't Stephen tell you . . . '

'Stephen didn't know.'

'I could have sworn — but maybe . . . ' He seemed almost to be speaking to himself. A feeling of dread was building up inside me. I knew something awful was coming and I wanted to get it over.

'Tell me,' I said.

He took a sip from his glass. 'She's dead.'

It would have been crass to match his own directness with anything less. 'What happened?' I asked.

'Ectopic pregnancy. It's when the fertilized egg doesn't get implanted in the uterus — '

'I know. It gets stuck in the fallopian tube and starts to grow there.'

'It wasn't diagnosed in time. She got peritonitis.'

'Oh God. I'm sorry.'

He leaned back into the sofa. There was still the same distant, enigmatic look on his face. He looked down into his whisky glass. 'People often feel guilty, don't they, when someone they love dies? They feel that it's their fault. Well, that's how I feel, but in my case it's true. I wanted a kid, Pat wasn't all that keen. She was doing it for me.' He closed his eyes. 'And in the end there was no baby, and no Pat either.'

Something was happening to his face. The lines around his mouth had grown deeper and his eyes were pressed tight shut.

He was crying.

I got up and took the glass from his hand. When I sat beside him, he turned blindly to me and buried his face in my shoulder. Hot tears soaked into my shirt. I don't know how long we sat like that, clamped awkwardly together, before his mouth sought mine. He pushed me gently back onto the sofa and the next moment we were necking like teenagers. Jim's hands were under my T-shirt, his unshaven face rasped against mine, his body felt dense and solid in my arms. We clung to each other as if we were drowning. We surfaced for a moment. Jim pulled back, pressed his face to mine and spoke into my ear.

'I'm sorry. I haven't got anything — have you — I mean is it all right . . . '

An image flashed into my mind: my diaphragm in its case in the drawer by my side of the bed at the Old Granary and anyway that wasn't enough, not these days.

'Just a minute. I must just . . . ' I pulled away, not knowing exactly what it was I had to do. 'I'll be back.'

Jim flopped back on the sofa. I staggered into the bathroom and opened the bathroom cabinet. There was a packet of condoms: a relic of the early days with Stephen. I took it out and stood holding it in my hand. I stared in the mirror. My face was red where Jim's stubble had scraped it and the plaster-dust in my hair made me look as if I'd gone prematurely grey. I asked myself if I was really going to go through with this? I'd like to say that it was conscience or love of Stephen that made up my mind for me, but it felt more like cowardice: the knowledge that this was a step that I could never go back from, no matter how much I might regret it. And strange to say, I knew full well that tomorrow I would regret not having done it. I'd gone too far to come out of this unscathed. Nonetheless my mind was made up even before I looked more closely at the packet of condoms and noticed the use-by date. They had expired three years ago.

I brushed some of the dust out of my hair and splashed water on my face.

When I went back into the sitting room, Jim was stretched out full-length and face down on the sofa. He was fast asleep. My first feeling was one of indignation followed swiftly by relief that no explanations were necessary and then compassion for this exhausted man. I put my hand on his shoulder, but he was so completely inert that he didn't stir. I saw that he had emptied his pockets and arranged the contents on the table. There was a white cotton handkerchief, neatly folded, and piled on it was a little heap of coins. His mobile phone was next to it.

I got a pillow and a blanket. He didn't move as I tucked the blanket round him. When I slipped my hands under his head so that I could edge the pillow underneath, he muttered something that I couldn't make out. Then he buried his face in the pillow and was silent. I stood looking at him. As so often when you see someone asleep, some of the adult personality had dissolved, leaving behind an innocence and a vulnerability. I put my hand on his forehead and stroked his hair. I had a strange sensation as though for a moment someone was in the room with us. I thought, I'm tired, I'm very tired, the words forming slowly in my mind as if I was articulating each one very carefully.

I went into the bedroom and took my jeans off, leaving on my t-shirt and my underwear. I laid down and slipped into sleep as if I was sinking into deep water.

17

No Name

'And there wasn't any attempt to use the credit cards, was there?' Jim asked. The contents of my handbag were spread out before us on the desk in his office.

I shook my head. 'I'd cancelled them, but in any case, that wasn't the point of them for Wendy.'

The useless credit cards, the driving licence, the hat that must have been bought at the same shop on Bridge Street, it was all so much like a small child tottering around in high-heels and pretending to be mummy. I remembered my flippant thoughts about her little girl name. Perhaps that had been a bit unkind, but I hadn't been so far off the mark.

'Is there anything missing?' he asked.

I scanned the table. Everything was in its own transparent plastic evidence-bag. What a lot there seemed to be when it was all spread out like this.

'Everything's here?'

'Seems to be.'

'Money?'

'Even that.'

A thought struck me. 'Will I get everything back?'

'Eventually.'

'I'm not sure I want all of it. I bet she used my make-up.' I saw Wendy staring into a mirror with narrowed eyes as she applied the lipstick that she hoped would transform her into me.

'Oh, but there's Grace's shoe,' I said, as my eye fell on it for the first time. 'I minded more about that than anything.' I felt a spurt of anger.

I looked at Jim and saw a tenderness in his eyes that made my heart turn over. I looked quickly away.

The day had begun with Jim waking me up with a cup of tea.

'I hope you don't mind my helping myself,' he'd said, not quite meeting my eye. 'I've had a shower and I've used one of the disposable razors in the bathroom.'

I propped myself up on one elbow and squinted at the bedside clock. It was eight o'clock.

'I'm sorry about last night,' he said quickly. 'I don't know what came over me.'

'Me neither.' The blood rushed to my face and I couldn't look him in the eye. 'Don't worry. Did you sleep all right?'

'Like a log. Haven't slept like that for ages. Look, I've got to go soon. If you hurry, I'll take you into the station so that you can identify the stuff in your handbag.'

And now here we were, standing in his office not much more than an hour later, almost as if nothing had happened between us. Almost but not quite: every now and then I had a flashback to the previous night and began to blush all over again. I didn't feel guilty yet, but I knew that I soon would and I couldn't kid myself that there was nothing to feel guilty about.

Jim cleared his throat. 'OK, so all your stuff seems to be here. But is there anything here that *doesn't* belong to you?'

I scanned the table.

'What's that?' I asked, pointing to one of the evidence bags.

Jim reached over and picked it up so that I could have a closer look. The bag contained a crumpled piece of paper about three inches square. On it were written in ink the numbers 1815.

'I don't remember that,' I said, 'and that's not my writing.'

'Do you recognize it?'

I shook my head. 'I'm not sure. It's harder when it's just numbers, isn't it? They're not as distinctive as actual writing.'

'Do the numbers mean anything to you?'

I stared at them. 'I have a feeling they do, but I can't quite think what.'

'It might come to you when you're thinking about something else. Go on looking at the rest of the stuff.' His eyes flicked away from mine and it came to me that he already knew the significance of those numbers, but before I could think any more about that, Jim was speaking again.

'What about this, Cassandra? I assume it belongs to your daughter.' He held up another evidence bag.

It contained a little plastic figure painted in red, white and black.

My mouth dropped open.

'What's the matter?' Jim said sharply.

'You found that in my handbag?' I saw myself dropping the little figure into Michelle's hand as we stood together in the entrance to the Fitzwilliam museum.

'It was underneath one of the book shelves,' Jim said. 'It looked as if it had rolled out when Wendy dropped the bag.'

'It doesn't belong to Grace. You see that wouldn't be suitable for a small child. They might swallow it,' I explained, as if that was the most important thing about it.

Jim was looking at me intently. 'You do recognize it though, don't you?'

306

'It's the Duke of Wellington. It belongs to Giles.'

And then I knew what was familiar about 1815. It was the date of the battle of Waterloo. What on earth was that doing on a piece of paper in my handbag?

★ ★ ★

Merfyn and I stood gazing out of my office window. The snow had completely disappeared. The rain swept in curtains across the court and the lawn was like a paddy-field.

When Jim had offered to arrange a lift home for me, I'd asked to be taken to St Etheldreda's. I wasn't ready to go back to an empty flat. Or rather the problem was that the flat wasn't empty enough: the air would still be thick with the emotion that had flowed between Jim and me. Better for a while to be part of the light and warmth and familiar bustle of the college. I left Stephen a text message. I wasn't ready to speak to him. But I did need to speak to someone and Merfyn fitted the bill. I told him everything except what had happened between me and Jim.

'Did the Superintendent tell you what he was going to do next?' Merfyn asked.

'Well, obviously he's going to want to talk to Giles and Michelle.'

'It's not looking good for either of them, is it? Someone must have let Wendy into the Institute after opening hours, so the circle of people who could have killed Wendy was small in the first place anyway. Now it's just got narrower. Unless of course someone wanted to throw suspicion on Giles.'

'Jim thinks that Wendy could have doubled back and hidden among the stacks, until after closing time.'

'OK, but the killer had to be there, too, didn't they? And they could only have got in with a key. How about this for a theory? Giles starts removing choice items from Una's collection, always being careful to keep ahead of Michelle's cataloguing. Even if Una noticed that a book wasn't where she thought it should be, it would be difficult for her to be certain that it was actually missing. Giles would bank on that.'

'And she'd be reluctant at first to believe that someone she trusted was a thief.'

'But Giles realizes that she *does* suspect. He's afraid it's all going to come out. He'll go to prison, lose his job. If that's not a motive for murder, I'd like to know what is.'

Merfyn turned away from the window and sat down in an armchair. He stretched his legs out in front of him.

Through the downpour I could hardly see

the copper beech where I had seen a shadowy figure on the evening that I ran into Wendy. Had it been Wendy following me? While I was getting the ice off my windscreen, there would have been ample time for her to cut through the college to the bus stop.

A trio of giggling girls with coats over their heads emerged though the veils of rain.

'Where does Wendy come in to it?' I asked.

Merfyn furrowed his brow. 'She could have known something that made her a danger to Giles.'

'Why didn't she go to the police?'

'Blackmail?'

'Oh no!'

'Why not?'

I turned away from the window and began to pace up and down. I tried to account for my gut reaction.

'It just isn't in character,' I decided. 'I mean, Wendy wasn't that clued up to the main chance. She was living in a world of her own.'

'Well, how about this then. She sees something, Giles removing a book, for instance, but doesn't realize its significance, she thinks he's allowed to do that. But maybe she mentions it to Una and the fat's in the fire. Una doesn't let her see that's something wrong: she needs to think about what to do.

Then later, after Una's death, Wendy says something to Giles, could be something quite guileless, and he knows that she knows. So she has to go, too.'

'I don't know. It sounds plausible enough, but . . . Giles, though, it's hard to believe.'

'Michelle, then. She was even better placed for nicking books.'

'Michelle committing two murders! It's unbelievable.'

'Strikes me that a lot of unbelievable things have happened lately and for goodness sake, sit down. You're making me feel giddy,' Merfyn said.

I sank into the chair opposite him. 'Tell me about it. Everything's going round and round in my head. I feel as if I've got vertigo. It's not just Wendy's death, but finding out that she wasn't what I thought she was.' And it was a shock too to find that Jim wasn't what I thought he was; and nor was I, come to that.

'And now you're thinking maybe nobody's what they seem?' Merfyn said.

I looked sideways at him. 'Don't tell me. You've been leading a double-life. In ordinary life you are self-effacing, scholarly Merfyn Jenkins, but when the call comes, you slip into a telephone box and — '

Merfyn grinned. 'Yes! It's Superdon! I know my secret is safe with you. Of course,' he added, 'one could argue it's never really possible to know anyone, even oneself. Perhaps oneself least of all.'

I groaned. 'Don't go all philosophical on me. I really *didn't* know Wendy very well. There was such a lot I took for granted.'

'And why wouldn't you? Ordinary social life couldn't function if we were constantly questioning everything. You'd end up paranoid, looking for the real meaning behind everything.'

Merfyn was following a new line of thought. 'One thing's for certain. It can't be a coincidence: two murders, and Wendy being Una's cleaner. That's assuming that Wendy was the intended victim. You must have wondered about that.'

'Of course I have. And so have the police.'

'You know, it does make more sense, if Wendy was killed in mistake for you. You're smart and you know about books, so it's much more likely that you would discover something that points to Una's murder, isn't it?'

'But I didn't!'

'Perhaps the murderer thought you did.'

I realized that I was chewing my thumb nail. I snatched my hand away from my mouth. 'Oh God, I wish I hadn't given up smoking.'

'Perhaps you know something without knowing what it is.'

'Then it's not much use to me, is it?' I snapped.

Merfyn leaned forwards and said, 'What would you do if you were stuck on some piece of academic work, couldn't see the wood for the trees?'

'With that kind of problem, a chronology can help. Putting everything in the order that it happened can help to get things clear, bring out connections and so on.'

'Do that. Write it down. Go on, girl,' he said.

I went over to my desk and I got a sheet of foolscap out of the drawer. I sat down. Merfyn came and looked over my shoulder.

'Where to start . . . ?' I murmured.

'Una's death?'

'That can't have been the real beginning. The changing of the will came before that, and Una's letter to me.'

'Put it halfway down then.' Merfyn glanced at his watch. 'Damn. I'm teaching in ten minutes and then I'm booked solid until this afternoon. Be lucky if I can grab a sandwich for lunch. Don't hang around too long, Cass.' He gestured to where the rain was still lashing at the window. 'If anything, I think it's raining harder. And did you hear the local news this morning? There's already been some flooding along the Backs.'

* * *

Half an hour later I pushed my seat back. I'd only filled in the space before Una's death, but it was enough to show me that I had over-looked something important. Once it was in front of me in black and white I couldn't think why I hadn't cottoned on before. Hadn't I suspected that Michelle was holding something back?

I didn't think the Institute would have reopened yet. I tried her mobile. The voice that answered was hardly recognizable as her's.

'Michelle? Is that you?'

'I'm waiting in the doctor's surgery.'

'You're ill?'

'I can't really talk. Oh, Cassandra, I want to see you.' She sounded as if she was about to burst into tears.

'I want to see you, too. Which surgery is this?'

'Huntingdon Road.'

'Can you walk down Castle Street to that Italian restaurant on Magdalene Street?'

'La Margarita?'

'That's the one. I'll be waiting for you there.'

There was hardly anyone in the café. I had a nasty feeling that most sensible people had headed for home. I was sitting over a cappuccino when the door opened and Michelle was blown in through the door, clutching her umbrella. A flurry of rain came in with her. Her eyes were red-rimmed and the hand she lifted to brush back her wet hair was trembling.

As soon as she reached my table, she blurted it out. 'They've arrested Giles. They think he murdered that woman. I couldn't tell you with all those people listening at the doctor's. The police came round to see me at home and they wanted to know about that figure of the Duke of Wellington. The one you asked me to put back on Giles's desk? They went away and later MaryAnne rang and told me that the police had come to the library and they'd taken him away!'

She was still standing by the side of the table. Water was dripping off her chin. Her lower lip was quivering.

'Sit down,' I said. 'Come on.' She obeyed. I reached for her hand and squeezed it. It felt icy. 'You'd better have a hot drink. Shall I order you a cappuccino? Or some hot chocolate?'

She looked at me as if she didn't know what I was talking about. Then she ran both

314

hands through her hair and nodded.

I beckoned the waiter over and ordered her a hot chocolate. 'Have you had anything to eat today?'

Michelle shook her head.

'You need some carbohydrates inside you. What could you eat? A pizza? pasta?'

'I couldn't — '

'Oh, come on. I'm going to have something.'

'Well, maybe some pizza.' She dabbed at her wet hair with a paper napkin. It didn't make much difference.

I ordered two pizza Napoletana. When the waiter had gone, we were silent. Then Michelle said, 'I haven't told you everything, Cassandra. About me and Una.'

'I know.'

Her mouth fell open and she stared at me. 'How did you find out?'

'I've made a list of everything that's happened, everything that could be relevant to Una's death, and Wendy's. The first entry in the chronology is 'January. Michelle goes to the Grange to catalogue Una's bequest to the Institute.' The second is 'March, Jane Pennyfeather notices that Una has had a shock.' They could be entirely unrelated, but they're not, are they?'

Michelle bit her lip and shook her head. 'I

didn't think Una would guess. But she did and I thought she'd be furious.'

At that moment, the waiter arrived with her hot chocolate. He took one look at our faces and retreated without a word.

Michelle said, 'I even thought I might lose my job. But it wasn't like that at all. She was so sweet and kind.' Tears were welling up in her eyes.

'Michelle, please tell me that you weren't pinching her books. That just can't be true.'

'Of course I wasn't!' She stared at me indignantly.

'So what the devil are you talking about? What did Una find did out about you?'

'I thought you'd guessed. Terence Carwardine was my father.'

★ ★ ★

It was a familiar enough story. Terence Carwardine had met her mother when they were both working in the archives at the Harry Ransom Humanities Center at the University of Texas at Austin. Michelle's mother had been a young postdoctoral student on a fellowship. She was in awe of him. He was flattered by her admiration. They had begun an affair that had continued when they returned to England. Michelle's mother had got pregnant. Terence was adamant that he wouldn't leave his wife, but she wanted the baby anyway. He set up a trust fund for Michelle's keep and for her education, and then there was no other contact. Later Michelle's mother had married and Michelle had three younger half-brothers.

'Of course, I've always known my stepdad wasn't my father,' Michelle said. 'I mean, I knew he wasn't my biological father, even though he's been a real dad to me in every other way. When I was eighteen, my mum explained all about it. She said she felt she owed me that, but it was too late, really, because by then he was dead.' She took a sip of her hot chocolate. 'I understand why she didn't.'

'You must have been curious about him. Was that why you came to Cambridge?'

Michelle bit her lip and nodded. 'I wanted to find out what he was like. That's why I took the job at the Institute. It wasn't *just* for that, I mean, I do want to be a librarian, but it was a way of getting closer. I didn't have a plan, I thought I'd wait and see what happened. I couldn't believe it when Giles told me that he wanted me to catalogue the books. To actually see where he'd lived — '

The pizza arrived. Michelle looked surprised to see it.

I said, 'You didn't intend Una to find out?'

'I'd promised my mum that I'd keep the secret. She said there was no point in upsetting the apple-cart now. To begin with I was angry with Una. Mum said that she didn't know about me, but I kidded myself that she did and that she'd stopped my father from marrying my mum. I was sure it was all her fault and I hated her.'

'How *did* she find out?'

Michelle pointed to her eyes. 'This funny thing in my eye? He had it, too. I didn't know how much I looked like him when he was young. I'd only seen photos of him when he was old. Una started asking me questions about my parents. I said I didn't know who my father was. She said, 'I think you do, my dear.' And that was it, I just started to cry.'

'You poor thing,' I murmured. And poor Una, too. No wonder everything changed after that. The discovery that her husband had an illegitimate daughter: that was the shock that had made Una embark on her spending spree and decide that she would do as she damn well pleased with Terence's library.

'I can't tell you how lovely she was.' Michelle was blinking back tears. 'I didn't think that she'd want me to keep coming to the house, but she did. And she talked to me about my father, too. Wasn't that nice of her?'

I nodded. It was more than nice, it was heroic. Never had I admired Una more than I did at that moment.

'You've got to tell the police about this,' I told her.

'I already did. This morning. Cassandra, I'm sorry I didn't tell you sooner. You see, it was my mum's secret and I hadn't told her what I was doing. I've told her now. She wants me to go home and I want it, too. The doctor says I've got post-traumatic stress disorder and I mustn't go into work.' Now she was crying openly. 'My dad's coming to collect me this afternoon. It was so horrible! Finding that woman and thinking it was you.'

'I know, I know.' I reached over and took one of her hands. She gripped mine tightly. 'It's the shock that's making you think like this. You'll feel better when you're at home.'

'I'd better go and pack.' She began to gather her things together.

'Will you be OK getting back to Chesterton? Can I get you a taxi?'

'There never are any when it's raining like this. Anyway there's a bus-stop just round the corner.'

She was about to leave when something else occurred to her. She fumbled in her bag and brought out a set of keys.

'Cass, please could you do me a favour? I can't face going back into the Institute. These are my keys. Can you give them to MaryAnne?'

'Does this mean . . . ?'

'Yes, it does. I don't want to go back. Not ever!'

18

Called Back

I reached Stephen's block of flats to find that the car-park had become a shallow lake. The pressure of water on my boots sent little trickles creeping in through their seams. My feet were soaked by the time I got to the entrance. Mr Walenski had banked it up with sandbags in readiness. It was on slightly higher ground so it was still above water level. As I slopped my way up the stairs, I said a silent thank you to Stephen for his prescience in buying a flat on the third floor.

I double-locked the door and put the chain on. Bill Bailey was on the sitting-room window-sill. I scooped him up and stood looking out. It was only four o'clock, but a premature twilight had descended. The rain was coming down in sheets, battering the trees in the wilderness, and bouncing back off the road on the other side of the river. Shadowy figures moved around in gloom, stacking sandbags against the doors of the houses that lined the road. The river was high and it wouldn't be long before it was slopping over the parapet.

It was time to prepare for a siege. I felt an urge to get everything in order. I'd managed to buy some food on the way home. I went into the kitchen and unpacked the shopping. I cut up some onions and sausage and set them to fry. I put the kettle on for some tea. In the sitting-room coffee-cups, a whisky glass, a plate with a piece of pizza on it were strewn around. Blankets and a pillow had been tossed onto the floor by the sofa. In the bathroom there were wet towels on the floor, and in the kitchen dirty tea-towels were lying crumpled on the kitchen work-top. I gathered everything up and loaded the dishwasher and the washing-machine. It was time to add lentils and water to the pan. I poked about in the cupboard and found a packet of dried oregano, so I added some of that. The soothing hum of the dishwasher and the click and whir of the washing-machine gave me a comforting feeling of being in control. It was like sitting in the engine house of a ship.

I sat down at the kitchen table with a cup of tea. Now that I had heard Michelle's story, I was able to fill in some of the blanks in the chronology.

I knew Una's letter by heart, but still I took it out and spread it out on the table, hoping that I would see something new in it:

I must know if my new suspicions are justified. If so, then I very much fear I've misjudged someone and I would hate that ... I don't want to commit any more to paper, but do you remember that grisly high-table dinner and what we talked about then? ... I really can't rest until I've got this sorted out, and if anyone can help me do that it will be you, my dear. I'm placing a great responsibility on you, I know that.

Suspicions of who? Suspicions of what? I was still no nearer to knowing what she meant by that. I groaned. It was beginning to look as if Una's faith in me had been misplaced.

I find it easier to think when I'm moving. I got up and roamed around the flat. I picked things up and put them down again without really seeing them. In the kitchen I stirred the soup. There was an idea in the back of my mind. I just couldn't quite grasp it. In the bedroom I was mildly surprised to find myself clutching *The Last Chronicle of Barset*. I perched on the edge of the bed and read a few pages at random. Poor distracted Reverend Crawley could not for the life of him account for his possession of the stolen cheque: he was half-crazed with shame and confusion. I clapped the book shut and continued my peregrinations.

Una, Una, I thought, why didn't you tell me everything in that letter. I'm just not as smart as you. I don't have your phenomenal memory. I heard Merfyn saying, 'She was bright, very bright. Was she at Bletchley during the war? I rather think she was.' What was it that Michelle had said that time in the orchid house? 'When she was my age it was the war and she was doing top secret stuff.' Something was nagging me, a connection that I hadn't made at the time. Bletchley Park was where the Enigma code had been broken, the breakthrough that had shortened the Second World War by two years. Had Una spent the war breaking codes? I remembered Jane telling me what a red-hot crossword addict she was.

What if there was more to that letter than met the eye? What if it was something hidden there in code.

I went into the kitchen, sat down at the table, and pulled the letter towards me.

And that was when all the lights went out.

* * *

The darkness was complete. It pressed against my eyeballs, rich, dense, and velvety.

It was if I had been struck blind. My first reaction was instinctive, unreasoning fear. Someone had done this to make me vulnerable. The next moment I remembered what Stephen had said about power-cuts.

Now that my eyes were adjusting to the darkness I realized that it wasn't quite complete. There was a blue flicker of gas light under the saucepan of soup. I got up and groped my way over to it and turned on all knobs on the hob. Circles of blue and yellow flames shot up, bathing the kitchen in an eerie light. Unfortunately the cooker was the only appliance that was fuelled by gas. The heating was electric and it wouldn't take long for the flat to start cooling down. But at least there would be hot food and drinks, and hot-water bottles, too, if I could find any. And no doubt Mr Walenski would be coming round to check up on us all.

I began to open drawers, looking for candles and matches. Just as I was giving up hope, I opened a cupboard door and there were two boxes of plain white candles with a box of matches. There was also a large flashlight and next to it a spare set of batteries. Something about the way those batteries were lined up so neatly on the shelf, and the foresight they presented, brought Stephen so vividly to mind that I felt a rush of longing for him.

I lit four candles and used hot wax to fix them in saucers.

I sat down and perused the letter. Could there be words hidden in the text in the fashion of a crossword puzzle? Then I turned it every way I could think of, but there didn't seem to be anything there. Maybe the whole letter was in code, in which case it was hopeless for someone as unmathematical as I am. And anyway I didn't really believe it: the letter seemed to flow so naturally, to be so uncontrived. And yet . . . and yet . . . I had that feeling that I was on the brink of discovering something, a kind of so-near-and-yet-so-far feeling. I was getting closer to the solution; I felt that in my water.

I got up from the table and took a candle into the sitting-room. Everything seemed different by its yellow light, softer, more deeply shadowed and there were reflections everywhere, from pans, from polished furniture, from glass. I felt different, too. You have to walk slowly and gracefully when you're carrying a candle or else it goes out. I could imagine myself trailing a long, rustling skirt.

It was still pouring with rain. I could see nothing except the wavering reflection of my candle, that seemed to hang in the darkness. I could have been the only creature in the world left alive.

A pressure against my ankle and a rumbling purr remind me that I wasn't. Bill Bailey was here and he wanted feeding. And perhaps I should feed myself too. I'd lost track of time and was surprised when I looked at my watch to see that it was six o'clock.

I put the candle down on the window-sill and picked up the cat. He pushed his head against me, his eyes gleaming in the light from the candle.

'It's all right for you,' I told him. 'You can see in the dark.'

His body stiffened and his head shot up. He'd heard something. And then I heard it too: a sound like a mouse scratching in the wainscoting.

But it wasn't a mouse. It was the sound of someone fumbling to get a key in a lock.

Someone was trying to get into the flat.

★　★　★

By the time I had raced into the kitchen and snatched up the flashlight, the door was open and straining against the chain. Bill Bailey had beaten me to it and had slipped through the gap.

I directed the powerful beam into some-one's face.

'What the devil!' said a cross and very familiar voice.

'Stephen!'

'Cassandra, what is going on?'

I hurried to unfasten the chain. My heart was still pounding like a piston. 'I could ask you the same thing. You gave me the shock of my life.'

'Get that light out of my eyes,' he complained. 'What were you planning to do, brain me with the torch if I managed to get over the threshold?'

'Something like that,' I admitted. The beam of light revealed that Stephen was dressed in something dark and shiny. Water was coursing down it. Bill Bailey, who had followed him in, shook his head and sneezed.

'Better come into the kitchen,' I said. 'It's the only room with any light.'

Stephen was revealed to be wearing a long black oilskin cape, a sou'wester, and a large pair of black wellington boots with the tops turned down.

'Call me Ishmael', I said, gazing at him in wonder. 'Or is it Captain Ahab?'

'What?' Stephen glanced down. 'Oh, the get-up. Martha insisted on giving me a pair of Dan's wellies and one of his oilskins. As well as a torch and a packet of sandwiches. Good job she did.'

A puddle of water was collecting around his feet.

'What you are doing here?' I asked. 'No, wait, let's get your things off first.'

I dumped the wet clothes and the boots in the bath. When I went back in the kitchen, Stephen was sinking down onto a chair.

'Come here,' he said, stretching out his arms. I sat on his knees and he pulled me in tight against him, As I hugged him, I had a flash of memory and felt Jim's arms gripping me. I winced and made an involuntary grimace. Even though my face was against his shoulder, I was afraid that he might guess something. It was one of those moments when you feel profoundly thankful that the other person can't read your mind. In the rush of events I hadn't decided what I was going to tell Stephen, or even if I was going to tell him anything at all.

Stephen gave a sigh and released me. 'Are you OK?' He scanned my face.

I nodded. 'Glad you're back.'

'It's good to be back,' he said.

'How did you get here? I don't understand.'

'I felt so worried about you. I couldn't settle. I hired someone Martha knows to drive me up. He didn't want to hang around, afraid of getting trapped by the floods. He dropped me off at the top of the road.'

'But Grace — '

'I know. It feels wrong that we're not all together, but don't worry. She'll be fine for a couple of days with Martha. They're getting on like a house on fire.'

'I don't want her to forget about me!'

'No danger of that.'

'You shouldn't be here,' I said without much conviction. I looked into his face. 'You're awfully pale.'

'I'm OK. I slept most of the way here. I couldn't relax in Devon, knowing you were here on your own. What's that wonderful smell?'

'Soup. We'd better have some.'

As we ate at the kitchen table, I brought Stephen up to date. I played down the collapsing gable wall as much as I could, but I don't think he was fooled.

'I keep wondering if I've missed something in that letter she sent me,' I said. 'It's been driving me crazy. I've even started wondering about invisible ink. What was it we used as kids? Lemon juice? Perhaps I should try heating it up.'

'Shades of Enid Blyton and the Famous Five. If you go wafting it over the gas ring, you're more likely to set fire to it than anything else. Let me have a look.'

I handed it over. Stephen positioned the candles to get a good reading light.

There was silence as he scanned the pages. I got up and pulled back the curtain from the kitchen window. For the first time in hours the rain had slackened off. It was no more than a drizzle. When I turned back, I saw that Stephen had returned to the beginning of the letter and was reading it more closely. When at last he raised his head, it was hard to read his expression in the strong shadows cast by the candle flames.

'Well?' I asked. 'Have you found something?'

He nodded and turned the sheet of paper round. He pointed to the heading of the page. 'I don't know what that represents, but it's not a telephone number. Not a Cambridge one anyway. It's got too many digits.'

I read out the number aloud. '01223 0020887. You're right. There's one too many. I can't believe I didn't notice that.'

'You didn't really read it,' Stephen said. 'Why would you? You knew what it said — or rather you thought you did — so your eye just slid over it. Whereas I read it word for word or number for number, in this case. That's what I'd do if it were a legal document.'

331

'What does it mean?' There was something strangely familiar about it, not the actual numbers but the rhythm of it.

'That I can't tell you.' Stephen held the paper closer to the candle, squinting at it in the uncertain light. 'There is one thing, though. Look here,' he angled the paper towards me, 'you can hardly see it, but doesn't there seem to be a bit of a gap here, between those two numbers, the sort of gap that you have when there's a decimal point.'

'A decimal point?' I stared at him with my mouth open. 'Oh, no, no, no. How could I have been so thick?' I put my hands up to my head and tugged at my hair.

'Cass, what on earth's the matter?'

'Stupid, stupid, stupid,' I groaned.

'Cass! Please!'

'One of Una's favourite Father Brown stories! In 'The Sign of the Broken Sword' Father Brown asks Flambeau, 'Where would a wise man hide a leaf?' and Flambeau replies, 'in a forest.' And that's the whole point of the story. In order to cover up a murder, a general instigates a battle that is bound to result in the needless slaughter of his own men. The body of the man he's murdered is just one of many left on the battle field.'

'I'm not with you.'

332

'Oh come on, the best place to hide a leaf is in a forest, the best place to hide a corpse is on a battle field, so what follows?'

Understanding dawned on Stephen's face 'You mean . . . ?'

'Yes, yes, the best place to hide a book is in a library!'

He frowned. 'But you've already worked that out. Weren't you looking through the books in Una's library?'

'Yes, but she didn't hide *The Prose Romances* in her *own* library. She hid it in the Institute and in this letter she tells me where. This is an accession number.'

'But didn't you say that she was crippled with arthritis? How did she manage it?'

'With difficulty,' I admitted. 'She could have taken a taxi there, but once inside it would have been a struggle. But I'm sure that's what she did. There was a night when Michelle saw a light there. It must have been then.'

'But how did she get in?'

This stopped me in my tracks, but not for long. 'Don't you remember at that dinner party, Giles told us that she was in charge of a team of ladies restoring books? Maybe she had a key and didn't get round to returning it.'

'It's all a bit tenuous,' Stephen objected.

'No, but listen. Don't you see? It could explain how Wendy got into the Institute. She was Una's cleaner. What if she got hold of her key?'

'You think she was after *The Prose Romances?*'

I shook my head. 'Maybe, but I doubt it.'

'Then what was she doing in there?'

'Probably just pretending to be me, sitting at my desk, looking at my papers.'

'But you see what this means, Cass? If you're right, someone else could have tumbled to the book being hidden there. If not Wendy, then the person who killed her. The book might not even be there any more!'

'There's only one way to find out.' I got up from my chair.

Stephen stared at me. 'What are you doing?'

'Going to the Institute, what else?'

'But how are you going to get in?'

'I'll ring Jim on the way and ask him to meet me there.'

'Why not ring him now?'

'Don't you see? He might not take me with him. If I'm already there . . . '

Stephen got to his feet. We confronted each other across the table. I willed him to understand. I had to know if I was right. I'd like to say that I felt I owed it to Una, but that was only part of it. I couldn't stop now, after all I'd done to get this far. If that book was there, I just had to get my hands on it.

'Are you going to come with me?' I asked.

Stephen shook his head. 'In this weather? It would be madness. I'm not going anywhere and nor are you.'

19

Taken at the Flood

Stephen and I walked with linked arms. Once we were clear of the car-park where water was ankle-deep, the ground rose, but water still flowed around our feet. It was hard to tell in the dark whether or not it was draining away. Here and there we saw candles in windows, and the headlights of an occasional passing car swept the street.

We'd agreed that we would walk up to Elizabeth Way — it wouldn't take more than ten minutes — and see how things looked from the bridge. Midsummer Common came into view. We stood side by side at the parapet and gazed in silence. The river had flooded its banks and the common was covered by a sheet of water. The night sky was streaming with clouds, and the moon was riding high. There was something so portentous about the brilliant night sky and the inky water gleaming beneath it, that I almost expected to see an arm with a sword emerge from the water.

Stephen broke into my reverie. 'I'm sorry,

336

Cass, we really shouldn't go any further.'

I nodded disconsolately. My feet felt damp and I was getting chilly. I turned away and that was when I caught sight of something over Stephen's shoulder, something large and as brightly lit as an ocean liner. It was a double-decker bus, throwing up sprays of water as it ploughed across the bridge towards town. Without even thinking about it, let alone conferring with Stephen, I raised my arm. The bus slowed down and I stepped on board. I looked back to see Stephen standing gaping on the road. I was afraid he was going to be left behind, but just in time he reached out an arm and hauled himself aboard. The doors hissed shut behind him.

'I'm only going as far as the bus station,' said the driver. He was a middle-aged man with sideburns and hair slicked back like Elvis.

'That's perfect,' I said, rummaging in my bag for the fare and trying to ignore the expression on Stephen's face.

'This is all very well,' he said, 'but if it starts to rain again — and it will, believe me, we haven't seen the last of it — have you thought about how we'll get back?'

'Oh, where's your sense of adventure? We'll cross that bridge when we come to it.'

He didn't reply, and when I looked at him,

I was struck by his pallor. It hadn't been so evident by candlelight.

'I'm sorry,' I said. 'We can go back if you like.'

'Never mind.'

I reached for his hand and squeezed it.

The bus station is little more than a stone's throw from the Institute. We arrived so quickly that I only just had time to ring Jim and explain the situation. I caught him at home where he had just that minute arrived. He wasn't pleased to learn that I was on my way to the Institute, but he didn't waste time on recriminations. He agreed to meet us there with the keys.

'One last thing,' I said as he was about to break the connection, 'Giles — '

'We've released him for now, but he can't get into the Institute. I've got his keys.'

We emerged from the bus into an unfamiliar city. There were no street-lights and the shop windows were dark. The moon had disappeared behind a bank of clouds. We turned into Downing Place, and even the lights of the traffic were left behind us. The laboratories rose like a dark cliff on our left. I felt the touch of rain on my face. We hurried to the Institute, and sheltered under the narrow ledge of the porch. Stephen switched off the flashlight to save the batteries and we huddled together against the wall like down-and-outs in one of those Victorian engravings of street life.

'How long do you think we'll have to wait?' Stephen asked, raising his voice. The rain was coming faster now, drumming on the roof above our heads.

I flicked the switch on my torch and looked at my watch. 'Depends on what the roads are like.'

'I'm not sure where he lives.'

'Somewhere out past Longstanton.' I felt rather than saw Stephen give me a sideways glance.

When I directed the torch onto his face, I saw that his skin had taken on a waxy texture.

'You're not well,' I said with compunction.

'I'll be OK.'

Even in their gloves my fingers were getting numb. I thrust my hands deep in my pockets and felt something hard at the bottom of one of them. I drew out a set of keys, the keys that Michelle had thrust into my hands as we left the restaurant. I lifted them up. 'I'd forgotten I had these. We can wait inside.'

I selected a key. It turned in the lock but when I pulled at the door, it didn't budge.

'Are you sure it's the right one?' Stephen asked. He was shivering.

'I felt the tumblers clicking. I think we

need to feed in the code into the key-pad.'

'And of course you don't know what it is.'

'I know it's got four digits.'

A picture came into my mind of Giles standing where I was standing now, keying in the code with a trembling finger. There had been a rhythm to his movements.

'Wait, wait!' I closed my eyes. 'I think the first digit was a one.' I could see Giles stabbing furiously at the top left-hand corner of the key-pad, but that was all I could see. 'That's not much good, is it?'

Stephen was pursuing his own line of thought. 'People choose from a disappointingly narrow range of options when they pick a user-code: wedding anniversary, kid's birthday. Of course in Giles's case that rules out a whole swathe of possibilities. But — '

'Stop! Don't say another word.'

I held the torch in one hand and with the other punched in a sequence of numbers.

'Voilà!' I said, as the door swung open. 'Or should that be open sesame?'

'But what did you — ?'

'1815. The most important date in Giles's life. The year that Wellington defeated Napoleon at the battle of Waterloo.'

And it was also the number on the piece of paper in Wendy's handbag, or rather, my handbag. I felt sure now that Wendy had taken the key and the security code from Una's house. Some further knowledge hovered on the edge of my mind, something that required my attention, but while I was helping Stephen inside, it slipped away.

★ ★ ★

Stephen sank down gratefully on the stone steps.

'We'd better not go any further without Jim,' he said.

'OK.' I sat down next to him.

I kept my little torch on. I was all too conscious of the weight of the dark, empty building at my back. There's something disquieting about a public place when it is deserted at night, especially a place as old and venerable as the Institute.

When my mobile phone rang, I nearly jumped out of my skin.

It was Jim. The reception was poor.

'I've been cut off,' I heard him say.

'What?' I got up and moved nearer the door to see if I could get a better signal.

'The Ouse has broken its banks. The A14 is under a metre of water. A state of emergency's been called. You'd better get home. Do you hear me, Cassandra?'

'Yes, I hear you.'

'I'll speak to you tomorrow.'

He rang off. Stephen looked at me enquiringly.

'He can't get here. He wants us to go home.'

'Oh no.' He heaved a sigh.

When I put my hand on his, it felt clammy. If I could only warm him up a bit, make him a hot drink, and then I realized that I could. I got to my feet.

'Come on,' I said. 'There's a gas ring for making tea and coffee in that little room that opens off the reading room. Not to mention sherry in Giles's office.'

We set off up the stairs, our torch lights dancing on the uneven stone treads, bowed in the middle from generations of feet. We'd only taken a few steps, when something occurred to me. I went back and checked that I had shut the door to the street. I wanted to make sure that no one could slip in and make their way silently up the stairs behind us.

When we reached the door at the top I fumbled with the keys and had tried two before I found the right one. I had to push the heavy door with my shoulder before it creaked open.

It was warmer up here and the dry aromatic smell of old books mingled with the slightly heady scent of floor polish.

Stephen swung his flashlight round. It lit up the gleaming mahogany of the issue desk. It moved on and stopped abruptly. A pair of eyes glowed in the dark. Stephen gave a gasp. My heart seemed to jerk in my chest. There was a welcoming little chirrup. It was Florence. I'd forgotten all about her. She jumped down and wound herself round our legs, delighted to have such unexpected company.

'I can't take much more of this,' Stephen hissed.

'Neither can I. I need a drink.' I found the knob of the door to Giles's cubicle and opened it.

It was typical of Giles that his sherry was in a cut-glass decanter and there were matching glasses. There was also a bottle of Plymouth Gin.

'Gin or sherry? Or shall I make you a cup of tea?' I asked.

'Gin. And make it a stiff one.'

'Don't have much choice. I can't see any tonic.'

I poured a healthy quantity into two glasses and handed one to Stephen. I took a swig and the hit was immediate. Fireworks seemed to go off in my head.

'I can't believe we're doing this,' Stephen hissed. 'It's probably illegal.' He knocked it back all the same.

'I could take you more seriously if you weren't still wearing that sou'wester, and why are we whispering?'

But really I knew why. The past seemed to press in all about us. The lives and thoughts and emotions of thousands of people were distilled into the books that crowded the shelves. It was easy to imagine the place haunted by long-gone librarians, vexed by overdue loans, or by scholars still trying to gather evidence for theories that had long been discredited. And then there was Wendy.

'What's that?' Stephen hissed.

'What?'

'I thought I heard something. Listen.'

There was a peal of thunder like a distant door slamming. I counted out the seconds aloud. I'd reached three when a flash of lightning brought the office and the issue hall into brilliant focus before plunging it into a darkness that seemed deeper than ever.

I took another gulp of gin. 'I can't hold out any longer. I'm going to look up the accession number.'

Stephen followed me into the issue hall. He held the torch while I riffled through the cards. They had been handled so much over the years that the edges were soft and grimy and slipped between my fingers. Finally I found the number that matched the one on Una's letter.

I let out a snort of laughter.

'Cass, what's the matter?'

'The title of the book: *Nooks and Crannies in Old France*, published in 1924. Brilliant! What's more outdated than an old travel book? I bet no one's had it out in years. And that's not the cream of the jest. You're not going to believe this. The book's in my room, the room where I've been working.'

'What? You mean it's been there all along?'

'All the time that I was wondering what it was, and where it was, all I needed to do was to go up there and pick it off the shelf.'

'If you're right.'

'I know I'm right.'

'Come on.'

'Cass, no, I don't think we should be doing this: we'll be contaminating a crime scene.'

'We'll wear gloves. You can wait here if you like.'

'Not on your life. We stick together. Haven't you seen what happens in those horror movies where the couple gets separated?'

'Are you drunk?'

'Maybe a tiny bit. Are you?'

'You bet.'

A combination of gin and darkness led to a

painful encounter with the table where the periodicals were spread out, and I was limping by the time we reached the foot of the spiral stairs. Stephen went up first and the steps rattled under his feet. He shone the flashlight down. I gripped the balustrade tightly, the mahogany cool under my hand. As I reached the top, there was a pattering of little feet behind me and Florence pushed her face against my leg. She sat down on the top step and began to wash herself vigorously.

Stephen led the way up the stairs to my room. He was breathing hard by the time we got to the top. It was colder up here, but that wasn't all that was making me shiver. Stephen ran the beam of his torch over my desk and I seemed for a moment to see Wendy sitting there.

'So where is it?' Stephen asked.

I moved in close to the shelves so that I could see the accession numbers, written in white on the spine.

'It's this shelf,' I said, and ran my hand along until I'd reached the number. As soon as I touched the book, I thought, what if the pamphlet isn't here. What if someone *had* got there first. At that moment I realized what I should have realized earlier. There was a key unaccounted for. Wendy had let herself in with Una's key, but it hadn't been found on her body.

'Go on!' Stephen's voice was tense.

The circle of light remained on my hand as I pulled out *Nooks and Crannies of Old France*. It sprang open. Between its bulging pages was a plastic envelope and inside it was a second envelope made of stiff paper. With trembling fingers, I fumbled both envelopes open and tilted them so that the contents slid out onto my gloved hand. And there it was: a tattered pamphlet with *The Prose Romances of Edgar A. Poe* printed on the cover. Below the title in spidery letters was written: 'To Virginia. Accept this token with all the devotion a husband can offer.'

'That's it?' Stephen asked. His breath was warm on my cheek. 'That's a million dollars?'

I nodded. I couldn't speak. For the first time, I truly understood the romance of book collecting. The little booklet, so drab and unassuming, contained a story that had launched an entire genre and it had been a gift from Poe to his dying wife. Poe had once held it in his hands as I was holding it now. The pathos of that inscription! And to think that if we hadn't picked up the clue in Una's letter, *The Prose Romances* might have remained hidden here for decades. And then something strange happened. Now that I'd got the pamphlet, I didn't want it any more. It lay in my hand like something malignant and ill-omened. I felt a wave of revulsion. Una had died because of it, I felt sure, and Wendy, too.

Everything seemed to happen at once.

Stephen made a noise between a gasp and a grunt and the beam of the torch jerked up to the ceiling. The torch hit the floor with a crash and went out. Darkness engulfed us. The pamphlet was plucked from my grasp. Retreating footsteps beat a tattoo on the bare boards.

Flailing about, I caught a hand. The hand gripped me back. It was Stephen. We clutched each other in the dark.

'Cass, are you all right?'

'Someone's taken it!'

'We've got to find the torch!'

We were down on hands and knees feeling around, when I remembered the pencil torch in my raincoat pocket. But I hadn't even switched it on before the room was bathed in a faint orange light. It was the street light outside. The power had come back on.

There was a shout and a hideous high-pitched yowl, followed by a boom, boom, boom, a crashing and clattering that seemed to last forever, then a sickening thud. The air around us quivered as if a huge tuning fork were vibrating.

'What the fuck?' Stephen said.

I knew what must have happened.

'Someone's tripped over Florence and fallen down the spiral staircase. Come on.'

We stumbled out into the darkness of the gallery.

Stephen switched on the flashlight and shone it down into the hall. A white face was caught in the beam.

'Oh, no,' I said. 'She's not — '

'No,' said Stephen grimly, 'she's not dead.'

Looking up at us, her face twisted in pain, was Eileen.

20

It Is Never Too Late To Mend

It was March and the cherry blossom was out on the day of Una's memorial service. There had been a turn in the weather and it was cold as well as sunny. There was even an occasional little flurry of snow. People were turning up coat collars and putting on gloves as they came out of Great St Mary's Church.

Once clear of the door, Stephen and I paused. Neither of us spoke. I was thinking of Una's last moments. She had tried to consign *The Prose Romances* to my care. Had it all been a blur of fear and pain after that, or had there been time for a final summing up? Had she forgiven Terence? Had the memory of their early days when they were young and in love been enough to set in the balance against the later betrayals? I hoped so and that she'd had time to feel glad that she had done right by Michelle.

Someone touched me on the elbow. I turned to see Giles.

'It was a good send-off, wasn't it?' he said. 'I think Una would have liked it.'

'Have you forgiven her?' I asked.

'Forgiven her? Whatever for? Oh, for changing her will? I came to terms with that ages ago. You know I've been short-listed for the new job?'

I nodded. St Etheldreda's had advertised for a librarian who would be responsible for taking care of the Carwardine collection and the building of the library that would house it. I'd be surprised if Giles didn't get the job.

'No,' he went on, 'the person I've really got it in for is Eileen. To think how that woman pulled the wool over my eyes. When that policeman let slip that all that money was missing — '

Let slip! Stephen and I exchanged amused glances.

' — I asked Eileen if she had any idea what Una could have spent it on. She strung me along. Had me burrowing around in the University library, when she knew all the time!'

'Not to mention that she was responsible for the deaths of two women,' Stephen said dryly.

'Oh, quite!' Giles nodded emphatically. 'It's poetic justice, what happened to her!'

Eileen had two broken arms, a broken leg and fractured ribs. The last I'd heard she was in the prison hospital. The case would take time to come to court, but there wasn't much doubt of the outcome. The police had traced some of books that she had stolen from Una's house. They had been sold on to other dealers. The rest would probably never be recovered: they were no doubt in the hands of collectors who had been happy not to ask too many questions. That would have been the fate of *The Prose Romances of Edgar Allan Poe*, if Stephen and I hadn't got to it first. Instead it was in a safe deposit box at the college bank. In due course it would be sold to provide money for a new library for the college.

'I could kick myself for not realizing that Una had still got a key to the Institute,' Giles said.

Eileen had seen Wendy turning into Downing Place late one evening and had mistaken her for me. When she saw Wendy letting herself into the Institute, she suspected that *The Prose Romances* was hidden there. Before Wendy knew what had happened, Eileen had come up, pushed her through the door, and stepped in behind her. She quickly realized her mistake, but when Wendy admitted that she was Una's cleaner, Eileen thought she knew more than she did. She killed Wendy when she wouldn't, or rather couldn't, tell Eileen where the book was.

We skirted the edge of the market, crowded as usual with stalls and people buying fruit, or fish, or second-hand books, or hats. Fortunately the flood waters hadn't risen this high. Elsewhere the cleanup operations still continued. We'd been lucky at the Old Granary. The outhouses and the surrounding land had been flooded, but the house itself was built on brick pillars and they had kept it clear of the water.

Outside the Guildhall, music students with brass instruments were busking and on Petty Cury a man in full highlander costume of sporran, kilt and bearskin was playing the bagpipes. The strains of *La Vie en Rose* mingled with *Scotland the Brave*.

'Love the Charles Ives effect,' Giles said.

'We're going to have some tea at Fitzbillies. Do you want to join us?' Stephen asked.

'I'd love to but I've really got to get back.' He nodded in the direction of the Institute. He had already turned away from us, when he paused and looked back. 'Cass, did you know that Michelle's coming back after all? Her sick leave's nearly up. She's going to work till June and then go travelling.'

I smiled and nodded. No need to tell Giles that this was the fruit of several long telephone conversations I'd had with Michelle.

Stephen and I cut through Free School

Lane and walked briskly down Botolph Street and into Trumpington Street. We didn't say much and it wasn't until we had settled ourselves in the café and ordered tea and chocolate cake that Stephen asked me if I felt OK about Una.

I nodded. 'I'm fine.' And I was. Knowing that in the end I had deserved Una's confidence had laid her ghost to rest for me.

Stephen pushed his hair back from his forehead and shot me a quick sideways glance.

'You were chatting to Jim before the service began.'

'He's about to leave for Chicago. A six-month secondment. Something to do with comparing policing methods.'

'Just what he needs, I should think. A change of scene will do him a world of good.'

'I think so, too.'

'And there's nothing to keep him here.'

'That's right.'

Stephen had taken a cube of sugar and was turning it in his fingers. He hadn't met my eyes, but now he looked up. 'Are you sure?'

'How do you mean?'

'That there's nothing to keep him here?'

I bit my lip. The moment I had been dreading had come. 'Yes, I'm sure. Stephen . . .' I didn't know what else to say.

He shook his head and held up a hand. 'Is it over?'

'It never got started. Not really.'

'That's all I need to know.'

There was something else I'd been meaning to say and this was as good a time as any.

I cleared my throat. 'I went to see Honoria this morning to ask her if I could do a four-day week. She was fine about it. I won't be in college on Wednesdays after the summer. That means I can spend more time with Grace, and if we did have another baby . . . '

I couldn't read his expression for a moment. Then I saw that he was suppressing a smile.

'Actually,' he said, 'I was just waiting for a chance to tell you. I've talked things over at work and I'm planning to stop work at two o'clock on Friday afternoons. I want to spend more time with Grace. And, as you say, if there was to be another baby . . . ' He dropped the cube of sugar and leaned across the table to take my hand. 'Do you really think . . . ? Look, I'm sorry that I put so much pressure on you. And it was tactless of me to say that there was no time to lose.'

'You were right though.'

He was gazing into my eyes. 'Do you have

to go back to work?'

'The book's more or less tied up. There's nothing that can't wait until tomorrow. Are they expecting you back at the office?'

'I said I'd be out for the rest of the day.'

'It wouldn't take fifteen minutes to walk home.'

'Five minutes in a taxi.' Stephen got to his feet.

I grabbed my handbag and stood up.

'The chocolate cake,' I said.

'Sod the chocolate cake.' Stephen got out his wallet, took out a twenty-pound note and flung it on the table.

As we went out of the door, I glanced back and saw the waitress standing by the entrance to the kitchen with a laden tray and a puzzled expression.

The Half-Sisters, by Geraldine Jewsbury
The Portrait of a Lady, by Henry James
The Way We Live Now, by Anthony Trollope
Great Expectations, by Charles Dickens
The Dead Secret, by Wilkie Collins
A Minor Accident, by George Moore
The Spoils of Poynton, by Henry James
Second Thoughts, by Rhoda Broughton
Stories of The Seen and the Unseen, by
Margaret Oliphant
Dr Jekyll and Mr Hyde, by Robert Louis
Stevenson
When It Was Dark, by Guy Thorne
The Story of the Treasure-Seekers, by E.
Nesbit
The Turn Of The Screw, by Henry James
The Two Destinies, by Wilkie Collins
The Secret Sharer, by Joseph Conrad
Ships That Pass in the Night, by Beatrice
Harraden
No Name, by Wilkie Collins
Called Back, by Hugh Conway
Taken at the Flood, by Mary Braddon
It Is Never Too Late To Mend, by Charles
Read

We do hope that you have enjoyed reading
this large print book.

Did you know that all of our titles
are available for purchase?

We publish a wide range of high quality
large print books including:
Romances, Mysteries, Classics
General Fiction
Non Fiction and Westerns

Special interest titles available in
large print are:
The Little Oxford Dictionary
Music Book
Song Book
Hymn Book
Service Book

Also available from us courtesy of
Oxford University Press:
Young Readers' Dictionary
(large print edition)
Young Readers' Thesaurus
(large print edition)

For further information or a free
brochure, please contact us at:
Ulverscroft Large Print Books Ltd.,
The Green, Bradgate Road, Anstey,
Leicester, LE7 7FU, England.
Tel: (00 44) 0116 236 4325
Fax: (00 44) 0116 234 0205

Other titles published by
The House of Ulverscroft:

STAGE FRIGHT

Christine Poulson

During her maternity leave, Cambridge academic Cassandra James gets involved in a production of *East Lynne* and soon discovers that there is as much drama behind the scenes as there is on stage. The director is desperate to revive his flagging career and the maker of a fly-on-the-wall documentary is equally desperate to launch his. When the leading lady, Melissa, disappears before the opening night, Cassandra suspects it is more than just stage fright, for Melissa has left behind her six-month-old daughter. Cassandra's struggles to uncover the truth lead her deep into a maze of deceit. Someone is not what they seem. Cassandra and her baby are in grave danger . . .

DEAD LETTERS

Christine Poulson

A painful divorce brings Cassandra James to Cambridge, where she takes up a lectureship in a women's college and moves into her new home, an isolated house deep in the Fens. Suddenly, her quiet life is shattered when she discovers the body of her head of department, Margaret, floating in a swimming pool. This death triggers a series of events that threatens Cassandra's job, her integrity, and her independence. She suspects that Margaret might have been murdered, and she is fearful that she herself might be the killer's next target. Will her skills in solving literary puzzles help her to unmask the assassin?